The tingling aftereffect of Luke's kiss clung to her lips.

Twenty-eight and never been kissed. But she couldn't help it. It had taken her years to overcome her fear of men, and still, Gaby had never overcome her fear of men's hands.

She'd tried dating a few times, but when she panicked every time a man tried to touch her, she'd given up on the idea. And there had never been anyone who'd made her want to face that fear.

Until now.

A multitude of emotions swirled through her. She'd liked the feel of Luke's lips on hers. They had been so soft, so warm, so…what? Shocking? Surprising? Wonderful?

Awe inspiring.

What was she thinking? She'd promised herself long ago to keep men out of her life. Not to let them in. But she couldn't stop the thoughts…and she didn't know if she wanted to!

Dear Reader,

Happy Anniversary! We're kicking off a yearlong celebration in honor of Silhouette Books' 20th Anniversary, with unforgettable love stories by your favorite authors, including Nora Roberts, Diana Palmer, Sherryl Woods, Joan Elliott Pickart and many more!

Sherryl Woods delivers the first baby of the new year in *The Cowboy and the New Year's Baby,* which launches AND BABY MAKES THREE: THE DELACOURTS OF TEXAS. And return to Whitehorn, Montana, as Laurie Paige tells the story of an undercover agent who comes home to protect his family and finds his heart in *A Family Homecoming,* part of MONTANA MAVERICKS: RETURN TO WHITEHORN.

Next is Christine Rimmer's tale of a lady doc's determination to resist the charming new hospital administrator. Happily, he proves irresistible in *A Doctor's Vow,* part of PRESCRIPTION: MARRIAGE. And don't miss Marie Ferrarella's sensational family story set in Alaska, *Stand-In Mom.*

Also this month, Leigh Greenwood tells the tale of two past lovers who must be *Married by High Noon* in order to save a child. Finally, opposites attract in *Awakened By His Kiss,* a tender love story by newcomer Judith Lyons.

Join the celebration; treat yourself to all six Special Edition romance novels each month!

Best,

Karen Taylor Richman
Senior Editor

Please address questions and book requests to:
Silhouette Reader Service
U.S.: 3010 Walden Ave., P.O. Box 1325, Buffalo, NY 14269
Canadian: P.O. Box 609, Fort Erie, Ont. L2A 5X3

JUDITH LYONS
AWAKENED BY HIS KISS

SPECIAL EDITION®

Published by Silhouette Books
America's Publisher of Contemporary Romance

To Connie McDowell, Kathy Jacobson and Debra Robertson.
Connie, without your support I never would have gotten beyond the first chapter.
And, Kathy, without your brilliant tutelage I certainly wouldn't have gotten to the last.
Thanks, guys, for helping to make my dream come true.
Debra, you're the fairy godmother in all this.
Thanks for that last wave of the wand.

 SILHOUETTE BOOKS

ISBN 0-373-24296-4

AWAKENED BY HIS KISS

Visit us at www.romance.net

Printed in U.S.A.

JUDITH LYONS

lives in the deep woods in Wisconsin, where anyone who is familiar with the area will tell you one simply cannot survive the bitter winters without a comfortable chair, a cozy fireplace and a stack of good reading. When she decided winters were too cold for training horses and perfect for writing what she loved to read most—romance novels—she put pen to paper and delved into the exciting world of words and phrases and, most important of all, love and romance.

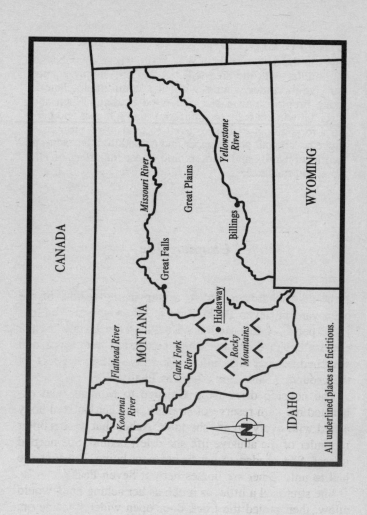

CANADA

MONTANA

WYOMING

IDAHO

Flathead River

Kootenai River

Clark Fork River

Rocky Mountains

Missouri River

Great Falls

Great Plains

Billings

Yellowstone River

Hideaway

N

All underlined places are fictitious.

Chapter One

Abigail Richards pulled to a stop in the middle of the open yard at Seven Peaks Ranch. All around her the majestic peaks of the Montana Rockies climbed toward the endless expanse of sky. She opened the truck door and stretched out her legs before carefully putting her feet on the ground. Thank God, she was finally here.

The nonstop drive from Chicago to Montana had exhausted her slim reserve of strength, and her battered body ached with every breath she took. Aches that were a bitter reminder of the abusive life she'd left behind. She needed to rest. She needed to get to her new home. But first she had to unload her six horses here at Seven Peaks.

She stretched a little, as much as her aching body would allow, then pulled the truck door open wider. "Come on, gang. We're here. Get out and move around a little." With a wave of her hand, she signaled her dogs out of the truck.

With pleasure, they bounded out, as thrilled to escape

the small cab as she. They were a mismatched lot, a German shepherd, a bloodhound and a border collie mix, but they were the best search and rescue team in the United States.

As they tripped over each other in their exuberance, Crash's brightly colored neckerchief came undone. Two steps later, the collie's bandanna fell to the ground.

Ignoring the constant ache of her ribs, Gaby bent over, picked it up and called the black and white collie to her side. While the dog sat at her feet vibrating with excitement to be off and running, she tied the kerchief around her furry neck and tried not to think about the scene with her brother-in-law four days ago. The man hadn't hesitated to take his anger out on her. Just as he'd never hesitated to take it out on her sister.

As she tightened the knot, the hairs on the back of Gaby's neck prickled in warning. Straightening, she rapidly took in her surroundings. Nothing. She spun around.

Her breath caught in her throat.

Twenty feet away a cowboy leaned against one of the porch's wooden pillars.

A shiver of fear ran up Gaby's spine.

He wasn't there to welcome her. Leaning against the rough pillar with his hat tipped low over his eyes, the thumb of one hand stuck in the band of his jeans, he radiated insolence and challenge like a gunslinger welcoming the county marshal to his town.

Luke Anderson. It had to be him, not his brother. She'd bought her little ranch from Luke, but he hadn't wanted to board her horses until she had stalls of her own built. His brother had offered her animals refuge, anyway, and it appeared Luke wasn't pleased.

Quickly, Gaby glanced at his feet. Cowboy boots. And a wooden porch.

He hadn't been there when she'd driven in moments before, and yet not so much as a whisper of sand on wood had alerted her to his presence. He'd meant to startle her. Meant to appear out of nowhere, full-blown and menacing.

His bad-boy attire only enhanced the illusion. His hacked-up denim shirt, sleeves ripped out at the shoulders and the front unbuttoned, exposed more bronzed skin than it covered, drawing her attention to the lean, corded muscle covering his chest and roping his arms. Strength and power. Arrogance and contempt.

Pure untamed, predatory male.

"Seen enough? Or would you like me to take something off so you can get a better look?"

Her mouth went dry. He meant to unsettle her, perhaps even frighten her with the lewd invitation. But she didn't let herself back up even an inch. Her ranch was on this mountain. Granted, it was on the other side, but still, this was her new home. She might have cowered before her brother-in-law's vicious attack four days ago, but she wasn't going to cower before *anyone* here.

"Don't bother. If I decide to beggar myself, I'll let you know."

A sudden stillness gripped the air. The calm before the storm. It was almost a relief when he finally moved, pushing up the brim of his hat.

For the first time she saw his eyes. A chill swept through her. They were a brighter blue than any sky she had ever seen. But even through their narrow slits she could see the winds of winter blowing in them.

Her heart pounded as he pushed away from the post and sauntered toward her, his step slow...deliberate... menacing. What had she been thinking to say such a thing? She knew better than to bait a wild animal. And this man was as wild as they came.

She didn't need the arrogant set of his shoulders to tell her he answered to no laws but his own. She'd dealt with his type all her life.

She'd come here to Hideaway, Montana, to her new home and the giant red mountain it was nestled beneath to avoid just that. She wanted peace. Quiet days and silent nights. Mornings filled with singing birds and evenings filled with singing crickets. Sweet-smelling grass growing slowly in the sun, and winter snows that covered the ground in a comforting blanket of white. Forever-lasting peace. She wanted it. She needed it.

And Luke Anderson was not going to stop her from having it.

Taking a deep breath, she refused to give in to the fear pounding at her temple. With a quick hand, she tested the fit of her sunglasses, making sure they hid her black eye. She knew the makeup she'd applied covered her bruised jaw and split lip. She'd checked just before she'd driven into the yard. She wanted no visible weakness for Luke Anderson to prey upon.

He drew nearer.

Her muscles tensed, and she waited breathlessly for him to stop. Her battered ribs ached with tension as every measured step brought him closer. But she didn't run.

The toes of his boots nipped her own. His heat warmed her. The smell of leather, soap and sweat filled her senses. And his stare bore into hers until she could feel the Arctic gales clear down to her soul.

She didn't dare breathe. Afraid even the tiniest movement would provoke him into violence, she stood motionless and waited to see which way the winds would blow.

The icy gales shifted and changed until they became a heated blaze that threatened to scorch her with his anger.

"Luke, throw the horses some hay, will you?" That was Matt Anderson's voice, Gaby recognized. Luke's brother.

Relief surged through her.

Turning, Gaby saw a tall, rangy cowboy standing in the barn door, the corners of his mouth turned down as he looked at his brother. But she didn't leave her attention on Matt for long. Not with Luke Anderson a hair's breadth away. She turned back to the angry cowboy.

A wry smile turned the corners of his lips. "Ah, your knight in shining armor. If you'll excuse me, I have hungry mounts to feed." He sauntered away, his stride the rolling gait that accompanies cowboy boots and a cocky arrogance.

The tension ran out of her. She turned back to the barn.

Matt headed her way, gravel crunching beneath his feet. He moved with the same Western roll his brother had, but his gait was easier, friendlier. And a welcoming smile sat upon his lips.

Her heart slowed its cadence and she drew a deep, steadying breath.

When he got close enough, Matt extended his hand.

Gaby's heart sped up again. Hands terrified her. Her earliest memories centered on hands and the agonizing pain they created. But in the outside world, shaking hands was a necessity. Ignoring the pounding of her heart, she stuck out her hand. "Mr. Anderson?"

Thankfully, Matt's quick handshake offered neither threat nor unwanted advances. "Abigail?" At her nod, Matt continued, "Call me Matt, please. We're informal out here. How was your trip?"

"The trip was fine, thank you. And please, call me Gaby. Abigail's a little too formal, too."

"Good enough. Let me show you your stalls. They were stripped and bedded down with clean shavings this morning. Your ponies should find them soft after their long journey.''

With the immediate threat of Luke gone, fatigue stole into Gaby's veins. Through a haze of exhaustion she followed Matt into the barn. She gave her eyes a minute to adjust to the light. It was a little dark for sunglasses, but she'd have to manage.

Matt pointed to a bank of stalls. ''These are yours until you're set up at your place.''

Automatically, Gaby stepped closer and peered inside. Clean, dry bedding met her gaze. Her horses would be comfortable and happy here. But dear God, what about Luke? Could she handle facing him again?

Matt seemed to sense her apprehension because he stepped closer to her and held out a tentative hand, as if he expected to have to catch her. ''Are you all right?''

She nodded quickly. ''I'm fine.''

He narrowed his eyes on her. ''No, you're not. Luke upset you.''

Too tired for subterfuge, she nodded.

Matt gave a soft sigh. ''Listen, I'm not going to apologize for my brother. He behaves like an ass sometimes, but he has his reasons. And they have nothing to do with you. Unfortunately, sometimes his sour moods spill over onto whoever happens to be around. But you are welcome here, Gaby. You and your horses. And if it's any consolation, you won't have to deal with him for the next two weeks. He's headed into the high country to bring down the steers we summer up there.''

His expression and tone told Gaby that although he acknowledged his brother's reasons, and perhaps understood them, he didn't agree with Luke's behavior. Still, he had stood up for the man.

Which could mean anything. It could mean Matt was

loyal to his family, or that he loved his brother, or even that his brother had some qualities worth standing up for. Whatever it meant, the bottom line was that for the time being she had to leave her horses here. And right now, Luke wasn't a threat. Exhaustion was. She had horses to get unloaded and very little energy with which to do it. The drive to the other side of the mountain she didn't even want to think about.

Mustering her energy, she gave Matt a smile and lifted a hand toward the trailer. "Shall we bring them in?"

Luke heard Abigail Richards's words as he approached the barn. Anger streaked through him. What the hell had his brother said to soothe her ruffled feathers? He'd had her on the run, and dammit, he meant to keep her that way.

He didn't want her here. Having to sell Seven Peaks' original homestead, the home and land that should have nurtured his own children, had been tough enough. That old house and the land that went with it had raised four generations of Andersons in good health and a mountain of love, and it should have raised several more.

True, after his ex-wife's betrayal, he never intended to set foot on the place again; the memories were too painful. And, true, Seven Peaks needed the fresh infusion of capital the sale had brought. But selling it outside the family had been like cutting off a part of himself. And when he'd been forced to sell it to another self-centered little rich girl just like his ex-wife, Tanya, the anger and frustration had almost eaten him alive.

And now, to add insult to injury, his blood was running hotter than a randy bull's. He gritted his teeth as he remembered the lovely heart shape of Miss Richards's bottom as she'd bent over her dog. Three weeks of watching nothing but bovine backsides had obviously impaired his judgment.

He clenched his fists in disgust. Why the *hell* did she feel it necessary to keep a kerchief on that dog, anyway? If she hadn't bent over to tie the bloody thing on the dog's neck, he'd be in a lot better shape right now. At least his heart wouldn't be pounding to beat the band...and his hands wouldn't be cold and clammy.

Hadn't he learned his lesson the first time around?

Beautiful, rich women who flaunted their wealth and played games with only their self-interest in mind made him sick. No. They made him angry. Deep down, soul-searingly angry. Because he knew they'd betray anyone to get what they wanted.

White-hot anger flared in Luke's chest as he remembered his ex-wife's final betrayal. He reached for it like a life preserver. Few things burned as hot as naked passion, but raw fury did. He only had to remember Miss Richards was as rich and self-centered as Tanya, and he'd be all right.

And he had plenty of proof of that.

This woman had had her lawyer call and offer whatever it took to buy the old homestead, but only if she could have it in five days. Five damned days. Just as the ranch was gearing up for roundup, with every hand working seven-day weeks, sixteen-hour days, she'd wanted him to drop everything to sell her a ranch she'd seen a year ago and been dreaming about ever since.

If she'd been dreaming about it for the past year, what was the damned hurry?

Her attitude clawed at his insides. The selfish, blind, uncaring attitude that allowed women like her to walk on anything and anyone to get what they wanted.

And if Miss Richards's methods of buying the ranch

weren't enough to convince him of her ilk, her comment about beggaring herself was.

It hadn't taken him long to figure out his appeal to Tanya had been his "lowly" life-style. Cowboy boots, the wail of the jukebox, drinking beer out of the bottle, and a man with trail dust still clinging to him had been her turn-on. She'd liked slumming it. For a while.

But the life-style had quickly paled. When she'd realized he intended to spend his life on the ranch, pushing cows and living in the modest homestead instead of living high on the hog in some godforsaken city on her money, their marriage had begun to disintegrate. And it had ended in bitter betrayal.

Yeah, anger would do it. Not an ounce of lust left.

He met Miss Richards and Matt as they headed out of the barn. "I'd like a word with you," he ground out, walking past his brother into the barn.

Matt stopped and raised a hand toward the trailer. "Go on, Gaby. I'll meet you at your rig in a minute."

Gaby, huh? So his brother was already settling Miss Richards in, nickname and all. Luke's temper simmered until *Gaby* stepped out of earshot. Then, he rounded on his brother. "I want her out of here."

Matt shrugged a shoulder. "I know you do. But it's not going to happen. The girl just drove across the country to get to a ranch *you* sold her—for a real pretty penny, I might add—and if she wants to leave her horses here, it's fine with me."

Anger seethed in Luke's chest like a pit of writhing snakes. "Listen, if you want to be a knight in shining armor, you could pick someone more deserving than a conniving little rich girl."

"Don't be ridiculous. I have no intention of usurping

your position. One knight—in slightly tarnished armor—
is more than any family can stand.''

Hell. That was a whole different argument. And Luke
was in no mood for it. If he wanted to spend his time
getting refugees out of the line of fire in war-ridden coun-
tries, that was his business. ''Don't start with that.''

''I didn't start it. You did.'' Matt stopped himself mid-
tirade and took a deep, calming breath. ''Look, I know
working for Life Move is important to you. And I think
it's great you're working with an organization dedicated
to keeping women and children as safe as possible in third-
world war zones. But we'd like to see you around here a
little more often. This is your ranch, too.''

Yes, it was. And he came home every year for the three
months when the ranch really needed him—two months
prior to roundup when they drove the herds down from
summer pasture and the final month of actual branding and
castrating and shipping to market. But the rest of the time,
it was easier to be somewhere else.

''Well, I'm here now, aren't I? And I'll be here for the
next few months. So can we have this fight another time?
Right now I just want that woman off this ranch.''

Matt shook his head. ''She's staying. I know this is a
bad time for you. Selling off the old homestead has to have
brought up bad memories. For that matter, Shanna and I
bringing Sarah home four days ago couldn't have been any
picnic, either.''

Pain seared Luke's heart, obliterating his anger. Shame
filled him. When Tanya ran away with another man after
their marriage had been on the rocks for months, Luke
hadn't been surprised. But when she'd told him she carried
another man's child, the child Luke had begged her to have
for him, her betrayal had taken on a whole other meaning.

Luke had vowed never to set foot on the old homestead

again. Never to come near the room where he and Tanya had shared a bed. The bed where Tanya had conceived another man's child while he'd been out on the range. And certainly Luke never wanted to deal with another woman whose riches had long since replaced her heart.

But he wasn't going to let any of that taint the birth of Matt's first child. "No, Matt. Don't let such a thought touch that sweet baby. I'm glad she's here. The only memories that little girl will ever be responsible for are good ones."

Relief flashed in Matt's eyes, but a wry smile turned his lips. "I'll remind you of that when she's ten and runs away on your best mount."

Luke looked forward to it. "I'll saddle him up for her."

"No, you won't. You'll probably read her the riot act for it. And she'll deserve it. But at the moment it's something neither of us has to worry about. Unlike the young lady standing out in the yard with six horses in her trailer."

The snakes started seething again. It would take a brawl to convince Matt to send the woman and her horses on their way.

Gaby Richards wasn't worth it. And as his brother had said, he'd be in the high country for the next two weeks. If he had to stretch it to four so the woman would be gone when he returned, so be it.

Luke gave in with an ungracious sigh and the bitter taste of defeat. "Let's get the damned beasts in."

Chapter Two

Frustration churned Luke's gut as he followed Matt out of the barn. He'd rather spend the afternoon in a pit of rattlers than help Gaby Richards unload her horses. Hell, he'd probably be safer in a pit of the venomous monsters, but it didn't appear to be an option. The best he could hope for was to unload the woman's horses and get her down the road before his pulse kicked up again.

He needed her out of here. Now.

A flash of gold caught his attention as he stepped into the sunshine. Looking to the trailer, Luke saw Gaby, her long, restless mane reflecting the sun's final rays. To him the golden tendrils seemed to dance enticingly on the evening breeze.

He gritted his teeth against the fire building in his blood and tried to ignore the grace with which Gaby climbed the short incline of the trailer's ramp.

But he couldn't. He imagined those long, lean legs

wrapped around him. The slow, silken glide of knee against flank. The pulsing heat of passion nestled between soft thighs. The fire in his blood burned hotter.

When Gaby finally disappeared into the trailer, Luke drew a calming breath. He definitely needed this woman gone. But even as the thought formed, Gaby backed the first horse out of the trailer.

Luke looked, and looked again. Even from fifty feet away, the size and sheer power of the horse stunned him. Never had he seen such a magnificent specimen of muscle and bone. Head high, the stallion peered around like a lord surveying his lands, and when the sun caught the sheen of his red coat, it turned to fire.

Just a few steps ahead of him, Matt had stopped, too.

Luke stepped even with his brother. "Want to throw a calf from the top of that brute?"

Matt shook his head, laughing easily. "Good Lord, you'd break half the bones in your body diving off that animal."

"Yeah," Luke agreed. "But what a ride."

Excitement fizzed in Luke's veins, becoming a slow burgeoning heat as the equine and human duo walked toward them in a sensuous dance that had Luke's belly tightening in response.

With ears pricked and head held at a regal angle, the stallion pranced beside Gaby in slow motion. His powerful gait suspended him above the ground so that he floated beside her. His mass dwarfed her, making her appear vulnerable and impossibly fragile.

And Gaby walked beside the stallion's powerful shoulder as though she were part of him, trusting him to keep her safe from both outside forces and his giant, flashing hooves.

Luke gritted his teeth at the sight. He'd let one woman fool him with her beauty. He wouldn't repeat the mistake.

This woman would not pull him in. Clenching his fists, he ruthlessly ignored the slow heat coursing through him.

As Gaby approached, her easy manner disappeared and she gave him a wide berth.

Fine with him.

Gaby held the lead rope out to Matt. "Would you please take him in for me, Matt? I want to get the next horse out as quickly as possible. This is Klaus. He looks like a monster, but he's a puppy dog. If he gets fresh with one of the mares, just tell him to stand down. He will."

With his own blood running hot, Luke couldn't imagine a stud of this power standing down once he'd caught the scent of a mare. And it inflamed him at gut level that someone would ask him to. But then, Tanya had spent the entire three years of their marriage trying to turn him into a trained poodle. Why would Gaby Richards be any different?

Disgusted at the desire pounding through his body, Luke strode purposefully to the trailer as Matt led the big horse away. Behind him he heard Gaby's softer tread following at a safe distance.

Good. With lust prodding him relentlessly the farther away she stayed from him the better. Climbing the trailer's ramp, he saw the next horse lying down in the small space allotted him.

The woman was not only spoiled, she was incompetent. No, he corrected himself, ignorant. She probably didn't know anything about horse training. Tanya had launched herself into dozens of projects because she thought they sounded like fun. He'd bet the ranch Miss Richards didn't know a horse's ass from a mule's. No wonder she'd walked so confidently beside the stallion. She hadn't a clue how easily those hooves could have crushed her. He turned to face her.

Like a wary animal she stopped at the bottom of the ramp, but she managed to pull her shoulders back and lift her chin.

He wasn't impressed. "Do you know how unsafe it is for horses to lie down in trailers? This is the best way I know to guarantee at least one horse ends up with a broken leg."

Her chin came up another notch, and a brow appeared above her dark glasses. "I just bought this horse, Mr. Anderson. He wouldn't have made the trip standing up. If I'd tied him, he would have hung himself. As for thrashing about, trust me, he doesn't have the energy."

A logical explanation, but was it hers? He doubted it. She was probably just parroting someone else's words. Turning, Luke unhooked the partition.

At the first sound of metal grating on metal, the horse surged to his feet. When the horse quieted, Luke swung the partition partway open. His stomach pitched. The horse's bones stuck out painfully, and deep lacerations crisscrossed the dull, fungus-eaten coat.

"Who did this?"

Coming up the ramp, Gaby took the partition from him. Opening it all the way, she secured it against the trailer's side and stepped in front of Luke to grasp the horse's lead.

Luke forgot all about the horse as his own body leaped to life. From collarbone to toes, Gaby threatened to bump into him with every move she made. One step would bring his body into contact with hers. His feet itched to take that step.

Gaby turned to him with a look of cold contempt. "His last owner did this to him, Mr. Anderson. Now, if you'd step away, I'll get him to his stall before he falls down."

Her look worked like a bucket of ice water, cooling his ardor and reminding him that he was trying to keep his distance from this woman.

Turning on his heel, he strode out of the trailer and waited impatiently for her to lead the poor animal out. A slow process. With the horse's weakness, each step was painstakingly won.

As he waited, Matt joined him. One look at the horse Gaby was leading out and Matt gasped, too.

Luke turned to his brother. "He'll probably die before the sun rises tomorrow, and then we're going to have to deal with getting a dead horse out of the barn." The sudden quiet caught Luke's attention. He glanced back at the trailer.

Gaby stared at him, her mouth compressed into an angry line. "He's not going to die, Mr. Anderson. He's going to live. I'll see to it."

The conviction in her voice surprised Luke, but it didn't fool him. As soon as she discovered how much work it took to save a horse this far gone, she'd abandon her task and leave the poor beast to decline in loneliness and misery.

Acid ate at Luke's gut. He didn't have time to nurse a sick horse in the middle of roundup. He wouldn't even be here to try. He'd be in the high country for the next two weeks. The animal would die, in *his* barn, because some spoiled little rich girl wanted to indulge in a Florence Nightingale fantasy.

Stepping the horse off the ramp, Gaby ignored him and turned to Matt. "The next two horses are fresh out of the pasture and barely halter broke. Neither one of them knows how to lead. If you want, I'll wrestle them in after I get Glock settled."

Matt lifted a hand toward the barn. "Don't worry about

it. Luke and I will get them unloaded. Just concentrate on getting that horse into his stall before he goes down.''

Luke scowled at his brother, injecting as much sarcasm as he could into his voice. ''Could this day possibly get any better?''

Getting one of the young, untrained horses in was more difficult than Luke had imagined. By the time he'd finally dragged the young mare into the barn, his toes had been tromped a dozen times. Shoving the beast into her stall, he glanced around.

He saw Matt wrestle the other young horse into a stall and then head out for the next horse, but where was Gaby? Anger pulled at him. If she thought she could sit around while they did her work, she could think again.

A soft cooing filled the silence. Following its source to the abused horse's stall, he peered in.

Gaby crouched next to the wary horse who looked as if he'd jump up and bolt if he had the energy. But Gaby spoke easily to him in a soft, gentle voice while she scooped water out of a bucket and offered it to him in her cupped hands.

As the horse cautiously drank the proffered water, Luke noticed the shaking of Gaby's hands and her slumping shoulders. Even her legs shook as she squatted beside the animal. Good Lord, she was as weary as the damned beast. Didn't she know there was an easier way?

''Why don't you just stick the bucket under his nose and let him have his fill?''

Gaby's back stiffened at his words, but she didn't bother to acknowledge him by turning around. ''He won't let me get the bucket anywhere near his head, and he's too tired to stand to drink. So for now, this will have to do.''

He looked at the bucket of water, at her small hands and at the size of the horse lying on the ground. She'd be there all night. "Fine. Have it your way. I'll bring the last horse in."

Now she turned to face him. "No, wait. I'll bring Dreamer in."

Luke pointed to the young horse he'd all but dragged in. "If I got that delinquent in here, I can handle the next one."

Gaby took a long breath as if garnering her strength and curbing her temper all at once. "Look, Mr. Anderson, I'm not trying to be rude or question your capabilities. Dreamer doesn't like men. Please, let me get her."

The mare didn't like men. Which told Luke that somewhere in the mare's history, a man had brutalized her. As someone had brutalized the horse Gaby now knelt beside. Was Miss Richards's mission to save lost equine souls?

Before the charitable thought could go any further, Luke squelched it. His priority was getting this woman on her way. If she wanted to unload the last horse, fine with him. "I'll unload the feed out of the back, then, and unhook the trailer. Then you can be on your way."

Grabbing the bucket, Gaby pushed herself up. It took much more effort than it should have, and she swayed when she gained her feet.

Unless Luke missed his guess, the girl was close to collapse. Apprehension washed over him as he swung the stall door open for her. He didn't want her to be weak or vulnerable or someone who might offer succour to a wounded beast. He needed her to be at her contemptible best, or all hell would break loose.

As Gaby headed out to get her precious man-eating horse, the sound of approaching hooves broke into Luke's thoughts.

Coming through the doors, Matt led a horse bigger than a mountain into the barn. "Luke, Shanna's hollering from the house. She needs me to hold the baby while she cooks dinner.''

Frustration curled in Luke's belly. He hadn't wanted Gaby Richards here in the first place. Now Matt wanted to leave him alone to take care of her. And if Matt's reason had been anything other than little Sarah, Luke would have made his objection painfully clear. But as it was, he had little choice other than to send Matt on his way. But he didn't try to hide his irritation. "So go hold her. I'll get your boarder settled in."

Despite Luke's assurance, Matt hesitated, his brows drawn down in worry. Clearly, he didn't trust Luke alone with Gaby.

Well, hell. Where was Matt's faith? Terrorizing women barely strong enough to stand went against even *his* tarnished standards. "Go take care of your baby, Matt. I promise not to eat Little Red Riding Hood."

Apparently satisfied with his promise, Matt handed Luke the giant horse's lead rope. "Tuck Killer here into his stall. And be nice to Gaby," he added as he turned to leave.

"Don't press your luck," Luke mumbled, watching his brother's retreating back.

Well, if he wanted Gaby Richards off the ranch, he would have to do it himself. Grabbing a wheelbarrow, he headed out to unload the feed from the back of her truck.

As he tossed sacks of grain down, Gaby unloaded the last horse, a lovely mare, black as midnight with an anxious disposition. Her head swinging nervously from side to side, the horse crowded Gaby with every step.

A fine thread of anger pulled at Luke that someone would abuse such an animal. But sadly, he knew such things went on all the time. And the mare wasn't his concern. She was Miss Richards's concern.

Forcing his attention back to his work, Luke finished

unloading the feed into the wheelbarrow. Then he parked her trailer alongside Seven Peaks's three big rigs and unhooked her truck. Driving back to the barn, he parked the pickup and retrieved the full wheelbarrow. With everything unloaded, he could send Little Red Riding Hood down the road.

Pushing the wheelbarrow into the barn, he stopped momentarily to let his eyes adjust to the darker interior.

Twenty feet ahead of him, Gaby stood in an open stall, soothing the timid mare. The soft sound of her calming patter whispered through the barn. With a gentle, sure touch, Gaby stroked the horse's silky neck, trying to get her to relax.

Heat surged through Luke, his hands tightening on the wheelbarrow's wooden handles. Like a voyeur, he stood motionless and watched.

The words were too soft to hear. But he could feel them. Oh, yeah, he could feel them. All the way down to his toes. And watching her hands…he didn't even want to *think* about what that was doing to him. But relaxation *didn't* cover it. Damn.

With desperate determination, he opened his hands and let the wheelbarrow drop to the ground with a definitive thud. "Are you going to stay in there all night, or are you going to feed these animals so Matt doesn't have to leave his baby again tonight?"

Gaby jumped at the noise and whirled to face him. Too much motion, too fast. The color drained from her face.

Cursing silently, Luke moved immediately, barely grabbing Gaby before she crumpled to the ground. Swinging her into his arms, he was shocked at her lightness and the way her bones dug sharply into his fingers.

Kicking the stall door shut behind him, Luke tried to ignore the chill that swept up his spine. How had he missed her depleted state before? Having spent the past five years in one war zone after another, recognizing the signs of starvation and extreme physical depletion had become second nature to him.

Gaby had most of them. Good Lord, she didn't have any more meat on her than her raggedy horse. Carrying her to a hay bale, he set her down and pushed her head between her knees.

In contrast to the sharpness of her ribs, her hair was soft against his fingers. A desire to stroke the silky strands to life rushed through him.

Realizing the bent of his thoughts, he snatched his hand back. "Breathe deep."

With effort, Gaby struggled to regulate her breathing.

Way down in Luke's gut, fear began to spread its malignant tendrils. This was bad. This was very bad. With his fingertips still itching with the need to plunge deeply into the depths of her golden hair, he needed her gone.

But he wasn't going to get it. Not tonight.

Spinning on his heels, he strode to the barn door. Gulping in deep breaths of the cool mountain air, he narrowed his eyes on the setting sun. Dusk had settled on the valley. Dark would fall soon. And Gaby Richards was in no shape to drive anywhere. She would have to stay.

He turned and walked back to her. She was sitting up now, her breathing more even and her color improved, though it wouldn't win any awards. Taking a long breath, he gave her the news that wasn't going to make her any happier than it did him. "Gaby, you can't drive home tonight. Your ranch is forty minutes away by road. You'd be asleep at the wheel before you were halfway there. You're going to have to stay."

Gaby wondered if the man had lost his mind. He'd been treating her as if she were the harbinger of pestilence. Did he really think she would stay?

Not in this lifetime.

Besides, she needed to make it to her new home tonight. If she didn't wake up tomorrow morning in a place where she could soak peace into her like a thirsty horse sucks up water, she wasn't going to make it.

She *needed* her mountain. And she couldn't wait one more day for it.

Pushing herself up from the hay bale, she whistled for the dogs and headed out of the barn. "Don't worry, I'll stay awake long enough to get there."

The dogs fell in beside her, and she walked determinedly to the truck, trying to ignore the sound of Luke's footsteps following. She reached for the truck's door and pulled it open.

In the next instant Luke shoved the door shut. Before she could pull in a breath to protest, he'd reached inside the open window.

He was taking her keys! Gaby lunged in the window after him and struggled to snatch the keys from his hand. As they pulled themselves from the window, her sunglasses got caught in the fray. She reached desperately for the flying frames.

And missed.

Silently she prayed it would be too dark for Luke to see the black eye.

But it wasn't. The second he caught sight of the bruised and swollen flesh, he came to an abrupt standstill, her keys clasped tightly in his grip. "Who hit you?"

Ignoring his intense look, she scooped the sunglasses off the ground and put them back on. "Give me my keys." Boldly she held out her hand.

He narrowed his eyes on her. "You're right. It's none

of my business. The keys, on the other hand, *are* my business, and I have no intention of returning them. On top of that, I want your spare set, too.'' He held his empty hand out as boldly as she.

She had four extra sets of keys. She could give him one and still drive away. But on sheer principle, she refused to hand even one of them over. This man had no power over her, and she had no intention of giving him any. She raised her chin. ''I don't have an extra set.''

''Bull. All women carry a spare set of keys. I think it's Girl Scout indoctrination or something.''

''Well, that would explain it. I was never a Girl Scout.''

Quick as lightning, he reached into the truck's cab and grabbed her purse. He dangled it in front of him. ''Maybe not. But you do carry a spare. Do you want to get them for me, or shall I do it?''

Gaby snatched her purse. ''You can't make me stay here against my will, Mr. Anderson. It's not legal. I'll call the sheriff.''

Luke's upper body disappeared inside the truck window again. This time she heard him punching out a number on her car phone. With the phone set on speakers, it was easy to hear the tone of each number. Grabbing the bottom of his denim shirt, she gave it a yank.

It had no effect until he'd punched in the last number, then he allowed her to haul him out of the window. Once his head cleared the truck, he turned to her. ''Trying to get me out of my clothes? Follow me into the house. I'll be more than happy to take them off for you.''

Gaby jerked her hands away at the crude suggestion and took a quick step back. The arrogant, insufferable—

Someone picked up the phone on the other end of the line. ''County Sheriff's Office.''

He'd called the sheriff's office! Add *audacious* to the

list. But he'd hoisted himself on his own petard this time. She stood silently, patiently, and waited for the right moment to cut him off at the knees. She knew the man whose voice crackled over her phone. Last year, during her search and rescue mission, she'd stayed with him and his family.

"Hi, Sheriff." Luke raised his voice so it would carry to the phone. "This is Luke Anderson. I have a young lady here who is too tired to drive. I took her keys away from her, but she's threatening to call you. Do you want to talk to her?"

Cute, thought Gaby. But she had a few tricks up her sleeve, too. "Tom? Is that you? This is Gaby Richards."

"Gaby, good to hear you. Luke told me you bought the old homestead. Congratulations. But what are you doing at Seven Peaks?"

"My horses are staying here, but I'm trying to leave."

"How tired are you?"

"Not that tired."

There was an extended pause and then Tom cleared his throat. "Luke?"

She gasped at the insult. He wasn't going to take her word for it? "Tom!"

"I'm sorry, Gaby. But I know you, and you drive yourself until you drop. You're a lousy judge of when you've had enough."

Panic clawed at her belly, and frustration brought the sting of tears to her eyes. She blinked quickly to keep them at bay.

Damn men and their macho games.

Well, let them play. She took a deep breath to calm her shaky nerves. She wasn't staying here tonight. Tomorrow morning, when the sun's first rays hit that red mountain, she would be there to see it. Even if she had to walk to get there.

"She's not gonna make it, Tom. She's shaking with exhaustion now."

Gaby sent Luke a scathing glance. She was shaking with anger, not exhaustion.

He ignored her pointed look. "Do you want to scrape her off the side of a tree? Because I don't."

Tom's voice crackled over the phone line. "Keep her keys. Sorry, Gaby. You can call tomorrow. I'll reserve fifteen minutes for your tirade on redneck, unjust, small-town sheriffs."

She was about to tell him what he could do with his fifteen minutes when Luke broke in. "She won't give me her spares."

A resigned sigh came over the line. "Gaby, you might as well hand them over. If you don't, he'll just take them. And if you try putting him on his back to avoid it, he'll put you on yours. Is that what you want?"

Tom knew the mere thought would send her running. She cursed him for using that knowledge against her. The idea of Luke looming over her while she lay helpless beneath him was more than she could stand. Angrily, she jerked her purse's zipper open, located a spare set of keys and slapped them into Luke's offending palm.

Then she jerked the truck's door open, snapped a curt good-night to Tom and disconnected the call. Slamming the door shut, she gave a quick hand sign to the dogs and stamped toward the barn, her canine cadre at her heels.

"Where are you going?" Luke hollered after her.

She didn't owe him any explanations. Ignoring him, Gaby continued on to the barn.

Luke's voice followed after her. "Shanna will have dinner ready in a bit. I want you to come in and eat."

She stopped in her tracks and turned to face him. If she just ignored him, he'd probably drag her in by her hair.

"Thank you, no. With a new baby to care for, I think Shanna has her hands full. And as you said, I'm tired. I'll just grab a couple of horse coolers for blankets and curl up on some hay bales."

He stared at her, assessing if she was being straight with him.

She stood absolutely still. Sweat broke out on her palms, but she resisted the urge to wipe them on her jeans. She was glad she'd replaced her sunglasses, because she had to convince him she meant exactly what she'd said. That she was going into that barn and going to sleep.

Finally he gave his head one curt, solitary nod. "You can have your keys tomorrow morning and be on your way."

She returned his blunt nod. Turning, she headed back toward the barn, the dogs trotting at her heels. She doused the lights and waited for complete darkness to fall.

Chapter Three

Half an hour later Gaby moved to the barn door and peered out. Frustration at Luke's high-handedness had kept her awake, but the adrenaline that emotion required exacted its own toll. Now sleep pulled at her like an intoxicating elixir. If she was going to leave, it had to be now.

The darkness of the night reassured her. She ought to be able to make it to her truck undetected. She glanced at the house. The lights were on, and the curtains were open. The living room was empty. She hoped they were all eating dinner.

Quietly, she took a set of keys from her purse and snapped her fingers to gain the dogs' attention. A quick hand signal brought them to her feet. Another signal and they followed quietly at her heels. Her heart pounding in her ears, she stuck to the shadows as she made her way cautiously to her truck.

When her hand closed over the truck's door handle, she

sighed softly with relief. So far, so good. Silently, she opened the door and signaled the dogs in. She cringed at the sound they made as they vaulted, one after the other, into the truck. But a quick glance at the house assured her she was still in the clear.

She crawled in after them and pulled the door closed gently behind her. She smiled and thanked Luke for pointing the truck in the right direction. Releasing the brake, she slipped the truck into neutral and waited to see if it would coast. She held her breath. Slowly, the truck rolled forward.

It didn't roll as far as she would have liked, but her choices were limited. She could start the thing and see if Luke came out to chase after her, or she could sit here not a hundred yards from the house and that man all night.

Maybe in her next lifetime.

Turning the key, she winced as the engine purred to life, but she saw no indication of discovery in the rearview mirror. She wouldn't have to argue with Luke again, after all. Slipping the truck into gear, she headed home.

Bumping down the road, she thought about her new home. She'd discovered it last year while working a difficult search and rescue mission here. Or, more specifically, she'd discovered the magnificent red mountain the small ranch nestled beneath. During the search, she'd spent her evenings in the shadows of that glorious mountain. And in the same way as the sun radiated warmth and light, that rock face had dispensed tranquillity to her during those agonizing days.

Now the mere thought of that butte brought peace, easing both mental and physical pain. She drew a slow, deep, calming breath and savored the languor stealing through her. Another half hour and she'd be there.

And not a moment too soon. Even the pain was losing

its power to keep her awake. And how she hurt. Swollen and aching, her eye throbbed in time to her heartbeat, and her ribs ached with every shallow breath she took. She'd forgotten how painful bruised flesh and broken bones could be.

The acrid taste of fear filled her mouth. She'd forgotten a lot of things since leaving her father's house thirteen years ago.

But her brother-in-law had been happy to remind her.

The heat of shame flushed her cheeks. She'd been so confident she would carry the day when she'd confronted Bill Clark…but she hadn't. Ten years in a dojo, learning the finer art of karate and self-defense, had all been for naught.

Bill had stripped her false courage and dignity with a single blow. In the space of a heartbeat, her mind had flown behind the walls she'd set up as a young child to endure her father's wrath.

And that was how the police had found her. Curled up like a coward on the barroom floor while Bill Clark took his fury out on her with an entire room of uncaring witnesses looking on.

Stop it! A spark of anger jolted her. She *would not* surrender the self-respect she had spent the last thirteen years working so hard for. She might have cowered under her brother-in-law's onslaught, but she'd won.

He was behind bars now, and when his trial came up, she'd go back and make sure he stayed there. Hell would freeze over before he got another chance to enchant a woman with his false smiles and empty charm. Her sister would be the last woman to fall into his deadly clutches.

Another wave of exhaustion hit her. An exhaustion that went deeper than fatigue, deeper than the need to rest. It was a weariness that gnawed at her soul and demanded not a place to sleep, but a place to heal.

And that place was waiting for her. She just had to stay awake long enough to get there. Forcing her melancholy thoughts away, she tried to remember what her new house looked like.

When she'd decided to start her new life here, she'd simply called a Realtor and had him handle the sale for her, so she hadn't seen the place in a year. Her memory of the two-story house was vague. But soon she'd know all the details.

She smiled at the thought of choosing the colors she wanted to paint the walls and the kind of furniture she would put in it. She'd never owned a home before. Never had a place she called home. Since she'd escaped her parents' house thirteen years ago, she had lived in a small, one-room apartment above the barn where she worked.

It had been convenient, inexpensive and safe. But home? She didn't think so. And *no one* would have called the house she grew up in a home.

This would be a home, though. She would make it one. For herself, her horses and her dogs. A tingle of antici-pation trickled through her. For the past ten years she'd saved every penny she'd made training and selling young horses. But all that scrimping, all that hard work had al-lowed her to buy her place. And now everything was ready at her new home. She'd had the electricity and the phone turned on two days ago. All she had left to do was move in.

Finally, like a beacon beckoning the lost, the tall yard light that lit the common area of her ranch came into view. Approaching her drive, she felt her heart pick up speed. Her own drive! Adrenaline bubbled through her veins as she came to a stop and shifted into Park. The dogs roused themselves from slumber. Scratching Susie's neck, she looked anxiously at her new home.

The light threw the three ranch buildings and surrounding terrain into shadowy relief. She was so excited, she didn't know which to look at first. She decided to save the house for last.

She pointed to the old barn. "Look, guys, that's the ponies' new house."

It was a typical old barn. Big and red with large double doors for an entrance. A small square hayloft door hung open above the lower doors. The whole thing needed a fresh coat of paint. Badly. But it looked strong and structurally sound.

A medium-size corral sat off to the side. At a quick glance the corral's fence didn't look as though it was missing any boards, but many of them were down. It would take a day or two with hammer and nails to make it horseworthy.

A slight turn of her head brought the large metal pole building into view. It was unremarkable in its appearance. Tan, she thought, but with only the farm light to go by, she might be wrong. It was bigger than the barn, longer and wider, but not as tall. And it had none of the older building's charm. But it would provide her with an indoor riding arena for the snowy, colder months of the year. She smiled with anticipation. Next year she would put gardens around it to soften its straight, utilitarian lines.

Now for the house. Her fingers flexed nervously in the German shepherd's coat. She closed her eyes, took a deep breath, and held it. She turned her head a quarter turn and slowly opened her eyes.

Her breath came out in a soft rush. Beautiful.

Its graceful old lines stood proudly against the night sky. A covered porch ran along the entire front of the house, its beautifully turned pillars welcoming all those who stepped beneath its canopy. Intricately cut gingerbread decorated eave and edge alike.

Perfect.

Tears stung her eyes, and this time she let them fall. She was home. It was an odd realization for someone who had never known a home before. But she knew it as surely as she knew her own name. Of all the places in the universe, *this* was where she belonged.

With hands that shook in excitement, she switched on the truck's map light and dug in her purse for the key the Realtor had mailed her. "Okay, gang, we're here."

Brushing the tears from her cheeks, she climbed from the truck. Holding the door wide, she waited anxiously for the dogs to get out. "Come on, Hank. We're going to sleep in a real house tonight!"

Her heart pounded and excitement expanded in her chest. She wanted to shout with it, but she didn't. Something about the quietness of the night kept her from disturbing the peacefulness. She quickly made the porch, grabbed the doorknob in one hand, and fit key to lock.

Her home. Her home. The words repeated themselves over and over in her mind. She was home. Closing her eyes, she turned the knob, thrust open the door and took one giant step inside.

The smell almost knocked her over. Her eyes flew open, and she gagged on her next breath. Pinching her nose closed, she felt around for the light switch. Finding it, she flipped it on. Bright light flooded the room.

She jumped at the picture of destruction around her. Broken furniture, discarded possessions and garbage littered the floor. The walls were covered in soot and dirt and other substances she didn't want to speculate on. The place was filthy. The last tenant's housekeeping habits went way beyond slovenly. And he'd left it all for her to clean up.

Her stomach turned again, and she fought the urge to throw up. She spun on her heels and ran from the house. Leaning against the porch railing, she pulled in long, deep breaths of air, but they didn't help the pain closing in on her chest.

Tears streamed down her cheeks, but they were no longer tears of joy. Clenching her fists, she crossed her arms over her chest and squeezed with all her might. This wasn't happening. This couldn't be happening.

A sob escaped her lips, and her next breath caught on the constriction in her throat. Lowering her hands to the railings, she tried desperately to calm her raging emotions. She had faced worse things in her life. She could deal with this mess. And somehow she would.

Her hands gripped the railing until the sharp edges bit painfully into her fingers. Finally she drew in a ragged breath. And another and then another. The blood began to slow in her veins. Raising her head, she turned to face the end of the porch. And there it was.

In the weak light of the half-moon, she could see the massive bulk of the red mountain in the distance. Even in the dark it called to her. She walked slowly to the end of the porch, her eyes never leaving its reassuring mass. *That* was why she had come. The house, the barn and the pole building had only been icing on the cake. If this piece of land had boasted only a miserly cave, she would still have come.

With her world on an even axis again, she took a deep breath and held it. Walking back to the door, she reached inside, flipped off the light and closed the door.

"Come on, gang. We're camping out."

Without a backward glance, she walked to her truck and

pulled out her sleeping bag. Then she fixed her eyes on her mountain and hiked up the small grassy knoll just beyond her house. Once on top, she laid the sleeping bag down, removed her socks and shoes, stuck her socks in the bottom of the sleeping bag so they'd be warm in the morning and crawled in. Gathering the dogs around her, she sought the peaceful arms of sleep.

Luke watched the first rays of dawn tinge the sky and tried not to dwell on why he was in a truck heading east instead of on a horse heading west. The answer would only burn his butt and he was already madder than a freshly branded calf.

But he needed to make sure Gaby hadn't wrapped her truck around a tree on the way home last night. Once he knew that, he was out of there. In fact, he would consider himself damned lucky if he never set eyes on her again. Because last night, he'd seen her every time he closed his eyes.

The image of her curvy bottom as she tied the kerchief on her dog had refused to leave his mind. Thinking of the silken feel of her hair teased him until the need to reach out and touch had almost undone him. And the thought of her poor bruised eye had made him want to kiss the pain away.

A much more dangerous thought than the previous two.

In short, it had been a very long night. But he might be lucky. So far he'd come across no wreckage, and the old homestead was around the next bend. In five more minutes he'd be turned around and headed for the high country.

There was enough light for him to see Gaby's truck pulled safely in the drive as he approached. Well, good for her. She'd made it. Now he could escape, body and soul intact. Whipping into the drive, he slammed the truck into

Reverse and glanced over his shoulder to back up. Then he saw her.

What the hell was she doing up there on the knoll? She should have slept till noon. But there she was, watching the sunrise.

She'd had her back to him when he first saw her, but now she turned in his direction. No doubt she wondered who'd pulled into her drive so early in the morning.

A wicked smile touched his lips. Once she figured it out, he would bet she'd hightail it into her house. Which was exactly where she should be. Sleeping. His smile got wider.

He shifted into Park, turned the engine off, grabbed his hat and stepped out of the truck. He pulled the brim of his hat low and walked toward the knoll. Yep, she was moving now. But what the hell was she doing?

Crawling on her knees, she frantically skimmed the grass with her hands. She seemed to be looking for something, and it didn't take her long to find it. Straightening, she slid the sunglasses on.

Oh, yeah, she needed those. There was barely enough light to see by.

She was pulling her last shoe on as he reached the base of the small hill. He was close enough now that he could make out more detail. Was she sitting on a sleeping bag?

She pushed up from the ground and hurtled his way, her stride long and definitely angry. "I want you off my property!" She pointed to his truck with a hand that shook with anger.

Ignoring the gesture and the enticing tangle of her hair, he walked by her to what had caught his eye earlier. He lifted the edge with the toe of his boot. Yep, a sleeping bag. Crouching down, he ran a hand inside it. Warmth enveloped his hand.

The knowledge that the heat had come from her body sent another type of heat straight to his groin. He gritted his teeth against the wave of desire and stuck his hand farther into the bag. Her socks were still tucked in the bottom of it.

She'd slept out here!

Turning back to her, he found her standing tall with her shoulders drawn back for battle and her hair falling in wild disarray around her shoulders.

His blood pounded heavily in his veins, and he tried desperately to ignore the incredible picture she made standing against dawn's first rays. But it was damned hard. With his jeans getting tighter by the second and his hand preheated with her warmth, he ached to grab hold of her and find out if he could turn her anger into heart-stopping passion.

But the snarl on her lips stopped him.

He glanced back at the sleeping bag. What the hell was going on?

"Who put a bee in your bonnet? And why did you sleep out here last night? Feeling sorry for the local bears? Felt they should have a late-night snack?"

"You know exactly why I slept out here last night. I slept out here because not even a self-respecting *pig* would sleep in that house. I'm going to have to shovel it out to decide if it's salvageable, or if I should just burn it to the ground. Now get off my ranch."

Was that what she was angry about? The fact that the inside of the house hadn't been cleaned? Hell, with five days' notice during this busy time of year, she ought to be glad she got the place at all. But then, it was important to remember what kind of woman she was. "What's wrong? A little dirt more than your lily-white hands can handle?"

"A little dirt? With the filth in that house, my guess is

whoever lived there last had no concept of what work was, hard or otherwise. Did he keep livestock in there?''

Luke could tell she held on to her control by the barest of threads. Just another example of how spoiled she was. If a few cobwebs and a little dust created such furor, he hated to think what real grunge would produce.

Still, maybe answering her question would calm her down. ''No, he didn't have livestock. He was a salvager. Why?''

A relieved breath sighed through her lips. ''Thank God. Maybe the barn isn't the pit the house is.''

''Pit?'' Luke headed toward the house. The man he had hired to check out the furnace and plumbing had said no woman in her right mind would live in a house in that condition. At the time he'd dismissed it as dramatics. Now he wanted to check it out.

Ignoring Gaby's protests, he strode down to the house and took the porch in one leap. With a quick turn of the doorknob, he pushed his way in.

He retreated just as quickly, slamming the door shut behind him. Stepping back onto the porch, he took a deep, cleansing breath. ''What is that smell?''

''Feel free to investigate and let me know,'' Gaby said from right behind him. ''It was more than I could handle last night. Am I supposed to believe you didn't know?''

The insinuation that he would do something so unconscionable triggered his own temper. ''I didn't.''

Swearing softly, he stepped back into the house. The smell was overwhelming. His gut twisted in anger as he stepped carefully around the abandoned refuse.

Damn. This ranch had belonged to him. Its condition was his responsibility. But after the end of his marriage five years ago, he hadn't come near the place. He had rented it out to the first party who'd come along and then washed his hands of it.

Shame on him.

Trying not to breathe any more than necessary, and gagging on what air he did inhale, he climbed the stairs, his anger growing with every step. This had once been a beautiful home. Now he understood Gaby's remark about burning it down.

The place had been thoroughly trashed. The stair railing had missing spindles. Huge gouges marked walls and floors alike. And there were bags of garbage and overflowing trash cans everywhere, as if the previous tenant had never taken the trash out in the five years he'd lived there.

The two upstairs bedrooms were as abused and debris-ridden as the downstairs rooms. Climbing over the trash, he opened the window of the front bedroom and stuck his head out. He gulped in the fresh, sweet air. A movement below caught his eye. Gaby was stepping off the porch and heading toward the barn.

"Don't go anywhere," he hollered down. "I want to talk to you. Stay there."

Gaby turned back toward him, her lips compressed into a narrow line. Rocking back on her heels, she placed her hands on her hips. "Mr. Anderson, as bad as my reflection looked the last time I peered into a mirror, I didn't notice four legs, a lolling tongue and a tail. If you think you can speak to me as if I were a recalcitrant pup, think again." With a sharp whistle, she called her own dogs to heel, signaled them up into the pickup bed, and then went on her way to the barn.

Oh Lord, he thought, the barn. A salvager might very well use a barn to store recovered items until they could be moved elsewhere. And if his house looked like this, Luke didn't want to think what the barn might look like.

Tripping over the trash, he left the house, trying to head Gaby off before she reached the barn.

The clean air cleared his lungs, but it did little to loosen the knot in his stomach. He wasn't going to get to the high country today where the chilly, brisk air would cool his body, and hours of hard physical labor would keep his mind from wandering to images best left untouched. He was going to have to stay and clean this damned mess up...right beside the person creating those heated images.

Unfortunately Gaby beat him to the barn. She was standing outside the open double doors, staring inside. He stepped up behind her. "I asked you to stay—" Catching sight of the interior of the barn, he stopped abruptly.

Damn. It was completely packed. From floor to ceiling, from wall to wall, from front door to back, every square inch was filled with something. Old tractors, old furniture, old machinery, and the inevitable bags of trash were stacked and piled and crushed, one on top of the other.

Swearing succinctly, he turned to Gaby, ready to face her anger. If he had paid as much money for a place as she had for this one, and he had arrived to find it in such a state, he'd be out for blood. What he found, though, was a single tear falling from beneath her sunglasses. She tried to hide it, spinning away from him, but she wasn't quick enough. He had seen. And worse, he knew it was his fault.

He grabbed for her shoulder as she walked away. "Gaby, wait a minute."

When she shrugged off his touch and sped up, he took one giant step and grabbed again. "Gaby, come here."

The next thing he knew, he was staring at the sky, and Gaby Richards had one of her knees planted on his chest and the other pinning one of his hands. She held his other hand in a surprisingly strong grip next to his head while her free hand was coiled into an impressively threatening fist right next to her ear. She was cocked for one hell of a wallop.

Would she really throw that punch? If he could see her eyes, he'd know. "Would you kindly take off those damned glasses. I already know about the black eye, and now that your makeup has worn off, the swollen jaw and split lip, as well." And he didn't like it one damn bit. Because it made her vulnerable. And he didn't want her vulnerable.

She leaned forward, digging her bony little knee into his chest. "Mr. Anderson, I'm not taking off my glasses. I'm not going to stay when you tell me to stay, and I sure as hell am not going to come when you tell me to come!"

That was it. His body leaped at the erotic challenge. The pain from her knee faded into obscurity. Her heat suffused him and the light trails her hair made against his throat and chest felt like silken whips against his naked skin. With her knees spread wide to keep him pinned, and her hair falling like an intimate curtain around them, images of naked, sweaty skin and heavy breathing filled his head.

Two seconds later, *Gaby* stared at the sky with Luke stretched out on top of her. He was playing with fire and he knew it, but like a moth drawn to the flame, he couldn't stop himself. Gently securing her hands over her head with one of his, he slowly, deliberately removed her sunglasses.

The fear he saw stopped him cold.

She expected a pounding. He could see it in her rich amber eyes. He glanced at her battered face. Someone had beaten her badly recently, but the expression in her eyes was older than that. More resigned than that. This wasn't her first black eye.

And she clearly expected him to deliver her next one.

In one quick move, he released her hands, rolled off her to his feet and hoped she didn't come up after him swinging. The thought of sporting his own black eye didn't appeal, but he could hardly defend himself when doing so would probably get Gaby hurt.

And that would only add to the resignation in her eyes. He'd be damned if he'd do that.

Holding his arms slightly away from his sides, palms forward—the least threatening position he could assume— he backed up a few steps, giving Gaby space.

But the trepidation in her eyes didn't change much. Her muscles remained tense, coiled for flight, and the desperation to flee shone brightly in her eyes. But she didn't move. She didn't even blink. It was as if she feared movement would precipitate an attack.

Anger tightened his fists. No woman should have that look in her eye for any reason. And he would love to get his hands on the guy who'd put it in Gaby's.

His knuckles itched to feel the crunch of bone as he taught the bastard that sometimes...sometimes victims had champions who would fight for them. Champions who were stronger and meaner and much more brutal than any bully could ever hope to be.

But those thoughts certainly wouldn't calm Gaby. He loosened his fists and opened his hands once again to hang noncombatively at his sides. Stepping back, he gave her more room.

''Get off the ground, Gaby, and let's talk about this mess.'' He waved a hand at the barn behind her.

Gaby's wary gaze remained pinned on him as she rolled to one side to get up—until she winced.

Guilt surged through him. Had he hurt her? His first reaction was to jump forward and help her up, but gut instinct stopped him. He didn't want her to mistake his help as an attack, so he stood quietly and let her pick herself up.

As she straightened, a stray breeze lifted the tail of her blouse, exposing the top of her belted jeans and the naked flesh of her waist and lower rib cage.

A giant bruise surrounded what he could see of her right side and disappeared beneath her shirt. A cold chill washed over Luke. No, he hadn't done that. Broken ribs had no doubt caused her pain. But even more disturbing than her injury was the pronounced way her ribs stuck out from her skin.

Grabbing the tail of her shirt and jerking it down, Gaby faced him with amber fire crackling in her eyes. She had apparently recovered her bravado. Good for her.

But then, he shouldn't be completely surprised. Thirty seconds ago she'd flipped him with very little effort. An amazing feat considering her obviously depleted state. He pointed to the ground where she'd tossed him only moments before. "Do you want to tell me where you learned to flip a man like that?"

She backed up a step and looked at him warily as if trying to decide if he was angry or not.

He didn't try to reassure her. Working with refugees who had been brutalized, he'd learned it was best to let people figure out for themselves who was safe and who was not. Words only reassured the uninitiated, and he suspected Gaby had left that rank long ago.

She watched him as carefully as a cornered rabbit watched a fox. "In a sweaty little dojo in downtown Chicago."

Ah, karate. That would explain it. "Got a belt?"

Her chin tipped up the barest of notches, and her gaze took on a hint of challenge. "Black."

He raised his brows at that. He was glad she hadn't thrown that punch. "Congratulations. Now let's move on to more pressing matters. Like why you're not eating. You have something against the four major food groups?''

Confusion widened her eyes. "No. I like to eat."

"Then why aren't you doing it?"

"I am."

"Is that so? When was your last meal?"

The confusion in Gaby's eyes turned to irritation. "Listen, I don't think I have to answer that question. I see neither a stethoscope hanging around your neck nor a medical degree tacked to the gun rack in the back of your pickup.''

A slight smile turned the corners of his mouth, but he didn't let the humor distract him. "You won't find a medical bag stuck under the seat of my truck, either. But after spending five years in every hot spot you can imagine moving orphans and refugees, I guarantee I'm qualified to spot starvation. And, lady, you're working on it. Now answer me.''

Annoyance flashed again in Gaby's expression, and she drew herself up to full height. But then she stopped, and he could see the realization in her eyes. "I don't remember. I think I ate something before I headed out here, but I'm not sure.''

When he only waited, she explained further. "Look, the last three weeks have been…bad. Sleeping and eating just weren't at the top of the list.''

He let his gaze rake her from head to toe. "You don't get this close to starvation in three weeks, Gaby.''

Expelling a short breath, she waved an impatient hand. "Well, the year before the last three weeks wasn't a picnic, either. But I hardly think I'm in imminent danger of starvation, Mr. Anderson, despite your expertise in the area.''

Luke placed a hand on his hip. "Is that right? Well, pay

attention, Miss Richards. You're about to get your first lesson in Nutrition 101."

He unbuttoned his denim shirt, held one side open and pointed to his ribs. "Your ribcage is an excellent indicator of how much meat you're carrying around. Meat brokers use it to grade livestock. Volunteers use it to gauge degrees of starvation in refugee camps."

Again he pointed to his ribs. "I don't carry a lot of fat around with me. You can see my ribs. But you'll notice they don't stand out. There is a healthy covering of skin and muscle over them. The muscle is round and dense. When you touch it, it has a giving quality to it."

He pointed to her midsection. "If you look at your ribs, you'll find they appear to be thrusting out of the skin. And when you press on them, there is no give from protecting muscle. Your body's too busy feeding important organs, like your heart and lungs, to worry about feeding your muscles."

Gaby looked at him as if she didn't believe a word he said. She obviously didn't get it. "You need a keeper. Go get your purse. I'm going to feed you, take you in for an X-ray, swing by the store for groceries, and then we're coming back here for one hell of a bonfire."

She raised her hands in protest.

Well, hell. Some people just didn't take instructions well. Apparently Gaby Richards fell into that category. He pointed to his shoulder. "You can walk, or I can sling you over my shoulder and you can ride. Your choice."

Chapter Four

Standing in front of her living room window, Gaby drew shallow breaths of fetid air and watched Luke climb into his truck. No way was she spending the night in this house. It still stank. But she had to stay inside long enough to convince Luke she was. He'd warned her—ordered her, actually—not to sleep outside because of the bears. If he came back and found her in the back bed of her truck, there would be hell to pay.

She glanced at her watch. As a precautionary measure, she'd give him ten minutes before she headed out. If he hadn't come back by then, he probably wouldn't be back at all. At least she hoped he wouldn't be back.

Despite his good qualities.

And in all fairness, she had to admit he had a few. Besides being a man of honor, something he'd proven by accepting his responsibility to help clean up the ranch, she'd discovered he was a caregiver, as well. She'd taken enough psychology classes while grappling with her own inner demons to recognize the signs. And Luke Anderson had them all.

He'd taken care of her. All day long. In fact, he'd escorted her from place to place as if his very honor were at stake. First he'd taken her to breakfast, then they'd gone to the doctor's to have her broken ribs taped. Next they'd picked up groceries at the store, and finally he'd brought her back to the ranch where he'd handled the heaviest and dirtiest of the work.

If he took care of the women he dated as well as he'd taken care of her today, she could well imagine all the single females of Hideaway, Montana, lined up to see who might catch his eye. A dry chuckle escaped her lips. Right. The man was drop-dead gorgeous. The women of Hideaway had probably lined up hoping for a date since he turned ten.

But she wouldn't be in that line. She wasn't interested in the dating game.

I love him, Gaby. Her sister's voice echoed painfully through Gaby's mind. How many times had she heard that plaintive cry, laced in disappointment and sadness after Bill had taken his anger out on her sister? A hundred? A thousand?

Love. Love had killed her sister.

She would never make the same mistake. Love was for fools.

She'd come here to her giant red mountain for peace and quiet and solitude. And that was what she intended to get.

She glanced around the room at the huge amount of work still to be done. Exhaustion swamped her. All the broken furniture, big bags of trash and other odd things apparently collected by salvagers had been carried out, but loose debris still littered the floor. Filth caked every surface. She had days of hard scrubbing ahead of her, and six horses to take care of on top of it. Peace and quiet might have to wait.

As for solitude, Luke Anderson would either be back, or he wouldn't. She'd hope for the latter and handle the former if it happened. She glanced again at her watch. Ten minutes. Long enough. She had a short night ahead of her.

She wanted to get to Seven Peaks early enough tomorrow morning to get Glock fed before the ranch woke up. She would need quiet and peace to coax the horse to her. Besides, she'd just as soon be gone before Luke wandered out to the barn tomorrow morning.

Scooping up the sleeping bag she'd hauled in to convince Luke she would stay in the house, she headed for the great outdoors. As she gulped in deep breaths of fresh, sweet air, the dogs joined her. Two minutes later she snuggled into the back of her truck, air mattress beneath her and the dogs around her.

Staring at the bright pinpricks of light overhead, she marveled that she could see the Milky Way. No city lights dimmed the beauty of the stars here. They shone clear and bright and true. Heaven on earth.

Luke drove over the dark, mountain road on his way back to Seven Peaks. He wished to God he knew which direction his last tenant had taken. He'd go after the slob and wring his scrawny little neck. For the entire day and half the night, Gaby and he had hauled trash out to a bonfire that had been so well fed it had grown into a living, breathing entity. But he had blown his chance for revenge. The man was gone.

Now there was just a woman who didn't have the sense to feed herself, trying to dig her way out of the aftermath.

She had the heart and determination of Ulysses, but she didn't have a clue as to how to take care of herself. If he hadn't been there to make her eat and rest, she would have worked herself into collapse long before noon.

Luke tightened his grip on the wheel and stomped down the tide of worry nagging at him. Unfortunately, he sadly suspected *someone* needed to worry about Gaby. And that was what bothered him, that tiny ache of tenderness that made him want to erase the shadows that lurked in her eyes. Erase the fear that flashed there every time he made a sudden move.

And his feelings scared him to death. He'd packed that part of his heart away when Tanya left him. And he had no intention of taking it out and dusting it off so it could get tromped again.

Luckily he had plenty of work to keep him busy for the next few months. He had animals to move down from the summer meadows, calves to brand, cows to vaccinate, and steers to ship to market. Then he'd get his butt on the first plane out of the country. As sick as he was of war and its pervading odor of death and hopelessness, it seemed infinitely safer than staying here.

Bent on escape, Luke strode to the barn early the next morning. His breath froze in the chilly predawn air, turning into tiny white clouds that ran before him. A sure warning that winter was on its way.

Good. If the temperatures were frigid enough, miserable enough in the high meadows, maybe he wouldn't spend all his steer-gathering time thinking about Gaby Richards. Because tucked in his warm bed last night, she was all he'd thought about.

Like a broken record his mind had turned endlessly on the same worries he'd held last night. Who would help her get her ranch cleaned up? Who would help her clean that damned barn out? Who would help her put the inside of that house back together? And those questions led to another familiar path.

Who would make sure she ate enough? Make sure she got enough rest? Make sure she didn't push herself too hard?

And that path led to pure temptation. Namely, wouldn't he just love to be the one doing all that for her? Because if he spent that much time at her ranch, sooner or later it would lead to her bed. He would make sure of it. And just thinking about that made him hot and hard and as restless as a bull in spring.

Ruthlessly he stomped on the tide of desire coursing through him. And his worries. Gaby Richards was one problem he couldn't afford to get mixed up with. The pull was too strong. The temptation too great. And before that pull got any stronger, he was hightailing it out of here.

He pulled the big barn door open, its well-oiled hinges silent and smooth. Light poured from the open door. Who on earth was in the barn at this ungodly hour of the morning? It wasn't Matt; he'd have heard his brother leave the house. And he couldn't imagine one of the cowboys being up this early. Sleep was more precious than gold during this time of year. And the sun wouldn't be up for another hour yet.

"Come on, son. Goodies." Gaby's voice floated to him over the still morning air along with the soft sigh of sifting grain.

Gaby. What the…? He strode to the stall where the sound of rustling straw gave away her location, and peered in.

Neither she nor the horse had heard him arrive. They

were so engrossed in each other a stampede wouldn't attract their attention.

Gaby leaned against the stall's far corner with a rubber feed tray propped between one hand and hip while she rhythmically sifted the grain in it with the other hand.

The poor, abused Glock stood a good three feet from her, his muzzle stretched toward her, his nostrils flared wide as he picked up the sweet scent of the molasses in the feed.

Luke jammed a fist at his waist and cocked a knee. "What the hell are you doing up?"

Gaby jumped at the sound of his voice. And so did Glock. Bunching his big, bony skeleton beneath his raggedy coat, the abused horse lunged to the far side of the stall, sending straw flying and slamming his body into the wooden wall as he tried to escape. His eyes wide and rolling, the animal huddled in the corner watching both humans anxiously.

Gaby gave Luke an impatient scowl from her corner. "I'm feeding my horse. Or I was trying to until you came in and scared the poor beast to death." She sighed in frustration. "I just spent the last half hour getting him that close. Now I'm going to have to start all over again."

Luke drew his brows together in thought, remembering the way she'd hand-fed the horse his water the day she'd arrived at Seven Peaks. Did she really believe she had to hand-feed this horse to get him to eat? "If you just put the tray on the ground, he'll feed himself. And you can go home. Which is where you belong. In bed. Resting, so your body can heal."

Gaby rolled her eyes. "I thought you had cows to get down out of the upper meadows?"

Luke raised a single brow. "If that's a subtle hint for me to mind my own business, forget it. Not until I find out why you're up at four o'clock in the morning *hand-feeding your horse.*"

She tipped her chin up and managed to look down her nose at him, despite his superior height. "You needn't say it as if it was the action of an unbalanced person. I came early because I wanted to be finished before people started wandering into the barn. And I'm hand-feeding him to teach him to trust me. He's afraid of being touched right now, but he's hungry. He'll come to me for food. Then when he realizes he's not getting hit and he relaxes a little, I can escalate the contact to a touch, and the touch to a pat, and so on.''

Luke looked at the battered horse, all but cowering in the corner, and thought about the way Gaby had cowered on the ground from him yesterday after their little tossing match. There wasn't enough trust in that stall to fill a shot glass.

And with his bones all but poking out of his skin, the horse needed that food. "Why don't you feed him first and then you can tempt him with an apple or other treat later?''

Gaby sighed, pinching the bridge of her nose as if she were warding off a headache. "You do have a thing about food, don't you? Do you really think I'd starve my horse to death?''

He looked her straight in the eye. "I have a thing about food because I've been in a lot of places lately where having enough food is the difference between life and death. And, no, I don't think you'd starve your horse to death. Not on purpose. But I'm not convinced you know how close he *is* to starvation.''

She met his gaze evenly. "You've made it clear you don't think I know anything about horses, period. But I do. I've supported myself by training them since I was fifteen. Believe it or not, I'm pretty good at it.''

Like mist in the night, dark shadows invaded the amber depths of Gaby's eyes. "As for how close he is to starvation, I know that, too. What *you* don't understand is that a treat later, after he's appeased his hunger, will never bring him to me. Glock believes, clear down to his soul, that if he gets within striking distance of me, his chances of getting beaten are damned close to 100 percent. Only real hunger, real need, will drive him to take the risk."

Luke's gut clenched at the story her words told. She was not mouthing platitudes. She understood intimately the horse's fear. The shadows in her eyes were proof of it. Standing in that corner for the past half hour waiting for the horse to come to her, instead of forcing her intentions on the horse, was proof of it. And if the shadows and her patience weren't enough to convince him, the bruises on her face were.

Her statement from moments before echoed in his head. Fifteen. She'd been supporting herself since she was fifteen.

He clenched his fists. No child ran away from home at fifteen if home life was good. But then, he'd suspected the fear he'd seen in her eyes had been old and ran deep. Now he knew.

He pictured a tiny girl with wheaten hair and eyes the color of ancient amber cowering in a corner, just as Glock cowered now. But the person hovering over that little girl wasn't a young woman with nothing to offer but comfort and a feed tray full of grain. It was an out-of-control adult with an angry look and bunched fists. An adult whose job it was to nurture and love, not terrorize and batter.

His stomach turned, and white-hot anger burned through him. He'd bet his half of the ranch that her father had been the main abuser in her house. Gaby jumped every time a man came near her. And the fear seemed as old as she.

Luke clenched his fists tighter. Wouldn't he just love to catch her father in an alley?

But if Gaby had left home at fifteen, who had given her this most recent beating? Had she run away from home only to end up with an abusive boyfriend? It was a common enough pattern. But it ate at Luke's gut to think Gaby had fallen into it.

An exhausted equine groan broke through his unsettling musings. He looked over just in time to see the quivering Glock crumple into the thick cushion of straw Gaby had liberally laid for bedding. Dried yellow straw jumped into the air and then settled gently around the heaving sides of the horse.

Damn. Would nothing go right this morning? He'd left early, determined to put as much distance between himself and Gaby as possible, only to run smack-dab into her. And now he'd frightened poor Glock into using up what little energy he had.

He turned his frustration on Gaby. "I suppose you're going to make him wait until he's rested enough to stand again so he can come get his damned breakfast."

Gaby gave him a pointed look and an irritated sigh of her own. "Don't be ridiculous. He was bolstering his nerve to come to me before you burst in and gave him a heart attack. I won't punish him for failing. I'll just have to go to *him* now."

Her irritation turned into a dark scowl. "Which is *not* my favorite way to build trust. Approaching him has a hint of threat in it, but it'll have to do. You're right about him needing the grain. And as calculated as it sounds, the more I'm able to touch him while he's too weak to fight, the quicker he'll learn I'm not going to hurt him."

She turned her attention back to Glock. Grabbing a

handful of grain, she let it sift through her fingers into the tray as she slowly straightened away from the wall.

Glock rolled his eyes in fear and struggled to rise to his feet, perceiving a threat as she slowly approached him. But exhaustion and his weakened condition made it impossible. Before Gaby made it across the stall, he settled back against the stall wall, his nostrils flaring, his sides heaving, and his eyes wide with fear of what was to come. The same look Luke had seen in Gaby's eyes the other day when he'd had her pinned on the ground.

An ache frighteningly close to Luke's heart throbbed as he watched Gaby approach the horse. She had to be exhausted damn near to the point of collapse with her depleted state and the work they'd put in yesterday. And he knew from experience, broken ribs ached and made it hard to breathe. But she was here, at four in the morning, trying to bring peace to this tortured animal.

A peace she knew damned little about herself.

A hollowness filled Luke's chest. Who would weave these fragile ties of trust for Gaby? Who would heal her ravaged soul?

And why did he want that "who" to be him?

He pushed that thought into a deep, dark closet and slammed the door on it. He'd given his home and care and love to a woman once, and she'd crushed them without a second thought or backward glance.

He wouldn't court that kind of pain again. He wouldn't give a piece of his heart or a chunk of his soul to anyone. What little he had left, he needed just to keep going.

He shifted nervously on his feet as Gaby squatted beside the horse, holding out a handful of the much-needed grain.

Turning her head at the sound of dirt crunching under his boots, Gaby glared at him. "Are you just going to stand there and watch?'' Impatience colored her words. Obviously she felt she'd do better without him.

And she was right. Absolutely right. For both of their sakes.

Chapter Five

Enjoying her lunch and the warmth of the midday sun, Gaby sat on her makeshift bed in the back of her pickup with two dogs' heads in her lap and the third by her side. The past four days had been a whirlwind of exhausting activity. She counted her blessings, though. She hadn't seen Luke Anderson since the morning he'd caught her hand-feeding Glock.

He'd saddled his horse and headed out quicker than a deadbeat with a collector after him. And she hadn't seen him since. She'd been left alone to commune each morning with her giant red mountain and fortify her spirits to attack the day.

And a frontal attack it had been. And promised to be for several weeks to come. But for now she was exhausted. After three and a half days of scrubbing with heavy brushes, heavy-duty cleansers and all the hot water she could carry and throw, her body had hit its limit. Rubbing one of Hank's warm, soft bloodhound ears, she enjoyed the soothing peace the action gave her and considered her next step.

Though the smell had been vastly reduced, the house still wasn't anything she could live in. But this afternoon, when the plumber replaced the toilet and sink, that should change. She wouldn't need a new bathtub. Through sheer intestinal fortitude, desperate desire and the donation of at least six layers of skin, she had saved the beautiful claw-footed tub.

Just thinking of sinking into a bath of hot water sent shivers down her spine. A quick sponge bath from the kitchen sink just wasn't the same. Having a new toilet would be an equal pleasure. Using the woods wasn't the same, either.

Closing her eyes, she tilted her head back against the truck and let the sun's rays warm her face. It felt so good. Arching her back luxuriously, she reveled in the sun's heat.

Settling back against the truck's cab, she grabbed a bagel and popped a bite into her mouth. She tore the rest into equal pieces and shared it with the dogs.

At the sound of a car pulling into her drive, she looked up, expecting to see the plumber. What she found was Luke Anderson sitting behind the wheel of his truck. Her heart jumped in her chest.

What was he doing here?

She glanced down. Her heart raced faster. She was sitting on her bed! If he found out she'd been sleeping out here...she didn't even want to think about it. In one quick move she vaulted over the side of the truck. Determined to find out what he wanted and to get him on his way before he discovered her bed, she headed him off halfway between her truck and his. Trying to control the shortness of breath her sprint had caused, she turned on her biggest smile.

"Why, good afternoon, Mr. Anderson. This is a surprise. I thought Matt said you would be up in the high country for the next two weeks." She cringed inwardly as Luke looked speculatively from her to her truck, but she didn't let her smile slip.

"Thought you'd be safe for a while, huh?"

Damn! She should have gotten out of the truck more casually. Her panicked flight probably looked suspicious. But she wasn't giving up yet. In a show of complete innocence, she shrugged a shoulder. "Safe? From what?"

"What indeed?" Luke placed his hands on his hips and looked straight into her eyes. "What do you have in the truck, Gaby?"

Her heart banged against her chest. She needed a diversion. Quick.

She waved a negligent hand toward the truck. "Just the dogs." She whistled sharply. Like a cavalry charge, the three dogs bounded over the truck's side and bee-lined for her feet. A quick hand signal settled the motley crew.

With the knuckle of his thumb, Luke pushed the brim of his hat up and lifted a lazy brow as the dogs fell into line and sat one after the other. When the last one sat quietly, Luke raised his blue eyes to hers. "An impressive display. But they're worthless watchdogs. Both times I've driven in they haven't uttered a sound. And the other night, they let me take the keys right out of your truck."

Gaby bristled at the rebuke. There weren't any better trained dogs in the United States. "That's because they're not watchdogs. They're rescue dogs. They're trained not to be protective. I only work one dog at a time in the field, but I bring all three for backup. Can you imagine what would happen if I sent a volunteer to get something out of my car and one of my dogs bit them?''

That news stopped him, and for a moment speculation sparked in his eyes. But then his brows drew together again. ''I can understand you teaching them not to bite, but do you teach them not to bark, as well? A little warning if a killer is coming up your drive doesn't sound like a bad idea to me.''

No, but killers walking up her drive weren't really her concern. Whereas getting him out of here was. ''We don't want them barking, either. Families of lost people have enough tension in their lives. The last thing they need is a bunch of yapping dogs in the background.''

He gave a short nod, apparently agreeing with her explanation. And then he turned his gaze back to the pickup. ''So what's in the truck?''

Blast. So much for diversion. She should have known better. She had found Luke Anderson to be many things the other day, but easily distracted hadn't been among them. Maybe a strong offensive would keep him from her truck.

''What are you doing here, Mr. Anderson? I thought you had cows to chase?''

Luke smiled approvingly. ''Nice try. Now, do you want to come with me while I peek into your truck? Or do you want to get a head start running in the other direction?'' Without another word, he walked around her.

Clenching her fists, Gaby admitted defeat and braced herself for his reaction.

When he got to the truck, Luke set his hands against the sides and leaned over to peer into the bed. With a slow turn of his head, his narrow-eyed glance pinned her where she stood. ''You have exactly thirty seconds to come up with a plausible reason for this bed being back here.''

She held his gaze and stood her ground, but she didn't answer. She knew too well nothing she said would appease him.

With an exasperated sigh, he turned back to the truck and plucked out the grocery bag. He glanced quickly into it and then raised his piercing blue eyes to hers. "These are the groceries I bought the other day." His tone challenged her to deny it.

She raised her chin a notch, but remained silent. The man did have a thing about food. Explaining to him that eating was low on her priority list would get her nothing.

Luke dropped the bag back into the bed of the truck, an irritated sigh falling from his lips. "If I go into the house, am I going to find any more food around?"

Lying was useless; he would only look. She shook her head.

"Gaby, there wasn't enough food in this bag for two days. We're going on four, and there's still bagels in there. Dare I hope you ate out sometime over the past three days?"

Now her irritation matched his. One glance at this place ought to tell him she had no time for frivolous outings. And she had six horses to take care of on top of it!

She didn't even try to keep the sting from her voice. "There's hardly been time for jaunting around the countryside, Mr. Anderson. You see, I made the mistake of buying a house sight unseen. Now I'm stuck with a mess I don't know if I'll ever dig out of. If I haven't had time to sit down and eat whatever your idea of three squares a day is, I'm sorry. But frankly, your wishes just aren't real high on my list of priorities."

Luke cocked a knee to the side, hooked a thumb in one of his belt loops and gave his head an exasperated shake before holding up the first finger on his right hand. "One, you look like hell, and in case you don't know it, you're about to fall off your feet. Two, you're going to have a hard time getting this place livable if you're dead from starvation because of it. Three, I understand it's my fault the house is in this condition. Four, I intend to remedy that. Five, if you call me Mr. Anderson one more time, I'm going to drive your truck into that pond.'' Luke pointed meaningfully to the small pond that sat just behind the outdoor corral.

"Six—" Luke reached over the side of the truck, snatched the air mattress from beneath the bedding and tucked it under his arm "—in the future, consider changing the priority of my wishes on your list. Until I see a real bed inside that house, and the air around it smells like roses, you're staying at Seven Peaks."

Anger coursed through Gaby. Lunging forward, she tried to grab the mattress. "Give that back."

Luke spun away just in time to keep her fingers from closing over the plastic. "Nope. Not today. Now collect your rescue squad and get in my truck. I'm taking you to lunch, and then we're going back to Seven Peaks where I expect you to rest."

Giving up on retrieving her bed, Gaby stepped back, shaking her head. Did he really expect her to bop off for a double cheeseburger with her house still in a shambles and her barn in even worse shape? She squared her shoulders and raised her chin another notch. "I can't. The plumber is coming this afternoon to replace my toilet and sink."

Luke's brows rose skeptically. "What? Are you going to help tighten the fixtures? Leave a note if you think he can't figure out where the toilet goes as opposed to the sink." Without another word, he strode to his truck.

Gaby stared after him. The temptation to ignore his dic-

tate almost overwhelmed her, but one look at his squared
shoulders and determined stride had her squelch the idea.
He'd threatened to throw her over his shoulder like a sack
of potatoes the other day. She didn't imagine for a minute
he'd hesitate today, either.

Grabbing her purse from the back of the truck, she
snapped her fingers to gain the dogs' attention. "Come on,
gang. It seems to be lunchtime."

Luke grimaced as he watched Gaby walk to the truck,
her dogs at her heels. What crazy piece of reasoning had
driven him out of the high country to check on Gaby
Richards? This was the beginning of roundup, dammit.
And if that wasn't enough to keep him occupied, he could
think of a million jobs safer than spending the day baby-
sitting this woman—like stomping through a minefield.

But despite the pressing needs of roundup, the frigid
temperatures and the long days, he hadn't been able to get
her out of his mind. He'd been inundated with images of
her. Erotic images. Dangerous images. Images that woke
him this morning with a hard-on that could have pounded
nails. Which he could have ignored if an image of her
haunted amber eyes hadn't picked that moment to settle
firmly in his mind.

Those lovely eyes full of exhaustion and old pain and
stubborn determination, he couldn't ignore. So here he
was, slogging through a minefield and praying to God he
came out the other side.

Frustration knotted his belly and something close to the
acrid taste of fear filled his mouth. He needed to get Gaby
fed, get her settled at Seven Peaks for a quiet afternoon
and then get the hell away from her.

From the side-view mirror, he watched her signal the
dogs into the bed of his truck. Once they were in, she

climbed into the cab, pulled the door shut and jammed herself as tightly against the door as she could.

Good Lord, what did she think he was going to do?

Unfortunately, he knew what she thought. She thought he'd beat her like the last bastard in her life. Disgust and anger consumed him at her lack of trust, but the more desperate side of him only thought to take advantage of the situation. If she feared him, she'd stay away from him. And he needed all the help he could get in that department. Shifting into Reverse, he backed the truck out of the drive.

As Luke drove over the twisty mountain roads on the way to the restaurant, Gaby stayed still and silent, as if she was being careful not to attract his attention.

She might as well save her energy. In the intimate confines of the cab, he was aware of every breath she took.

Finally they arrived at the small house that served as Hideaway's one good restaurant. At the restaurant's door, Gaby stopped, reached into her purse, pulled out her dark glasses, and put them on.

Luke rolled his eyes. "That's ridiculous. How are you going to see the menu to order?"

Gaby's chin tipped up a notch and both brows rose imperiously above her sunglasses. "What would be the point? You're going to order the biggest thing on the menu for me, anyway, and then complain when I can't eat it all."

A smile tugged at Luke's lips as he swung the restaurant's door open and waved her in. "You're right. After you."

He'd barely closed the door behind them when a familiar voice rang out. "Hey, hey, the prodigal son has returned. And with him the angel of peace and mercy."

Both Luke and Gaby turned toward Sheriff Johnson's voice. Luke winced at the speculative look in Tom's eye as his gaze bounced from Luke to Gaby. And when Tom's mouth turned up in a knowing grin, Luke wanted to groan.

Tom was worse than an old lady when it came to match-making. And Luke had been at the top of his list for years. Now the anticipation of triumph gleamed in Tom's eyes.

Apprehension twisted Luke's gut. Before he left this res-taurant, Tom would feed him a list longer than his damned horse's tail of Gaby's good qualities. And he didn't need that. He already knew she placed an animal's comfort be-fore her own. He already knew she would offer peace to a weary animal despite the fact she had none of her own. He already knew he was attracted to her more than was good for either of them.

He didn't need any more shining qualities heaped before him. What he needed was a good solid reason to stay away from the woman. And Tom sure as hell wasn't going to give him one.

But it was too late to escape. Tom was already pulling a chair out for Gaby. "Where are the dogs, Gaby?"

With an easy smile, Gaby sat in the offered chair. "In the back of Luke's truck. You'll have to say hi when you leave."

Tom nodded and sat down, his gaze narrowing on Gaby's face, his expression turning serious. "I'll do that. But for now I'd like to hear an explanation for those bruises. And are you hiding another one behind those hideous glasses?"

Cool satisfaction ran through Luke as he sat in the last empty chair at the table. Not being any of his business, he'd never asked Gaby who'd hit her. But he *wanted* to know.

Gaby leaned back in her chair with a sigh of disgust, unhappy about the turn of conversation. But eventually she pulled off the sunglasses and flipped them on the table. "I found Bill."

Tom's brows snapped together as he assessed Gaby's damaged eye. "Bill?" Tension filled the man's six-foot-two-inch frame. "Is he behind bars?"

Gaby nodded. "Yeah."

"Will you have to testify?" Tom asked, concern lacing his words.

"Yeah. The Chicago D.A. called a few days ago. The trial begins early February. He's going to let me know the exact dates he'll need me so I don't have to be gone from the ranch longer than necessary."

Tom nodded, and some of the tension appeared to run out of him. He reached across the table and gave Gaby's hand a gentle, reassuring squeeze.

So Tom had known Gaby's assailant. Now Luke wanted to know him. "Bill?" he prompted.

Gaby waved a hand in dismissal. "It's not important."

Tom looked Luke in the eye. "Her brother-in-law."

Luke swung his gaze to Gaby. "Your brother-in-law?" He didn't even try to keep the shock from his voice. How did anyone get themselves into a position where an in-law gave them the kind of beating Bill had given Gaby? And where had her family been? Where the *hell* had her sister been?

Pain flashed briefly in the amber depths of Gaby's eyes. But determination quickly replaced it. "This subject is closed." She emphasized each word with a definitive tap of her finger on the tabletop.

Damn. Luke wanted to know what had put her in the path of her brother-in-law's vicious fists, but her expression clearly said even thumbscrews wouldn't elicit the answer. And then the waitress interrupted, and the moment disappeared. He would have to ferret out the answer another time.

After everyone ordered, Tom picked up the conversation again. "Nancy and I are glad to have you for a neighbor, Gaby. Nancy's thrilled at having someone next door she can gossip with. Plus, it's good to see the land go to someone who loves it."

Tom turned to Luke, the matchmaker gleam in his eye. "Did you know that last year, when Gaby was here searching for Timmy Danner, I dropped her at the grassy knoll every evening? Rain or shine, she'd go up there and just sit, staring at that big old red mountain. Remember when your granny used to do that?"

Luke nodded. When his grandmother was alive, she'd had an affinity for that mountain. She'd spent countless hours up on the knoll staring at it. And though the family never understood it, they all agreed there was an uncommon peace about her when she returned.

Luke glanced at the woman across from him with her bruised face and the sad shadows in her eyes. If that old red mountain could offer her even the smallest portion of the peace it had given his grandmother, he would laud its graces.

But he wouldn't succumb to Tom's machinations. He wouldn't let Tom run on and on about how much Gaby loved the land. Land Tom knew Luke considered part of his soul. Land Tom thought he could use to form a bond between Luke and Gaby.

With a warning glance at Tom, Luke turned to Gaby and deftly changed the subject. "So, you helped work the Timmy Danner case?"

Gaby nodded, a gentle smile coming to her lips. "That case was a miracle. I don't think anyone who worked it walked away thinking a Supreme Being hadn't reached down and saved that little boy.''

Tom unfolded his napkin and placed it in his lap. ''Yeah, well, God had some help on that one.''

Gaby shook her head. ''Trust me, Tom, without divine intervention, neither the handlers nor the dogs would have meant a thing.''

Tom lifted a shoulder, dismissing Gaby's comment. ''Maybe. But trust *me,* without the handlers, one in particular—'' Tom gave her a pointed look ''—divine intervention wouldn't have meant much, either.''

A hint of red climbed into Gaby's cheeks and she looked away. ''Tom, you're not going to embarrass me here, are you?''

''Embarrass you?'' Tom gave Gaby a look of exaggerated innocence.

The look almost gagged Luke. He thought he'd moved the subject onto safer ground. Now he realized he'd walked right into Tom's little trap. Gaby had obviously been the one to find Timmy Danner, and Tom wanted Luke to know it.

Luke didn't even try to hide his aggravation. ''Of course he's going to embarrass you, Gaby. It's his specialty. But you'll live through it.'' Whereas his chances were damned slim.

Tom's two favorite hobbies were matchmaking and storytelling. It looked as though he'd hit the jackpot today. He could combine the two for a full frontal attack.

And a full frontal attack was the last thing Luke needed. He was having enough trouble fighting Gaby's pull on him as it was. He took a giant swig of water, wishing like hell it was a tumbler of Jack Daniel's, and braced himself for the onslaught. ''Go on, Tom. You have my complete attention.''

Tom gave him a Cheshire-cat grin. "Glad to hear it."
But to Luke's surprise Tom didn't continue. Instead, he
turned to Gaby. "Gaby, this is really your story. Why
don't you tell it?"

"Tom." Gaby shook her head.

But Tom didn't let Gaby off the hook so easily. He
waited silently with a patient and expectant look on his
face until Gaby had to say *something*.

Shaking her head in exasperation, she gave a sigh of
defeat. "There's not a lot to tell, actually. Timmy's dad is
a reporter for Billings's big paper, and his mom is a pho-
tographer there. They were doing an article on the fire on
Aspen Hill last year when their son, Timmy, wandered
away from them."

Luke had been out of the area during the case, but he'd
heard snatches of it when he'd returned. "The parents took
a five-year-old to an active fire while they reported on it?"
Disbelief and a tinge of anger tightened his gut.

Gaby nodded, a dark shadow of sadness appearing in
her eyes. "I've been working rescue for ten years now.
You'd be amazed where people take their children." She
shook her head slowly. "So careless."

The last two words were a bare whisper, and in them
Luke heard the shared pain of a fellow survivor. Pain he
was sure Gaby would have been appalled to know he had
heard. Pain he couldn't do a damned thing about.

Wouldn't do a damned thing about. Best to move this
conversation along. "But you found him, didn't you?"

She blinked, pulling herself out of the past. "Yeah, but
it took us four days."

"Four days?" Luke couldn't imagine anyone staying
alive in the fires that had ravaged Aspen Hill for four
whole days.

Gaby nodded, acknowledging the astonishment in his

voice. "That was the miracle. We found him in an old bear cave, scared, dehydrated and hungry, but not a scorch on him, despite the fact that the area around him had been burned to a cinder.

"I still don't know how it happened. Not a tree, not a bush, not a blade of grass escaped the flames for twenty acres around that little cave." Wonder softened the lines of her face.

Luke steeled himself against the tender emotions her expression evoked. All he had to do was get through this lunch and then run like hell for the high country. And stay there this time.

A smile, puzzled and joyful, as if she still couldn't believe the scope of the miracle, turned Gaby's lips. "The cave was tiny—three feet by four maybe, set in a small outcropping of rocks. It should have gotten hot enough to roast a turkey in there. Certainly the fire should have sucked all the oxygen out of it. But there he was, tiny Timmy Danner tucked into this cave sound asleep with barely a smudge of dirt on him."

Luke mentally shook his head at his ironic turn of thoughts. Four days ago he'd condemned this woman because he thought she was like Tanya. Today he'd give anything if she were.

He could resist a woman like Tanya no matter how beautiful. But this. This concern for little ones whose parents didn't take enough care, and this open awe of miracles? *This* could kill him. From the corner of his eye, Luke caught Tom's gaze.

A knowing smile curved Tom's lips and a devilish light sparkled in his eyes.

The knot in Luke's gut tightened. Things were about to get worse.

With a wink of warning, Tom turned up his smile and

swung his gaze to Gaby. "Yeah, it was amazing. But it wouldn't have meant anything if you and your dog, Susie, hadn't found him. The firefighters had left the area behind the day before, along with all the other search and rescue teams."

Tom shook his head like a sad ol' hound dog. "*You* and Susie were the only team that offered to stay. Hell, half the teams went home the first day because they weren't willing to work in the dangers a live fire presented. And the other half left the night before when they hit the end of their three-day limit. Only you stayed, Gaby."

So Gaby had been one of only a few who'd been willing to risk their lives and that of their dogs in the fire. And she'd been the only one to stay for the long haul.

And she'd saved a little boy because of it. Mercy and tenacity all rolled into one bruised little angel.

He had to get out of here. Now.

Standing up, Luke pulled his billfold from his back pocket and extracted enough money to cover the tab. Tossing it down onto the table, he gave Tom a narrow-eyed look. "I have steers to get down out of the upper meadows. Since you're here, you can see Gaby eats. Then I'd appreciate it if you'd take her to your place to rest. And she needs a bed to crash in at night until she gets her place livable. She's been sleeping in her pickup."

Satisfied with Tom's unhappy look at that news, and positive the sheriff would make sure Gaby didn't spend another night in her truck, Luke turned to Gaby. "Don't worry. I'll put your dogs in Tom's cruiser. They'll love the plush seats." Turning on his heel, he strode for the door and safety.

Tom's voice came to him across the room. "Are you going to do some thinking while you're up there?"

Without breaking stride, Luke let his words float back

over his shoulder. "Yeah. I'm going to rethink my list of friends."

Gaby watched the door slam behind Luke and turned to Tom. "What are you up to?"

Tom gave her the same innocent-eyed look he'd been sporting since she sat down at his table, and totally ignored her question. "I think Luke had a good idea. You look beat, and Nancy would love to see you."

Gaby shook her head. "Has it occurred to you that Luke Anderson is *not* my keeper?"

Tom leaned back in his chair and fixed Gaby with a *Father Knows Best* stare. "You could have worse men looking after you, you know? He's a good man, Gaby."

Gaby thought Luke probably was a good man. But she'd made up her mind not to have a man in her life long ago. Good or bad.

Tom's brows pulled together at her silence. "You're not afraid of Luke, are you?"

Surprisingly, that question took Gaby little thought. "No, he doesn't scare me."

Tom smiled. "Good, because he's going to be back, you know."

A tiny smile found Gaby's lips. She did know it. And even more surprising than her lack of fear was the tiny flutter of anticipation racing through her veins. She shook her head at the foreign emotion and chalked it up to practicality. After all, she had a barn to empty, and four hands were better than two.

Chapter Six

Luke sat on the old porch swing and sipped at his steaming cup of morning coffee. He drank in the hospitality of the enclosed porch and familiar swing as greedily as he did the warming brew. The last two weeks in the high country had been cold and windy and comfortless.

Joining him with his own cup, Matt sank into a porch chair and stretched out his legs. "How many strays you pick up?"

Luke took a sip, enjoying the warmth of the steam as it wafted up from the cup. "About a hundred and twenty. I left them on the second level. I'll work the south peaks the next time I go up, but that won't be for a bit."

Matt's brows rose in question. "Oh?"

The tone of that *oh* caught Luke's attention. He narrowed his eyes suspiciously on his brother. "Tom didn't happen to stop by while I was gone, did he?"

Matt took a sip of coffee and looked Luke right in the eye. "As a matter of fact, he did."

A silent groan echoed through Luke's head. So, Tom had recruited help in his matchmaking campaign. Luke stretched out his own legs and gave Matt his most quelling look. "Don't look so smug. Tom suggested I do some thinking up there, and I did. End of story." Luke took a sip of his coffee, hoping his brother would take the hint and close the subject.

But of course Matt didn't. "And?"

Exasperation pulled at Luke, but Matt would keep harping until he had his answers. "And I came to some conclusions. Including the fact that it's my responsibility to get that mess Gaby bought looking like a ranch again. At least I have to get that junk out of the barn for her. Unless, of course, she's managed to hire someone to help her do it?" Luke raised a brow hopefully.

Matt shook his head. "Nope. She's got flyers up advertising for help, but you know she's not going to get anybody this time of year. They're all punching cows. She told me Nancy helped her paint the inside of the house, though, and arranged the furniture that came yesterday."

Matt gazed out over the vista, an easy smile coming to his lips. "You should have seen her. She was as excited as a kid about being able to sleep in her own bed, in her own house. It's a first, apparently." Looking back to Luke, his expression became dramatically somber. "I hope she takes advantage of it, because the shadows under her eyes are as big as a coon's."

Oh, yeah, perfect. Matt knew how to play him like a bloody violin. But still he couldn't ignore the insinuation that Gaby hadn't been taking care of herself. Luke narrowed his eyes on his brother. "Is she eating anything?"

Matt gave an overly negligent shrug. "How would I

know? I'm out on the range all day just like you are. The few times I wandered in before sunset, she was in the corral working horses. Which is a sight to see. I have never seen anyone work with horses as well as that girl does. You should see her with her stallion.''

Yep, played like a bloody fiddle. But there was damned little Luke could do about it. If he wanted news on whether or not Gaby was taking care of herself, and he did, he'd have to listen to the story on what an incredible person she was first. Tom was going to pay for this one. Big time.

Matt took a leisurely sip of coffee before continuing his story. ''Shanna and I sat out on the porch the other night with Sarah and watched them. It was like watching a dance. That big old horse can suspend his trot so far off the ground, he looks light as air. We wondered if he would ever touch the ground again. And Gaby sits up there so quiet, you wonder if she's using telepathy to give him instructions. It is an awesome show. You should see it sometime.''

Luke took another sip of his coffee and stared out over the Montana Rockies. Obviously Gaby hadn't starved to death while he'd been gone. Maybe if he just ignored Matt, he'd go away. But when the silence not only stretched out, but became uncomfortable, he looked back to his brother.

Matt stared at him, his expression speculative and brooding.

''What?'' Luke asked defensively.

''Did you forget why you went up there in the first place?''

''I went up there to find strays. We *are* approaching roundup, remember? Trying to figure out my feelings about that woman was only secondary, believe me.''

''Does that mean you didn't resolve anything?''

''Oh, no. I resolved plenty. One, I'm not ready to have

anyone in my life. Two, I may *never* be ready to have anyone in my life. Three, I can't stop thinking about her. Four, or worrying about her. Five, every time I think of her I get hot. And I'm not talking about my temper. Six, I don't like the implications of three, four and five worth a damn. So I intend to get that barn cleaned up as soon as possible—keeping my hands as deep in my pockets as they'll go—and then I plan to finish roundup and get on the first plane heading out of the country. Now, would you like to answer *my* question for a change?''

Matt shrugged indifferently. ''If you're so worried about how the girl is taking care of herself, why don't you go look for yourself?''

A damned good idea. It would certainly be a lot quicker than sitting here listening to his brother go on and on.

Giving Matt a black scowl, Luke set his mug down on the wooden floor, grabbed his hat and headed out to his truck. Driving down the gravel road, he thought about the past two weeks. They had been long. Almost as long as last night.

Despite being in a soft bed for the first time in two weeks, he hadn't slept at all. And he could lay his restlessness at Gaby's feet. Or at the door of a specific part of his own anatomy quite a distance from his feet.

Even now, that part of him readied at the thought of seeing her. He gritted his teeth against the all-too-familiar reaction and tried to imagine himself in an icy mountain stream. Not that it did much good. He'd spent the past two weeks immersing himself in the real thing and the cure had lasted only as long as he stood waist-deep in the rushing, freezing waters.

He shook his head. Keeping his hands in his pockets might prove to be as futile as tilting at windmills. But he had to do it. He'd meant it when he told Matt he wasn't ready to have anyone else in his life.

Tanya had left him so little of his heart and soul, he would be hard-pressed to claim he had either. And what little remained he refused to put at risk.

No, he'd keep his hands in his pockets, or busy with the task at hand, but he *wouldn't* sink them into the rich, gold strands of Gaby's wild mane, or test the softness of her nape with them, or—

Cursing his wayward thoughts, Luke pulled into Gaby's drive. He shoved the gear into Park and gave the barn a nasty look. If not for that barn, he wouldn't be worrying about keeping his hands in his pockets. He'd be herding steers in the high country. Flipping off the ignition, he caught the sound of a chain saw. He cocked his head and listened.

Yep, a chain saw. Could Gaby have gotten a hired hand, after all? He looked around hopefully for a vehicle other than her own. Nothing. Grabbing his hat, he slid out of the truck and headed behind the buildings toward the sound.

Coming to the end of the metal building, he caught sight of her. His heart stopped and then slammed against his ribs before trying to jump directly out of his throat. Gaby was waving the chain saw over an old dead tree that had fallen down years before. It would make great firewood if she was alive long enough to burn it.

Adrenaline crashing through him, Luke strode toward her as quickly as he dared. He stretched his strides until they ate the ground like a racing leopard, but he didn't run. He didn't want to scare Gaby. With the way she handled the saw, her chances of losing a hand or leg before he got there were high enough, anyway. If he startled her, she'd lop off a limb for sure.

A verbal warning would be the safest way to let her

know he was there. Over the buzz of the saw, it wouldn't be loud enough to startle her. He hoped. He filled his lungs and hollered her name. Relief swept through him when she looked up without doing any harm to herself, but the steady chatter of the saw kept his stride steady as he closed the space between them. Her expression, at first surprised to see him, changed to one of pleasure as he stepped up to the opposite side of the tree.

She swung the saw up in front of her and Luke jumped back on a second jolt of adrenaline as the deadly end swung within inches of him. With an incredible show of will, he managed not to reach out and snatch the damned thing before she killed one of them. But only because if she put up a fight about it, the saw would win. So he hung his hands at his sides as casually as his racing heart would allow and waited for Gaby to look at him again.

Switching the saw off, she held it aloft. "Do you know how to use one of these things? I can't seem to make it cut right. Either it goes too slow and gets stuck in the cut, or it goes too fast and cuts through the tree and into the dirt before I can stop it."

Luke nodded his head. His throat paralyzed, he couldn't have spoken if he'd wanted to. Eyeing the saw in Gaby's hands, he took in its stats. A brand-new, top-of-the-line Stihl's, it was a saw that would have thrilled Paul Bunyan. But anyone smaller than the legendary hero hadn't any business with the damned thing. It was *not* a lady's saw. And anyone who sold it to a dead beginner ought to be drawn and quartered.

His fear subsided now that the instrument hung dead in Gaby's hands, and anger began a slow burn in his belly. She wore no safety goggles, no gear to protect her hearing and no cutter's chaps to keep an out-of-control saw from cutting through her legs. She did have on gloves, but they were the thin riding type. They would offer little protection for cutting wood. The slow burn became a good-size fire.

To top it all off, she obviously didn't know which end of the damn thing she held. "New?" His throat had relaxed just enough to get the word out.

Gaby nodded.

"Nice saw. Where'd you get it?" Luke had a pretty good idea, but he wanted to be sure.

"Down at Carlson's Lumber and Hardware."

Luke nodded. He thought so. "Who sold it to you?"

He tried to keep his tone pleasant, but Gaby noticed the questions seemed a bit specific for casual conversation. Wariness clouded her next answer. "One of the boys who works there helped me out. I didn't ask his name. Why?"

Luke ignored her question. "Blond?"

"No. Brown hair. A good-looking kid. What difference does it make?"

"It doesn't. I just wondered." He made a mental note to have a meaningful conversation with that boy. "Did he show you how to use it?"

Gaby nodded. "He showed me where the on button was, and how to pull the cord."

A very meaningful conversation. "Did he tell you you're supposed to wear safety gear when you use those things? Goggles, protection for your ears, chaps for your legs, good strong gloves?"

Gaby shook her head.

What the hell, he would just beat the crap out of the kid. Anyone that stupid would never be impressed by something as benign as a meaningful talk. Luke held out his hand. "Here, let me see that for a minute."

Despite her confusion at his questions, Gaby handed the saw over almost cheerily. No doubt she thought he'd show her how to use it. A silent, humorless laugh vibrated in his throat. Not a snowball's chance in hell.

"This—" Luke tapped the bright orange motor casing, trying to keep his voice pleasant "—is a very dangerous piece of equipment. It should only be used by people who know how. The first rule is, you *never* get a blade that is longer than your arm."

He traded the pleasant ring in for a warning growl. "The second rule is, you *never* buy a saw that is stronger than you are!"

Gaby's previously cheery expression disintegrated into one of mulish disregard.

Righteous anger bubbled in Luke's veins. The hell with it, he could talk until he was blue in the face and the next time he came over, she'd still be waving the damned thing with whatever limb was left. He glanced quickly around him. His gaze settled on her pond.

Perfect.

Turning on his heel, he headed for the small body of water behind Gaby's barn with the same ground-eating strides he'd used only moments before. He kept an attentive ear tuned toward Gaby.

Halfway to his destination, her piercing words rent the air. "Luke! Don't you dare!"

Luke smiled wickedly, but didn't turn around. He had no intention of stopping. He kept his stride straight and true until he stood at the edge of the pond. He spun around twice like a discus thrower, letting the weight of the saw carry his arm out straight from his body, and the next time the pond came into view, he gave one final thrust and let the saw fly.

Pure satisfaction washed through him as the saw sailed through the air and landed with a great splash near the middle of the pond. A hell of a throw.

With the saw safely taken care of, Luke turned to check on Gaby. She stood about thirty feet from him, her arms flailing as she stopped her forward momentum, and then she stood frozen in a state of outraged shock.

Quickly shock turned to anger. Fists bunched at her sides, strands of golden wheat hair streaming behind her, she strode toward him with the light of battle crackling in her eyes. An avenging Valkyrie.

God, she was beautiful.

A small smile pulled at the corners of his mouth. He much preferred this angry warrior to the woman who had cowered beneath him only a few weeks ago. Now, if her curled fists were merely a sign of her frustration and not the readying of a weapon, he'd be a happy man. But just in case, he braced himself.

Gaby kept coming until he could see the individual flecks of gold melting in the flames in her eyes. Until he could feel her heat against the exposed skin of his chest. Until the golden strands of her hair reached out to tantalize his sensitized skin. "You puffed-up, autocratic, macho...cowboy," she finally spat as if the latter were a dirty word.

Luke smiled a little wider. "I would call that description a little one-sided but not totally inaccurate."

Gaby's eyes widened at his nonchalant dismissal of her insult. With an outraged gasp she took several steps toward the pond and jabbed a finger toward the middle. "That was an eight-hundred dollar saw!"

She was magnificent. Bold and brave and full of fire. He shrugged a shoulder. "Don't worry, I'll reimburse the money. But don't buy another saw with it, or it'll be following that one into the drink."

With an infuriated huff, Gaby jammed her fists at her waist and narrowed her eyes as if she were drawing a bead on him. One definitive step at a time she closed the distance between them again. "You low-bellied, self-righteous, meddling...Neanderthal!"

Meddling? *Neanderthal?* Well, hell, even magnificence had a limit to its appeal. Now the question was how to stop her before her insults got any lower.

The perfect solution popped into his head with the clarity of divine providence. Like a hawk after his mouse, he swooped down and took her by the shoulders, capturing her lips with his.

Gaby startled, for just a moment, but then her muffled words died against his lips and she became utterly still.

With the touch of her warm, smooth lips beneath his, the fire he'd been keeping in check for the past two weeks leaped out of control. His blood heated and boiled and raced to a central destination. His nerve endings chattered like a buzz saw and his control spun out of reach.

His hands tightened involuntarily on her shoulders. He'd thought of her, dreamed of her, fantasized about her, and now he had her. But not enough of her. Her lips remained closed against him, and he wanted *in*.

He ran his tongue along the crease between her lips, savoring her taste as he tried to gain entrance. But her lips didn't part for him, didn't allow him the more-intimate caress he wanted. He tried again. This time with a soul-searing kiss that should have opened the gates of heaven.

Nothing.

Absolutely nothing.

He lifted his head and looked down at Gaby.

She looked back at him, her eyes wide with confusion and...wonder?

"Gaby?"

"Your lips are soft." Her whisper was so faint, Luke

had to lower his head to hear it. "I never thought lips would be so soft. And warm...so warm."

Luke's head jerked back. *Please God, don't do this to me.* But Gaby's expression told him it was a wasted prayer. "Gaby," he started cautiously, "please tell me you've been kissed before."

Still caught in a shroud of confused wonder, Gaby shook her head. "I don't like to be touched. And I've never wanted to be in love. Avoiding the whole thing seemed like the best idea."

Luke knew she never would have uttered the words if she weren't so stunned. And now he wished she never had. *A virgin.* What did he do with a virgin? He released her shoulders and stepped back so she could regain her wits.

She raised her hand to her lips and slowly stroked them, her eyes taking on an amazed, slumberous expression.

Desire surged through him. He knew what he wanted to do. He wanted to show her, in exquisite detail, what sensual wonders lay down passion's path. And with the look of dawning desire on her face, it was a damned hard desire to resist.

Stomping a booted foot in frustration, Luke turned away and stared at the red mountain that had brought Gaby to this spot. He did *not* need this. He had promised to keep his hands deep in his pockets. And how the *hell* would he do that if she kept running her fingers over her lips as though she was discovering paradise?

Blocking his carnal thoughts, he turned back to Gaby and grabbed her wrist. "Come on, girl, before I take your look as an invitation." Heading toward the house, he dragged Gaby behind him. "Something tells me it's going to be a long morning. I need some coffee. You do have coffee, don't you?"

At the house he pulled the still-silent and acquiescent

Gaby up the stairs and through the front door. And he would have continued to pull her through the house to the kitchen if the sight of the dining room hadn't stopped him dead in his tracks.

Gaby pulled free of his hold. From the corner of his eye he could see her watching him. Her brush with passion obviously forgotten, a mischievous smile pulled at her lips. She swung a hand wide to encompass the rooms before them. "Pretty nice, huh? Nancy helped. Didn't she do a great job?"

Luke looked around him with stunned appreciation. Just two weeks ago he'd worried Gaby would burn the place down. Worse, he thought it might be the only feasible alternative.

Now it was beautiful.

The wainscoting in the rooms he could see was painted a blue-gray, and above that each room had its own unique color. The room where they stood carried a light wash of beige. And next to them, the living room was a dusty rose.

But the staircase leading to the bedrooms upstairs caught his attention most. Gaby had replaced the missing and damaged spindles and painted it like the outside of an old Victorian house. Using the blue-gray as the main color, she'd accented the cutouts and carvings with the rose and beige.

He walked over to the staircase and ran his hand down the rail's shiny new surface. As a kid, he slid down these stairs. A week ago, he feared no kid would ever slide down them again. Now Gaby had turned them into a thing of beauty. Joy warmed him. Someone loved this house again.

"I would say Nancy did a hell of a job." He turned from his admiration of the stairs and looked Gaby right in the eye. "And so did you."

She seemed confused by his compliment, and after

watching her mull it over for a minute, he felt obliged to reassure her. "Don't worry. When I walk into the kitchen and find nothing but a can of coffee, I'll return to my autocratic old self."

That snapped her out of it. She glanced quickly at the kitchen, and he could see her mind working like crazy. "That's right," she said. "You wanted some coffee. Why don't you have a seat on my brand-new sofa, and I'll go fix you some."

Well, it was a nice try. He gave her a teasing smile. "Do you have any eggs to go with it?"

She tipped her head to the side. "Well, no. I don't have a fridge yet."

He nodded knowingly. "How about some toast? That doesn't require a refrigerator."

She hesitated before smiling triumphantly. "Well, no. But it does require a toaster. And I don't have one of those, either."

He nodded his head. She wasn't fooling him. "How about bread?"

Her shoulders slumped in defeat. "Well, no. I'm missing that part, too."

"Uh-huh. Lilah's? Or shall we splurge and go all the way into Hideaway and eat at the truck stop?"

Gaby shifted restlessly on her feet. "Luke, the last few nights have been pretty cold. And that barn is—"

"Gaby, if you're not up to walking, my shoulder's available." He'd seen her mentally preparing her case to avoid taking time out to eat and decided to save them both the time and trouble.

With a huff of exasperation, she placed a hand on her hip and gave him an annoyed stare. "Does this mean I don't have an option?"

Undaunted, he winked. "Don't let anyone tell you, you aren't a smart lady," he said, striding toward her.

Before he got close enough to grab her, Gaby turned on her heel and rushed ahead of him. At the door, she stopped with her hand on the knob and turned to him. "You know, Anderson, winter is almost here, and if I don't get my barn done, my horses are going to be staying at Seven Peaks *all* winter. I would think you, of all people, would want to make sure *that* doesn't happen. And it's going to happen if I spend my days eating at restaurants instead of cleaning out my barn."

"As it happens, we're going to do both. We're going to eat at restaurants until you get a stove and refrigerator, at least, and we're going to get your barn cleaned out, too."

"We?"

He smiled at her nervous croak. Before they could work together, they needed to clear some things up. He rocked back on his heels. "Yes, we. But in light of what just happened out there, I think we'd both feel better if we set some ground rules."

She flushed a becoming shade of red, and he marveled at the phenomenon. He couldn't remember the last time he'd been around a woman innocent enough to blush. And that thought alone sent his blood racing. After Tanya's calculated manipulation and the degradation he'd seen perpetrated on the battlefield, Gaby's fresh innocence pulled at him like the sweetest siren's song.

And it would drown him just as surely. What the hell had he gotten himself into? Did he really think he could spend the next few weeks with Gaby without showing her how nice touching could be? And then what? Where would that leave him, and where would it leave her?

He knew where it would leave him. Harder, hotter and hornier. Because in the time it would take to clean her barn, he couldn't even scratch the surface of what he would want to teach her. And he didn't have the heart for the long haul.

As for Gaby, she deserved a guy who had more to offer than a quick tumble and a quicker goodbye. She *needed* more than that. And he didn't have anything more to give.

Luke shoved his hands in his pockets. And then he shoved them deeper. "I take full responsibility for what happened out there, and I promise it won't happen again. Rule one, we'll keep this on a purely professional level. Just look at me as your hired hand, and in the future I'll try to behave like one."

She lifted a sardonic brow at him. "Does this new rule begin before or after breakfast?"

Luke had to laugh at that. "We'd better make it after breakfast. If we started now, you'd nix breakfast and I'd have to break my rule thirty seconds after I made it and haul you out to the truck, after all. A bad precedent, wouldn't you agree? Now, would you like to walk or ride?" He pointed meaningfully at his shoulder.

Gaby shook her head and swung the door open. "I'll walk. For all their impressive muscle, your shoulders are probably bony as hell."

Gaby sat in Luke's truck and watched the pines pass outside her window in a soft, green blur. The hot flush of embarrassment still clung to her cheeks as surely as the tingling aftereffect of Luke's kiss clung to her lips. God, he must think her an idiot. Twenty-eight and never been kissed. But she couldn't help it. After leaving her father's house, it had taken her years to overcome her fear of men, and she had never overcome her fear of men's hands.

She'd tried dating a few times, but when she panicked every time a man tried to touch her, she'd given up on the idea. And there had never been anyone who'd made her want to face that fear.

Until now.

A multitude of emotions swirled through her, leaving her hands cold and her stomach doing a persistent rumba. She'd liked the feel of Luke's lips on hers. They had been so soft, and so warm, and so alive, and so...what? Shocking? Surprising? Wonderful?

Awe inspiring.

Oh, God, what was she thinking? She bit her lower lip to erase the ghostly touch that lingered there.

She'd promised herself long ago to keep men out of her life. Not to let them in. But she couldn't stop the thoughts. She didn't know if she wanted to. For one brief moment a warm breeze had blown across her soul. It felt good over the frozen layers fear had laid down year after year.

And Luke didn't have to know how she felt. She could keep her feelings to herself. So what would it hurt to indulge in a little private fantasy?

She deserved something for herself, and she was going to take this.

Chapter Seven

Gaby stood in the chill morning air and stared at the stepladder leaning against the barn wall. A dozen emotions swirled inside her. The barn was clean. Today she and Luke would get it ready for stalls to go in. If she didn't think of something, it would be the last time she'd see him.

An acute sense of loss assailed her. She shook her head at the irony of the situation. A month ago she'd moved here to get away from men and their brutality. Now she would do anything to keep one specific man from leaving her to her solitude.

She'd tossed and turned all night trying to think of a convincing argument to get him to stay and help her build stalls. An argument that wouldn't tip him off to the real reason she wanted him to stay.

As promised, she'd kept her interest in Luke to herself. She'd kept her glances secretive and her thoughts silent.

But every day it became harder. The moment he stepped out of his truck each morning, strange, exciting currents began to flow between them. Currents that intrigued and pulled her, the way the moon pulled the tides.

She sighed with frustration. It had been twelve days since he'd kissed her—not that she was counting—and the memory hadn't had the decency to dim one whit. In fact, it had haunted her until she *knew* no one's mouth could be so soft or so warm.

No matter how she tried, she couldn't get that kiss out of her mind. Every time she looked at him, her eyes were drawn to the chiseled perfection of his lips. And she ached to feel their touch.

He felt the pull of the currents that ebbed between them as strongly as she did. The half-closed eyelids, the smoky look in his blue eyes, the tension in his work-hewn muscles left no doubt in her mind about that. But he ignored them with the tight-lipped determination of a monk.

She should be grateful. Uncertainty and fear still galloped about at the mere thought of letting a man get close enough to kiss her.

But she wasn't grateful. She would never have the courage to instigate anything on her own, and if Luke wouldn't, she'd never know if his lips were as soft as she remembered. And she *wanted* to know.

And blast him, he wanted to show her. But he wouldn't. Oh, no. The man had a will of iron. She'd seen his fingers *twitch* with need, but then he would grit his teeth and stick his hands in his pockets and head to the other end of the barn.

So where did that leave her?

The same place she'd been three minutes ago. Tired, anxious, sad and still wondering how to convince Luke to stay. Well, she wouldn't find an answer standing around.

She might as well get a jump on the day. She glanced up at the cracked ceiling strut overhead. It was as good a place to start as any.

She rubbed her hands together to warm them, grabbed a ladder and dragged it under the damaged strut. Then she snatched a bag of barn spikes, stuck a hammer in her back pocket and climbed the steps, while her mind worked frantically to come up with a plausible reason to keep Luke coming back.

On the last step before the top, she tossed the bag of long nails on the top platform. When she straightened, a cobweb tickled her forehead. With a light brush of her hand, it gave up its tenuous hold on the weakened beam. Steadying herself, she reached up to position the nail so it would go from one side of the crack to the other and pull the damaged board back together.

"Blast." She needed to be higher. Prudently, she eyed the absolute top step and then glanced downward. The hard-packed earth waited ten feet below. She shrugged a shoulder. As long as she didn't fall, there wouldn't be a problem, so she didn't really need to wait for Luke and his taller ladder.

She moved the nails to a lower rung and stepped onto the top platform. Much better. With steady, sharp strikes, she worked at getting the five-inch spike pounded into the ancient oak beam. Now, if luring Luke to stay could be so easy.

"Gaby, get off that damned ladder and let me do that!"

Startled, Gaby grabbed the top beam with both hands to keep from falling headfirst from her precarious perch. When she regained her balance, and her heart left her throat for its rightful home in her chest, she noticed the shaft of light streaming into the barn. She shook her head. She was in bad shape if she hadn't heard the barn door open. It squeaked loudly enough to wake the dead. That squeak now echoed through the barn as Luke closed the door, the shaft of light disappearing.

"Get off that ladder."

Gaby smiled at Luke's staccato demand. Why did she want to keep this guy around? He had to be the bossiest man on earth.

But she knew why. She turned her head to peer at him over her shoulder. Her stomach tightened at the heart-stopping picture he presented in his open, hacked-up denim shirt, his whipcord lean muscles blatantly exposed for her covert pleasure.

She gave an involuntary shiver. And not just from the thrill of anticipation his presence invariably brought. She didn't know how he kept from freezing to death. The November temperatures hovered around freezing this early in the morning. But she'd never seen a goose bump on him. And she knew from experience if she got near him, she'd feel the heat wafting off him as if from a wood-burning stove.

Did she face a winter without that heat? She blocked the melancholy thought. She wouldn't let anything spoil today. Because today might be the last day she had with him. She took in Luke's scowl. She wouldn't let him spoil the day, either.

Nor would she let him think he was the boss. A trait she'd been trying to curb—however unsuccessfully—for the past twelve days.

With a spark of mischief, she realized her unplanned position of power. What could he do to her up here? Dropping her hands from the beam overhead, she turned easily on the top step and gave him a wicked smile. "Good morning, Luke. How are you today?"

"A lot better than you're going to be if you don't get your butt off that ladder right now."

Gaby smiled wider. She'd started teasing him one day when his overly autocratic nature threatened to rain on an already gloomy day and discovered, to her surprise, that he could sometimes be teased out of his bossy ways. She climbed down a step and sat on the top platform.

Perching her elbows on her knees, she swung the hammer carelessly between her legs. "You know, Luke, for almost two weeks I've been trying to figure out why you think you're the boss here. Did you see my new sign this morning when you drove in?"

After he'd left last night, she'd stayed up to finish the sign she'd been working on for the past week. Then, flashlight and shovel in hand, she'd stayed up until 1:00 a.m. putting it up. Now the large, hand-painted sign, with its giant picture of her red mountain, announced her ranch: Peaceful Shadows.

Luke rocked back on a heel and planted his hands on his hips. "Yes, I saw it. Beautiful artwork. Did you do it?"

Oh, dear, Gaby knew that tone. She wasn't impressing him a bit. But she didn't give up. She gave him a single nod.

He gave her a single nod back. "Nice job. But if you're trying to tell me in your own subtle way that I'm *not* the boss, save your breath. God could own the place for all I care, and if he was up there on the top step of that ladder, I'd tell him to get his butt down, too."

He took a single step closer. "Now, I love your new name for the ranch, and I hope to hell you find all the peace you want here, but if I don't see those cute little feet of yours come tripping down that ladder in the next thirty seconds, you sure as hell are not going to find it today."

And then there were days when teasing didn't work worth a damn. It looked as if today was one of those days. Grabbing hammer and nails, she started down the ladder. But she didn't turn around; she stepped down it as one would a staircase.

She'd learned early on not to turn her back on an angry man. Not that Luke was angry. Ticked maybe, but not truly angry. And she didn't think he'd hurt her. But still, old fears tightened a thread of warning around her heart.

Irritation flashed in Luke's eyes and he gave an exasperated huff as she descended the ladder.

A tiny trickle of her own irritation bubbled through her. After the first few days of working together, she'd seen this reaction every time they had an argument and she'd backed down. And it annoyed her. Why should he be angry if he got his way?

Except she knew why. Her capitulations annoyed him because they came from fear. And because they showed a lack of trust in him. But didn't he know how hard it was for her to be close to a man?

She wanted his touch, and she craved being close to him, but that didn't mean the years of abuse just disappeared. Every single day she fought against old memories, old fears that warned her no man was safe. Didn't he know that?

A silent sigh sounded in her head. No, he didn't know. He didn't know anything about the first half of her life. He suspected, but he didn't *know*. And she didn't want him to know. Living through it had been degrading enough. She didn't need the added humiliation of sharing the story.

When her foot hit the bottom step, Luke closed the distance between them.

She sank back onto one of the ladder's steps, trying to put as much distance between them as she could.

Luke ate the space as quickly as she gave it, jostling the ladder as he stepped directly up to it. Grabbing the ladder just above her head, he leaned over her and pointed an admonishing finger at her. "Stop it."

She jumped at his sharp tone. "Stop what?"

"Stop looking at me as if you expect me to tear you limb from limb for my greater entertainment. It's irritating as hell to have someone look at you like you're Attila the Hun all the time."

The heat from Luke's bare arm warmed her cheek. The heat of desire flowed into her veins to join the tiny thread of age-old fear.

Fear and desire. The two emotions warred inside her until her heart pounded in her chest and she couldn't pull enough air into her lungs. She closed her eyes against the riot of emotions. She couldn't stand this anymore. She had to make a choice. She either had to give in to the fear and ask Luke to leave, or she had to take a deep breath and reach for him.

Squeezing her eyes as tightly closed as she could, she drew in a long, shaky breath. Then she raised her chin and looked Luke right in the eye. "Kiss me."

Every muscle in Luke's body jumped as if a cattle prod had struck him. His nostrils flared, and he drew in a deep breath as if testing the air for her scent. His eyelids dropped to half-mast and his sky-blue eyes darkened to twilight. The hand beside her head tightened on the ladder until she couldn't believe the wood didn't splinter under the pressure.

An unnatural stillness came over him, and she knew only a thread of will much more fragile than the cobwebs she'd brushed away earlier stopped him from kissing her.

Heat and fire ran through her veins, but her palms broke out in a cold sweat. Every cell in her body screamed at her to snatch the words back. But she didn't. She *wanted* this. And for once in her life she wouldn't let fear rob her. She lifted her chin a notch. "Please."

The thread broke. Luke's strong, work-roughened hands cupped her face. Not gently, but in a hard, possessive grip that frightened her in its intensity.

A spiral of memories flashed in her mind. Her father's big hands reaching to grab her, an open palm slapping her face, Bill's doubled fist smashing into her jaw. Panic flooded her and her heart raced out of control. The hands. She had to get away from the hands. *Now!*

She jerked her head from his grasp and blindly pushed his hands away, fear pounding through her.

Knocked hard from her struggles to get away, the ladder fell, entangling her legs in the rungs. Luke's hands grabbed at her everywhere. Scrambling and fighting, she frantically tried to extricate herself from the ladder and Luke's hands.

Finally she managed to step free of the ladder and pull away from Luke. A few fine strands of her hair were tangled in Luke's fingers and jerked from her head, stinging her scalp painfully, but she was free.

She spun to face him. She feared he'd still be coming after her, but he stood right where she'd left him, his hands held at shoulder level, palms toward her like someone under arrest, making it clear he had no intention of touching her.

Relief rushed through her, but then his expression registered. Her stomach plummeted. All traces of passion were gone. In its place was the iron mask of restraint she'd been looking at since he last kissed her.

Oh, God, what had she done? She dropped her hands and shook her head frantically.

I didn't mean it! She wanted to scream the words, but only an incoherent wail broke through the tears clogging her throat. She reached for him, silently pleading for him to understand. But it wasn't going to help her.

Pushing his hands back into his front pockets, Luke stepped farther back from her. "I can't help you, Gaby. You need more than I can offer. Deserve more than I can offer." He looked quickly around the barn before settling his eyes back on her. Eyes that seemed as sad as her heart. "The barn's clean now. You won't have any problems getting stalls in."

He gave her one last long look as if trying to memorize the moment, then he gave his hat brim a single, sharp pull.

A cowboy's farewell.

Gaby stared at his retreating back, blinded by her tears. She wanted to scream at him not to go, but she couldn't pull the breath into her lungs or push the sound past her throat. She reached toward him, but caught only air. The door opened, flooding the barn with light. A shadow passed through the sunny shaft, and then the door closed behind him.

He was gone.

Pain stabbed her, knocking her to her knees. Clutching her chest, she curled up against the unbearable ache. Why had she run away?

The answer seared through her. Fear. Pure and simple. When Luke had raised his hands to her face, she'd panicked. No matter how hard she tried, she was still the frightened little girl who'd hidden in the closet with her sister to avoid being hit.

And she would never be anything else.

Luke sauntered into the dingy bar and grill. The place wasn't much to look at, but they had the best steaks around, and their brew was colder than most. Leaning against the marred wooden bar, he ordered a draft and a shot. He had every intention of drinking himself into oblivion. He'd tried everything else to forget Gaby, but nothing had worked. This would work. It might take a bottle or two, but oblivion would come.

"You drinking alone these days, Anderson?"

Luke turned at the voice. Tom sat not far from him at a table for four, but he was the only one occupying it at the moment. Propping his elbows on the bar behind him, Luke leaned against it. "Tonight I don't care how I drink. Alone, with company, upside down or hanging from a tree. The only important thing is that the booze keeps coming."

A loud thunk announced the arrival of his drinks. Luke turned and dropped the shot glass into the beer mug. The foamy amber liquid sloshed over the top. Before it settled, he raised the drink to his lips and drained it in one long swallow. He slammed the empty mug back onto the bar and called for another. He turned back to Tom while he waited for it to arrive.

Tom's brows were raised in unimpressed disdain, but he pushed the chair opposite him away from the table with his foot, inviting Luke to join him. "Yeah, well, I'd heard you'd had a long two weeks. Guess that confirms it. Matt tells me the men, horses and even the cows have decided you're too mean a sonofabitch to work for."

"Is that right?" Luke ignored the invitation, deciding it *did* matter how he drank tonight. He wanted to poke at old wounds and lick his new ones all by himself. In short, he wanted to brood alone.

Tom just smiled cordially, took a more conservative drink from his own mug, and kept on talking. "Yep, that's what I hear. Too mean, too cussed and too stupid."

Luke looked at him warily, irritation and a foreboding

of dread scratching at his hide. Tom had a bone to pick. If he turned around, the man would just keep talking to his back, hollering his business across the bar, and he didn't want *that*.

His drink arrived with a double thump. He dropped the shot glass into the mug. Well, hell, he'd best get on with it. Grabbing his drink, he strode to Tom's table.

He set the drink down, flipped the chair around and straddled it. "What else you hear?"

Tom took another slow, leisurely sip of his beer. "I hear your mood is caused by a woman."

Luke's eyes narrowed. He knew it. Tom wanted to talk about Gaby. Hell, the woman had so many damned knights in shining armor milling around her, she ought to be blind from the glare.

He erased all hint of irritation from his voice. If he didn't sound absolutely innocent, this talk would go on all night. "What woman would that be?"

"Rumor has it my new neighbor put a burr under your saddle."

"I don't allow burrs under my saddle. Miss Richards bought my ranch, and I helped her clean it up. She doesn't see me, I don't see her, end of story." Perfect. You couldn't get more innocent than that.

"Is that right?"

"That's right." Luke lifted his glass to his lips, proud of how conciliatory he sounded. He'd come here so he wouldn't have to think about Gaby. And now Tom—his damn self-appointed conscience—wanted to cram her down his throat.

Tom leaned back in his chair, his brows raised in mild surprise. "Well then, my grapevine must be wrong. Because I heard that you chucked her saw in the pond." Luke slammed the half-empty mug down on the table, the shot glass rattling against the mug's sides. "Yes, I did! What would you like to hear? That I care? Okay, I care. I care if she hacks off an arm or leg. I care that some bastard in her past has beaten her and left shadows of fear and sadness in her eyes. But I can't help her with that. I'm not going to be around long enough to do a damned thing about any of it."

Tom nodded, his expression solemn. "Ah, so you care. Just not enough to stop your endless running?"

Luke narrowed his eyes at the slur to his character. "Running?"

Tom shrugged a shoulder, but his eyes challenged Luke to deny it. "You have another name for it?"

No, he didn't have another name for it. He *had* been running for the last five years. At first he'd run away from the pain of Tanya's betrayal. Then, when he'd realized he would never risk his heart or soul in such a fashion again, he'd simply stayed on the move so he wouldn't notice the emptiness of his life.

He'd risked life and limb to keep families threatened by war together while ruthlessly ignoring the fact that he had no family of his own.

A circumstance that fit him perfectly.

Luke fixed Tom with a steady gaze. "I like my life, Tom." *It's cold and barren, but it's safe.* "And I think Gaby probably likes hers just the way it is. I don't think she'd appreciate your interference."

Tom rolled his eyes. "Gaby doesn't know what she likes. She's spent her life trying to keep the jagged edges of an abusive upbringing from opening an artery when she wasn't looking."

The allusion to Gaby's past snagged Luke's attention. Gaby had never spoken about her past. The few times he'd tried to broach the subject, she'd sidestepped the issue like a wild horse dodging the lasso. But he'd always wanted to know.

And it looked as though Tom had some of the answers.

Luke crossed his arms over the chair's back. "Tell me about Gaby's past."

Tom shrugged. "If you want to know about Gaby's past, ask her. What I know came out of police reports, and they're confidential. I won't share what's in them."

"You were happy to tell me about Bill Clark the day we all had lunch," Luke pointed out, his temper strained.

Tom took a sip of his beer as if he didn't have a care in the world. "Bill Clark is in jail waiting trial. Everything about him is public record."

Luke narrowed his eyes on Tom. "Including why he hit Gaby?"

"That's an easy one. Bill Clark hit Gaby to avoid being arrested for murder. And because he's a coward and bully who likes to hit women."

The hairs on the back of Luke's neck stood up. "Murder?"

Tom nodded. "A year ago Bill Clark beat Zoey Richards—his wife and Gaby's little sister—to death in a fit of rage. When the authorities couldn't find him and refused to spend any real time or money tracking him down, Gaby went after him."

The hairs on the back of Luke's neck all but started to dance. His fingers tightened on the chair's back. "She went after him? Knowing he killed her sister? Knowing he was just as likely to kill her? *More* likely since he had a murder charge to avoid?"

Tom tipped his head and looked Luke right in the eye. "She was going to get justice for her sister any way she could. Just like she's going to fix that ranch you sold her any way she can. It would be nice, however, if for once in her life she didn't have to do it alone.''

Oh, God. After suffering through a childhood of abuse, Gaby had escaped only to lose her sister to the same nightmare that had haunted the first half of her life. A cruel, brutal man.

And still she'd asked him to kiss her.

And what had he done? Had he given her a sweet, gentle kiss like any girl's first kiss should be? Hell, no. He'd grabbed her face and moved in for the kill with hormones raging. He'd crowded her into a corner and grabbed her with all the finesse of a fifteen-year-old after his first grope.

And he'd scared her to death.

Just like every other bastard in her life.

A cold knot formed in Luke's stomach, and he rubbed his eyes with the heels of his hands. Had he protected his heart and soul so well over the past five years that he had lost them along the way? Had he become so callous that he could now wound others without even realizing it? Was that the kind of man he had become?

Was that the kind of man he wanted to be?

He gave a deep sigh. There was a time, he knew, in every man's life, when he had to stand up and be counted or forever slink away in shame. For the past five years he'd wallowed in his pain and his misery and his self-pity until it was all he could see. Until it had blinded him from anyone's pain but his own. Enough was enough.

He had an apology to make. A big one.

And then he had a kiss to deliver. A sweet one. One with all the gentleness and care his last bungled attempt should have had.

He waited for the panic to set in that would have swamped him two weeks ago at the mere thought of giving in to his desire to kiss Gaby, but it didn't come. Only anticipation and need flooded his chest.

He wanted this kiss, not just for Gaby, but for himself. In a little over a month he had a plane to catch out of the country. He wanted to get on that plane, knowing his soul wasn't dead. Knowing he'd shown Gaby Richards that all men weren't born bastards. *And* that kissing could be very, very nice.

Chapter Eight

Luke rose early the next morning, but he didn't rush over to Gaby's. Instead, he took a cup of coffee out to the porch. Sometime during the night, snow had begun to fall, so he pulled the collar of his sheepskin coat up and burrowed down into its warmth. Settling into the porch swing, he sipped at the scalding brew and wondered if he'd be able to bring Gaby around.

Putting a new pump in her barn and helping her get her stalls up seemed like a fair trade for a few dates with him, but wasn't sure Gaby would see it that way. Not that he wouldn't put the pump in and help her with her stalls even if she refused the dates. But she didn't have to know that. Not right away, anyway. Because he had a feeling he was going to need some kind of leverage to convince her to let him closer than the proverbial country mile.

He grimaced, thinking about Gaby's fear of men. Since her day of birth, men had abused Gaby and those nearest and dearest to her. No wonder she didn't like being touched. She probably acquainted not being touched with surviving until the next day.

But that was going to change.

Starting now.

Draining the last of his coffee, he set the mug on the porch and headed out to his truck. He ducked deeper into his coat as the stinging ice crystals assaulted his ears and cheeks. The winds were becoming vicious, blowing angry white swirls in every direction.

Halfway to Peaceful Shadows, he leaned forward over the steering wheel and fought to see through the condensation on his window and the blowing snow outside. The storm had turned into a full-blown blizzard. The drifting snow made the road more impassable by the minute.

An hour later he pulled into Gaby's drive, damned glad he'd made it at all. Jamming his hat down tight, he jumped from the truck. He took the porch steps in one leap and banged on the door. When it didn't open after thirty seconds, he pounded louder.

Open the door, woman. I'm freezing out here.

He reached forward to see if the door was locked, but just as his hand settled on the knob, Susie and Crash came bounding around the side of the house. They were covered in snow and ice. Crash, with her thin mongrel coat, shivered against the elements.

He strode around the side of the house and peered into the driving snow for Gaby. Nothing. He couldn't remember seeing the dogs without her right on their heels, or vice versa. To see the dogs alone, their coats matted with snow, made the hairs on the back of his neck stand up. Stomping back to the door, he gave the knob an urgent twist. It turned beneath his hand.

He shoved the door open. "Gaby!"

No answer. The tingling at the back of his neck got stronger.

Stepping into the house, he held the screen door wide and waved the dogs in. Crash bounded past him into the warm interior, but Susie sat resolutely in the snow.

"Come on, girl. Get in here. Let's find out what your mistress is up to. Give her hell for leaving her friends out in this mess." He turned back toward the house and looked anxiously around for any sign of Gaby. Nothing.

His heart picked up its beat. This wasn't good. He could feel it in his bones. Since Susie refused to come in, he shut the door, sprinted to the staircase and took the steps two at a time. At the top he swung himself around the door-jamb into her bedroom. No Gaby.

His heart raced out of control. She had to be on the ranch. Her truck was here. But if she hadn't followed the dogs to the house, something was wrong.

Pounding down the stairs, he slammed out the front door. Like a statue, Susie sat in the blizzard waiting for him. Of course. Why hadn't he seen it sooner? He'd bet his eye-teeth the dog knew where Gaby was. "Where is she, Susie? Where's Gaby?" The dog's eyes lit up at mention of her mistress's name, but she didn't move. He tried again. "Where's Gaby?"

Why didn't she get up and lead him to Gaby? She raised a paw in supplication and whined with obvious worry, but she didn't move. Damn. He didn't have the right command word. Quickly he tried several, but none of them worked.

With a frustrated growl and a sense of urgency clawing at him, he stepped off the porch. "Never mind, Susie. I'll find her myself."

Magic. Susie sprang into action, racing ahead of him with definite purpose. Of course! *Find*. The dog found people. It was the obvious command. He hollered after the retreating dog, following her as quickly as the snow allowed. "Find Gaby, Susie. Find Gaby."

Susie raced ahead of him, thankfully stopping to wait when he fell too far behind. It was obvious she had a specific destination in mind. She raced ahead of him, her path straight and true. Unfortunately she ran toward the forest's edge as opposed to one of the buildings. Which meant Gaby was out in this treacherous weather somewhere.

Please, God, don't let her be hurt.

In this cold an injury could be fatal. But even as he prayed for her safety, he knew better. He doubled his efforts to stay close behind Susie.

When the dog stopped in front of a huge downed tree, Luke's heart stopped pumping. Fifty feet from him, the tree's massive body lay in a broken heap on the ground, the raw wood of its newly cut trunk all too visible.

Gaby had bought another saw! A rage so pure and hot blazed through him, he couldn't believe the snow didn't melt under his feet. And then fear exploded inside him, driving him harder.

Pumping his legs against the knee-high snowdrifts, he prayed she wasn't under the tree. Finally he skidded to a halt next to Susie. Carefully, the dog pawed the snow from Gaby's body. Horror arrested him. She *was* under it. Partially covered by snow, Gaby lay trapped under the giant tree.

Adrenaline screamed through his system. He dropped to his knees and dug into the snow with the dog. "Gaby!"

No answer.

His hands moved faster, snow flying from his efforts. He had to get the snow away from her to know what he fought against. He held his breath as he worked. And he prayed.

The bottom half of her body and her right arm were trapped under the tree. The pristine color of the snow reassured him. She wasn't bleeding. At least not externally. With the size of the tree, she could easily be hemorrhaging internally. Her waxy coloring and unconscious state scared him to death.

His heart pounding and his mouth dry, he gently nudged her shoulder. "Gaby."

Slowly her eyes opened.

He practically collapsed with relief, but it didn't last long.

Her eyes were cloudy with confusion, and it took her some time to recognize him. When she tried to smile, her muscles responded awkwardly, turning the smile into a sad twist of her lips. And then she closed her eyes and drifted back to sleep.

He'd been worried about hypothermia all the way out here. Her sleepy state and the uncooperative muscles of her face—all classic signs of hypothermia—confirmed his fears. And he could probably add shock to the list.

He jerked his jacket off and dropped it over her torso, ignoring the icy bite of wind and ice as it blew through the thin layer of his shirt. Acid and urgency ate at his gut. If he didn't get her out of the snow soon, there would be little point in the exercise.

Jumping up, he kicked through the snow, working his way to the base of the tree until his toe connected with the saw's metal casing. He snatched it up with hands grown clumsy from cold. Struggling to make his numb hands work, he refused to think how long Gaby had already been in these chilling temperatures.

Turning back to her, he found Susie laying half on and half off her. Smart dog. "Good girl, Susie. Keep her warm. We'll have her out in a jiff."

Yanking the starter cord, he brought the saw to life.

His heart pounded faster with every passing second, each beat reminding him time was running out. Working against that unforgiving clock and the raging elements, he cut away at the tree until he feared to go further for worry of cutting Gaby, as well.

He tossed the saw aside and tried to lift the remaining section off her. It didn't budge. Howling his fury into the wind, he tried again, straining muscle and bone with every ounce of strength he possessed. Nothing.

Frustration and rage boiled inside him. He wasn't going to let her die, dammit. With a ruthlessness honed on too many battlefields, he went over his options. They were damned few, and all of them ugly. He'd never get help here before she froze to death. She was gray and getting grayer by the minute. To chop the huge section of tree to little bits without cutting her would take nearly as long. The other option sent a cold chill down his spine. He could roll the tree off her, and pray that whatever he crushed in the process she could live without.

Tears stung his eyes, but he closed his mind against them and the crippling pain in his chest. He could save part of her, or none of her. With brutal purpose, he shut off the part of him afraid of hurting her. Then he closed his eyes and prayed for a miracle of epic proportions.

Opening his eyes, he straddled her, placed his numb hands against the bark, braced his arms for the push, dug his feet into the ground, and shoved with all his strength. Slowly, the tree section began to roll. Even in the arctic temperature, with the wind whipping him, sweat trickled down his back as he strained against the heavy tree round. Peripherally, he caught glimpses of Gaby's limbs being uncovered. First her hips, then her knees, and finally, the giant piece of wood rolled off her feet. He rolled the tree an extra turn to make sure it didn't roll back on her, then braced himself for the worst and turned back to Gaby.

He fought his instincts to scoop her up and carry her into the house's warmth. He couldn't move her before checking for injuries. He dropped down beside her, relief surging through him. No blood. He hadn't thought he'd glimpsed any earlier, but it felt good to have his hope confirmed. Neither her hips nor her legs appeared mangled, and her toes and knees seemed to be pointing in the right direction. It seemed impossible she hadn't sustained major damage, but prayed that was the case.

Shielding Gaby from the wind, he nudged her shoulder. "Gaby! Wake up."

No response. He nudged again, not so gently, and called her name again, but the result was the same.

The clock beat faster, ticking off the minutes of Gaby's life. He would have to rely on what his hands could feel and his eyes could see to ascertain her injuries.

He started at her hips, closing his fingers over the bones. Her bones felt solid. A trickle of hope ran through him. He had expected a consistency closer to mush. Squeezing harder, the solid form of the bone held. He carefully moved his hands down her leg. A short sigh of relief escaped his lips as he reached her ankle. Everything seemed intact.

He'd prayed for a miracle. Maybe he'd gotten one. Having completed his examination of her right side, he stood up to step over her so he could examine the left.

And fell flat on his face. Scrambling back up, he brushed the snow from the obstacle that tripped him. A ghostly shiver ran up his spine. Lying directly next to Gaby, from ribs to toe, ran a long red finger of rock. It protruded from the ground just high enough that it had supported most of the tree's weight. Gaby would probably carry some hellacious bruises, but little else. That tiny finger of distinctive red rock had saved her life.

Luke turned toward the house, and there, just behind it, playing hide and seek through the blowing snow, stood Gaby's giant red mountain. Another shiver ran through him. "You old bastard."

He knew clear down to his bones an examination of her left side wasn't necessary, but he did it, anyway. As expected, he found no injuries. Tucking his coat more tightly around her shoulders, he scooped her up and struggled through the raging storm with his precious cargo, Susie at his heels.

By the time he finally fell through Gaby's front door, he couldn't feel his hands. Not an auspicious sign, considering how long Gaby must have been outside. He kicked the door shut behind Susie and laid Gaby on the sofa. He jerked off his snow-covered hat and flung it out of the way as he strode to the telephone. Snatching the receiver, he crammed it between his ear and shoulder and started dialing. Silence filled his ear. The line was dead. With a vile curse he slammed the receiver back into its cradle and returned to Gaby.

He grabbed her hand from the canine noses nudging it and tried to warm it between his own. A mirthless laugh escaped his lips. Trying to warm ice with ice. That ought to work. He tried to arouse her once again, calling her name and pushing at her, but she remained ominously silent.

He needed to get her stripped down and tucked into a warm bed with lots of covers. Better yet, an electric blanket. He removed his coat from her shoulders and attacked hers next. His numb hands fumbled with the jacket zipper, but eventually he got it and carefully pulled the wet garment from her. He glanced down at her stiff, snow-encrusted jeans. Those were next.

The snap and zipper teased his clumsy fingers, but he managed them. He tucked his fingers inside the top waistband and gently pulled the jeans over her hips. Scrambling over the dogs, he moved to her feet and pulled her boots off before stripping the jeans completely off.

He grabbed the afghan from the back of the sofa, threw it over her, scooped her into his arms, carried her up the stairs amid a flurry of canine feet and laid her on her bed. Pulling the afghan aside, he divested her of her wet flannel shirt. He gritted his teeth as the wet pink bra followed. The panties, he didn't even think about. Pulling the covers from underneath her, he tucked her in, snugging the edges of the quilt and down comforter close around her.

He frowned at his handiwork, desperately afraid it wouldn't be enough. Though pretty, the top quilt wouldn't offer much warmth. The down comforter beneath would retain what heat was emitted into it, but Gaby wasn't making any. He'd sell his soul for an electric blanket. Anything that would actually make heat.

If he didn't warm her up soon, he would lose her. She hadn't made a peep since he'd dragged her in. A deep, deep sleep claimed her.

With hypothermia, sleep came just before death.

His heart pounded and the icy hand of fear squeezed the breath from his lungs. He couldn't panic now. He had to think rationally. And warming this damned house up would be a good first step. Lord, he could see his breath. He pounded down the stairs to the thermostat and tried to turn it. It didn't budge. He looked closer. It had already been cranked all the way up.

Damn!

With a trail of obscenities, he stomped down to the basement. Sure enough, the pilot light was out on both the furnace and hot water heater. He spotted a pack of matches and went to work, trying to light both pilot lights. No luck. Either she had a block somewhere in her gas line, or she had no gas.

He'd hoped things were looking up. But this changed the whole ugly scene. Desperation riding his shoulders, he stormed back up the steps, snatched his coat off the floor, and headed out into the storm. Pushing against the winds, he made his way to the white gas tank. He popped the lid and looked at the gauge. Empty. His gut tightened.

If the line had been blocked, he might have been able to fix it. Now, they would have to do without. A cold shiver that had nothing to do with the sub-zero windchill racked his bones. He trudged back to the house, cold determination settling in his belly.

He pushed through the front door and stomped the snow off his boots on the way to the living room. The house had no heat, no hot water, no firewood in the hearth and, temporarily, no phone. He could already see his breath. In another six hours the temperature inside would match the one outside. He ran back upstairs. Gaby hadn't moved.

He searched Gaby's room for more covers or anything else he could use. He tossed the afghan on her, and threw the robe hanging on the back of her door over her, but nothing else presented itself. The drawers in the only dresser in the room weren't big enough to hold blankets, so he headed for the closet.

Nothing. He checked the spare room next. Empty. Absolutely empty. Where the hell did she keep all her stuff? Had she left it all in Chicago until she got more settled? Returning to her room, he yanked off his sheepskin coat and settled it over her shoulders.

He shook her shoulder, trying again to bring her around. "Gaby."

Nothing.

Damn! The blankets weren't working. Luke glanced down at himself. A warning bell sounded in his head. Gaby would have a fit if she woke up with him beside her. His glance settled on her gray pallor. Hell, let her scream. A good shot of adrenaline would help get her blood pumping.

Practically pulling the buttons from his shirt, he jerked it off. Posthaste, his boots and pants followed. His hands hesitated at his wet, icy briefs, but then with grim determination he stripped them off. His wet socks, he chucked just before he lifted the covers and crawled in with Gaby.

Refusing to acknowledge any thoughts beyond those necessary for the task at hand, he turned Gaby on her side, facing away from him, and snuggled in behind her. He jerked away, his belly and lap tightening with cold. Her panties were as cold and wet as his briefs had been.

He gritted his teeth and pretended the sudden heat curling through him and the shaking in his hands was a normal occurrence. He swiped the panties from her in one smooth motion. Closing his eyes against the graceful curve of her spine and the enticing twin globes of her bottom, he tossed her panties on the floor and snuggled back up.

Heat exploded within him. Blood raced to his sex. His hands closed convulsively on her shoulders and he strained a quick, indrawn breath through his teeth. What the hell had he been thinking? He moved away from her again. God, he felt like someone trespassing without permission.

His hand moved down her arm and a fresh coolness chilled his fingers. Reality sank in. She was freezing to death right here in this bed with him. And that was the hottest part of him. He shifted forward, fitting bottom to lap, ignoring the sexual surge this time. The more heat he made, the more she got.

To preserve as much heat as possible and to capture the warm air escaping their lungs, he pulled the covers over their heads. Plunged into darkness, the world disappeared around him. Now skin against skin, the fresh scent of soap and sunshine became his only reality.

Knowing better but not giving a damn, he buried his nose in the silky strands of her hair and drew in a slow, deep breath. He reveled in her scent before exhaling into the tendrils of silk. His breath bounced off her nape, warming his lips and tickling his nose, bringing sunshine with it. His chest rubbed against her back, the goose bumps on her skin abrading his nipples. Fresh heat surged to his lap.

A frustrated moan escaped his lips. The tiny space throbbed with intimacy, and before he could stop himself, he'd nuzzled through her hair and settled his lips on her nape. She was cold as ice.

What was wrong with him? This wasn't a damned game. Pulling his lips away, he redirected his thoughts and tried to get some blood circulating by rubbing her arm vigorously. Once the skin there warmed up, he moved his hand to the hard, smooth contours of her flank and began to rub. The soft flesh of her bottom felt as good as he'd imagined the first day he'd seen her bending over her dog.

Another jolt of pleasure raced through him. Yep, between the friction the massage created and the furnace he was becoming, he ought to have her heated up in no time. In fact, her skin did seem to be getting warmer.

Five minutes later a tiny groan came from her lips. Hope soared through him, but he kept up the light, fast massage. Another tiny groan. And a few minutes later another one, stronger this time. A triumphant smile broke out on his lips and he wanted to whoop with laughter. But he didn't.

Gaby would be shocked enough to find him in her bed; he didn't need to scare her into consciousness on top of it.

A bit later the groans were pretty steady and she began to shift restlessly in his arms. No doubt the pain of thawing out had begun to pierce her unconscious state. A good sign. It meant her body was starting to warm itself up. As it continued to do so, the discomfort would get worse. A pang of regret ran through him at the thought of the pain she would go through, even as he prayed for the warming that would cause it.

Pain. A slow, dull, throbbing pain pulled at Gaby. She shifted against it. It went away and she drifted quietly, half asleep and half awake, enjoying the comfort of her own bed and the warmth surrounding her. No, more than *enjoying* the warmth. *Reveling* in it, as if she would never get enough.

The pain returned, stronger this time and concentrated more in specific areas. Her feet hurt, and her hands. She shifted again, trying to stretch her legs out, but something stopped her.

A pang of frustration tweaked her. Something was wrong. An important memory pulled at her, but she couldn't pinpoint it. And before the thought could completely coalesce, the pain slid away and the heat surrounded her. She snuggled deeper, soaking it in like a desert floor sucking up the first spring rain. It felt so good, but as she began to reach the upper realms of consciousness, something still bothered her.

She couldn't move, and she needed more air. She drew in a deep breath. Or tried to, but the air was too heavy. And humid. Awakening, she struggled purposefully against the covers and whatever seemed to be holding her down.

Suddenly something in bed with her moved, and the blankets whooshed away from her head. Frigid, oxygen-rich air assaulted her head and shoulders.

"Wake up, Sleeping Beauty."

Fear shot through her, and Gaby practically jumped out of her skin as she struggled to get away from the male voice at her back. Her arms and legs flailed helplessly, refusing to respond correctly to any command. Her heart pounded in her ears, and with fear and panic driving her, she fought harder against her restraints.

"Ouch! Dammit, woman, hold still!"

A hand on her shoulder flipped her to her back. A strong arm and a heavy leg landed over her, capturing her arms and legs. But she'd already stopped the struggle. She knew that voice.

"Luke?" Her fuzzy brain worked slowly, despite the shot of adrenaline. But one thing registered clearly. Luke had come back. Joy warmed her heart. For the past two weeks, she'd awakened each morning hoping to see Luke again, but knowing she never would. And now he was here.

She looked at his precious face above hers and thought it the most beautiful sight on earth. So handsome and strong...and worried. She tried to draw her brows down in question, but her facial muscles didn't seem to be working any better than the rest of her. A hint of panic returned. What was wrong with her?

Luke must have seen her confusion; his lips pulled back in concern and he tried to soothe her. "Easy. Everything's all right. We got you out from under the tree. Remember the tree?"

The tree? A kaleidoscope of images spun in her head. A new chain saw. Pulling the cord. The loud buzz of its engine. The scary power of the saw as it cut into the huge tree. Tiny wood bits flying in every direction, stinging her cheeks as the blade cut deep. Her cutting and cutting and cutting, and the tree still refusing to fall. And so, finally, she'd pushed it.

Like an instant replay she could see the tree falling again. Not away from her in the direction she'd pushed it, but toward her. An icy shiver ran through her. She'd known then she'd never get out from under it before it fell. Her hands awkwardly clutched at the covers, and she pulled them tight against her, trying to hoard the warmth they gave.

She'd been knocked out when the tree fell on her. She'd come to with it lying on top of her, the storm raging around her and her bones aching with cold. And then so much later, past the point when she'd given up and decided she would die under that tree, Luke had come. An angel in sheepskin and denim. The memory was hazy, like something seen through a veil, but it was there.

And now he was here. Wrapped around her, protecting her from the world. Warm and strong...and...and.... She moved against him experimentally, horror dawning. *Naked.* Her heart leaped in her chest, and she exploded into action. She had to get out of this bed!

Her escape didn't get her any farther than it had last time. Luke just tightened his arm and leg, subduing her awkward movements with little effort.

"Easy. You're all right. I'm not going to hurt you."

"But you're naked!"

Blood surged through her veins, but she couldn't have said what from. Fear or desire. Part of her wanted to wallow in the heat and feel of his skin against hers. Frostbite still nipped at her, and he was *so* warm. The soft hair covering his chest and legs felt wonderful, gently coaxing the feeling back with a rub and tickle. And his arms and legs, wrapped tightly around her, brought an unfamiliar feeling of security. But the feeling was too alien to trust, and the tendrils of fear, so much more familiar, began to rule her emotions.

"Gaby, I am not here to hurt you or terrorize you in any way. And if you start looking at me as though I am, I'm going to throw you out that window and back into the storm."

Luke pointed at the window, but Gaby didn't remove her eyes from his. She gulped past the lump in her throat and tried desperately not to notice how hard the muscles under his skin felt. Instead she concentrated on how his chest hair tickled her shoulder. Did she like it or not? The idea so captivated her that before she could stop herself, she rubbed her body against his to find out. And then she felt the hard length of his arousal.

She froze. Her breathing stopped. Her heart stopped. The whole world stopped. Every drop of blood in her body careened to her toes, and then came crashing back to her cheeks with a force that set her face on fire. Her fingers closed on the covers until not an ounce of air could be found between feathers and material. She closed her eyes in embarrassment.

"Now, Gaby, don't panic. We're not going to do anything about it."

She squeezed her eyes tighter and fought for composure. Useless. Panic edged every word. "You've got to get out of this bed. Now. *Now!*"

Luke sighed with a hint of exasperation. "Look, I'm sorry you're frightened or embarrassed about being naked in bed with me. But before you go ballistic and shriek the rafters down, think about this. When I dragged you in here and stripped your clothes off, you were unconscious from hypothermia. And you're not out of the woods yet. The roads and the airways are impassable. Nobody's coming to rescue you. And you haven't got a drop of heat in this house. Not a stick of wood or a whiff of gas or a decent blanket to keep you warm. You ought to thank your lucky stars you've got a hot-blooded man willing to share his heat with you. Now, roll over and try not to screech like a banshee when I snuggle up to you.''

Gaby's mind raced like lightning. She understood now why they were in bed together. If she'd found a victim with hypothermia and had as few supplies as Luke thought he had, she would have done the same thing. Stripped them both naked and put them in bed together to generate as much body heat as possible. But thankfully she'd never had to perform such a heroic act. Because she couldn't have pulled it off, any more than she could lie here with Luke and pretend a nonchalance she didn't feel.

She tried desperately to pull her thoughts together. Not easy when the only thing that seemed to matter was the long, hard heat of his arousal poking her in the hip. But she made a valiant effort to organize her thoughts.

Careful not to move *any* other part of her body, she tipped her head toward her nightstand. ''There's a heating pad in that bottom drawer. And there are two sleeping bags in the storage under my staircase. If you plug in the heating pad, pile the sleeping bags on me and fix me a cup of hot tea, I'm going to be better off, Luke.''

His expression had turned hopeful when she'd mentioned the heating pad and sleeping bags, but it had become decidedly black when she mentioned the tea.

He pulled his lips into a stern line. ''If I could heat water for tea, you'd be swimming in it. Remember, you have a gas stove, and you're out of gas. And why the hell you let your gas tank run out in the middle of November will be

our first topic of conversation when you're all thawed out.
But for now—"

"I didn't let my tank run out." Gaby prickled at his
admonishment. "I filled the thing two weeks ago. I don't
know what happened. But you can still make me tea. I had
to replace my old stove, remember? I had an electric one
put in."

Luke's eyes popped open. "You have an electric stove
down there?" He didn't wait for an answer, he just leaped
out of bed.

Pushing herself awkwardly to a sitting position, she prepared to flee if Luke tried to return to the bed. But the
sight of Luke stopped her cold—broad shoulders, a narrow
waist, an expanse of bronze skin and sculpted muscles, and
two of the tautest buttocks she'd ever seen. Her mouth
went dry, and her hands began to sweat.

Totally unaffected by his nudity, Luke snatched his
pants from the floor and turned back to her.

With an astonished shriek, Gaby pulled the covers over
her eyes.

A chuckle filled the room along with the sound of wet
denim being pulled over long, strong legs. The whisper of
a zipper sighed across the room, and then, like a shot in
the dark, the decisive sound of a snap being closed. "You
can come out now."

She peered over the blanket. The purely male deviltry
in Luke's smile stopped her heart. Suddenly she wanted
him back in her bed with his hot skin and his soft hair and
his sexy smile. And, oh, God, where did that leave her?

Wanting and afraid.

A wave of pain stopped her thoughts. She closed her
eyes and gritted her teeth against the throbbing in her feet.
"Hurt?"

She nodded her head at Luke's question.

His expression turned grave. "It's going to get worse."

A lot worse. She nodded her head again. "I know."

He said nothing else until she looked up and he caught her gaze with his own. "Are you going to let me help you with it?"

Her heart flipped in her chest. What was he asking? Was he giving her another chance? She didn't know why he was here. But if he was giving her another chance, she was going to take it.

She smiled sweetly. "You'd like that, wouldn't you?"

An answering smile turned the corners of Luke's mouth. "More than you can imagine."

Chapter Nine

Four hours later, Luke lowered Gaby into the big chair he'd dragged into the kitchen from the living room. When he'd found out about the electric stove, he'd moved them, dogs and all, into the kitchen immediately. He'd closed the door between the kitchen and dining room and switched all the burners and the oven on. With the oven door open, it hadn't taken long for the kitchen to heat up. Now, the little room, with its small eating nook off to the side, was positively toasty.

It had been a long day for Gaby. The pain in her feet had gotten so bad she'd cried for an hour as he'd held her against his side and helped her walk around the kitchen to get the circulation going. But the tears had abated a while ago, and pain no longer pulled at her expression. Now, she looked exhausted.

He dropped the heating pad into her lap, piled the

comforter on top of her and snugged the edges tight. "Better?"

She nodded her head.

"Warm enough?"

She nodded again, stifling a yawn behind the comforter's folds.

He pointed a finger at her. "You're tired, and a nap would be good, but you can't have one until we're positive your temperature is stable. I want you to drink a cup of coffee. It'll help you stay awake."

"Does that mean we're out of chicken soup?"

He laughed at the hopeful look on her face. Not that he blamed her. The three cans of chicken soup he'd forced down her in an equal amount of hours would gag anyone, but it wasn't his fault it had been the only choice in her cupboard.

"Yes, you're out of chicken soup. And it looks like you could use a bit of caffeine. Don't go to sleep while I fix it. Okay?"

She nodded, but immediately snuggled deeper into the chair and closed her eyes. He'd best brew it quickly. He looked around for the coffeepot, which was nowhere in sight.

"Gaby, where's your coffeepot?"

She didn't even open her eyes as she answered him. "I don't have one. Instant coffee's in the freezer."

"In the freezer?"

"Yeah, it stays fresher that way."

Fresh instant coffee? Now there was a frightening concept. He shook his head as he pulled the coffee out of the freezer, set it on the counter, and began the search for mugs. Gaby's idea of what qualified as sustenance needed a major adjustment. That first day when he'd helped to clean up the barn, she'd showed up with what she considered lunch. Two cans of ravioli, opened but not heated, with spoons stuck into the gelatinous mass.

He'd eaten it, but only after she'd polished hers off with a disinterested nonchalance that told him it hadn't been a joke. The next day, when she'd shown up with cans of tuna, he'd drawn the line. They'd eaten lunch at restaurants every day after that.

Sticking two cups of water in the microwave, he cranked the knob and waited for the water to heat.

He glanced back at Gaby. "Don't go to sleep on me."

She shook her head back and forth, but didn't answer. He mixed the drinks quickly and then brought them over to her. Nudging her knee, he handed her a steaming mug.

Opening her eyes, she smiled easily and wrapped her hands around it as if to soak up every ounce of heat. Then she raised her eyes to his. "Thanks."

He gave a half bow. "Anytime, ma'am."

She chuckled softly. "'Anytime' you will fix me a cup of coffee? Or 'anytime' you would drag me out from under a tree? I was thanking you for both."

He narrowed his eyes in warning. "Gaby, soon you and I are going to have a serious discussion about that tree and your penchant for chain saws, but now is not that time."

She got the message. She nodded quickly and took a quicker sip of coffee, dismissing the subject. Then she gave him a teasing smile. "So, tree aside, why *did* you come over here?"

His muscles tensed. It was the perfect opening. He took a long swallow of coffee, choosing his words carefully. "I came over here to make a deal with you."

Gaby's eyes widened in surprise and then narrowed with suspicion. "In *this* snowstorm you came over to make a deal?"

He gave her another pointed look. "And aren't you glad I did?"

She laughed sheepishly, nodding her head. "Yes, I am. But I want to hear about this deal."

He smiled and held a finger up. "Good change of subject." He glanced around for a comfortable spot. Negotiations could be tricky. He'd brought three sofa cushions in and thrown the sleeping bags over them to make a bed for Gaby. That would do. Settling down on them, he stretched his legs out and crossed them at the ankle. Taking a leisurely sip of coffee, he mentally put his ducks in a row.

"How's the barn coming?" he asked.

Gaby raised a shoulder. "I haven't been working in there. I've been putting in paddocks. I figured I could put the stalls in anytime, but if I didn't get the fence posts in before the ground froze, I'd be out of luck until spring."

Luke raised his brows in surprise. "I didn't see any new fences out there."

With a wry laugh, she looked out the window at the swirling snow. "Can't imagine why."

Luke smiled with her. "Yeah, neither can I. Okay, how is the fencing coming?"

She cocked her head to the side, trying to figure out what he was getting at. "As of yesterday, done."

"Good. Stalls next?"

She nodded.

"Ever built one before?"

"Dozens."

Too bad. He needed something where his help would be indispensable to her. But he wouldn't worry yet. He still had the pump up his sleeve. "Good. How are you at digging out wells and replacing the insulated casings? The pump in your barn has frozen for the past eight years. If you don't dig out the old casing and replace it with a new one, you're going to have to haul water from the house all winter.''

Gaby's eyes widened in horror. "The pump in my barn doesn't work in the winter?" Her voice positively squeaked with distress.

Oh, yeah, the perfect ace. He shook his head, trying not to smile. "Nope. And you still have your indoor arena to get ready, right?"

She was beginning to catch on now. She narrowed her eyes. "Are you volunteering to help with all that?"

Smart lady. "Well, yes, I am. But there's a price."

She nodded knowingly. "Ah, finally we've come to the deal part."

Luke nodded.

"Well, get on with it. What do I get, and what do you want?"

He pointed to his chest. "You get me to replace the casing on your pump. And to help you put up stalls. And last, I'll bring the tractor over from Seven Peaks and get your indoor arena done. Sound good?"

"And you get?" she prompted, brows raised.

Tension gripped him. This was it. He drew in a slow, deep breath. "I want you to go out on a few dates with me. To be specific, for every day I work, you go out on one date with me."

Gaby's breath left her in a whoosh, and her eyes doubled in size. "Dates?"

He nodded, watching the play of emotions on her face. Surprise gave way to something close to wonder, and his heart gave a joyful leap. She liked the idea. Now he had to convince her it was safe to take a chance on dating him. With her background and his major blunder in the barn two weeks ago, he would need just the right words.

"I'm not talking about modern-day dating. I'm not interested in swapping financial stats and social rankings to be followed by a sexual coupling to make sure every notch and cog fit before we advance to the next date. I'm talking about old-fashioned dating. We'll go for picnics ''

Gaby glanced out the window as if he'd lost his mind.

He chuckled, setting his coffee cup down as Hank wandered over and made himself comfortable, laying his big bloodhound head in his lap. "Never been on a winter picnic?"

She shook her head, her eyes still wide with disbelief.

Automatically he grabbed Hank's ear and began to rub it between his fingers, enjoying the warm, silky texture. "Well, there are tricks to winter picnics you'll like. I promise. And we'll sit on the porch swing at Seven Peaks in the evening when you're done with your horses and talk. We'll go on Sunday drives and I'll show you vistas that will knock your socks off. And then we'll stop for hot chocolate on the way back. I'll take you to dinner and a movie, and we'll steal secret kisses in the back of the theater and again on the porch when I bring you home."

A pink flush tinted her cheeks, and excitement sparkled in her eyes. But then her brows pulled together and shadows of uncertainty moved in. "You'd be getting the short end of the stick, Luke. I'll bet you build a fine stall, but I don't know anything about secret kisses."

Luke's heart knocked inside his chest. Such innocence. "I know you don't. That'll be part of the deal. I get to show you. But you'll set the pace. We'll go nice and slow."

Indecision warred within her. The darkness of fear and uncertainty stalked relentlessly across her features. But the piquant light of want and curiosity marched there, too.

He held his breath. *Come on, Gaby. Say yes.* He sent

the mental message across the room like a shot, his eyes glued to hers, as if he could will her to give him the answer he wanted.

Silence stretched between them, but her eyes never left his. He fired the message again. *Say yes.*

Finally she gave a sigh of mixed emotions and leaned back against her chair. "Luke?" A pink flush bloomed on her cheeks, but she leveled her gaze on him and forged ahead nonetheless. "Just for the record, I'm not looking for a relationship that goes any deeper than a few dates. I decided a long time ago I would never do the couple thing."

Like a chimera in the desert, a shimmer of loss slid over Luke's heart, catching him off guard and making him wonder why he felt the tiny pain. He wasn't looking for anything deeper, either. Was he?

Before he could look at that question too closely, he slammed the door on that voice and reassured Gaby. "It's okay. I understand about not wanting to get tangled up in relationships, believe me. And I'm not asking for that. All I'm asking is that between now and when I have to leave the country again, you and I fix up your ranch together and take a little time for ourselves, as well."

Gaby's brows pulled together in question. "You're leaving the country? Again?"

He nodded. "In five weeks, to be exact. I work for an organization called Life Move. We zip into places of political unrest and try to get civilians out of the way. Try to get medicine and medical assistance to those who need it. Help with famine relief. That kind of thing. Roundup will be finished by then. It'll be time for me to leave."

She cocked her head and gave him an assessing look. The fact that he would be leaving before long seemed to reassure her and finally she gave him a pleased grin and stuck out her hand. "Okay, cowboy. You have a deal."

Joy exploded inside him, and he moved Hank so he could crawl the few steps to Gaby's chair. Taking her hand in his, he gave it a single, hearty shake. "Deal." He wanted to seal the deal with a kiss, but he hadn't earned that right yet.

Soon though. Very, very soon.

For the next hour, Luke force-fed Gaby coffee and paced from one window to the next as he watched the storm rage on and the snowdrifts pile higher and higher.

Gaby watched him with a mixture of shy anticipation and ingrained wariness. Getting close to her without sending her into flight mode would be tricky. It would be a lot easier if he knew exactly what form her boogie men came in. If he could get her to tell him a little about her past, it might help.

Luke glanced out the window again at the blowing snow and ice. A smile played across his lips. What better atmosphere for sharing old stories and confidences than being stranded together in the midst of raging elements? He turned back to Gaby, careful not to trip over Hank who seemed to think it his duty to follow Luke from one point of observation to the next.

A cautious smile turned the corners of Gaby's mouth. She looked so damned adorable, he wanted to scoop her into his arms. But he didn't. They'd made a deal, and the only way to build her trust would be to stick to it. A day of work for a single date. And he hadn't done a lick of work yet.

A loud growl from her stomach caught his attention.

He pointed his finger at her. "Food. You need food."

He strode toward the stove area intent on fixing them some dinner.

But Gaby pushed herself out of her chair with a groan and waved him off. "No, I'm tired of watching you and Hank pace around the kitchen. I'll fix something. You sit back down on your little bed and pet Hank. It'll keep you both quiet."

Luke watched her slowly straighten as she walked to the kitchen area. She was stiff and hurting. Moving around a little might be the best thing for her. He resettled himself on the cushions and pulled Hank down beside him. "You're going to be stiffer tomorrow, and worse the day after that."

She nodded. "I know. Usually after I strain my muscles, I try to repeat the same activity the next day. I can avoid a lot of stiffness if I re-stretch the muscles. But I don't think dropping another tree on myself would have the same effect. Do you?"

Well, hell. If she could joke about it, so could he. He chuckled dryly. "No, I wouldn't recommend it."

Gaby smiled back at him. "What do you want for dinner? I have a can of stew and tuna. I always have a cabinet full of tuna. I think—"

"Stop! Right there. I'm not eating anything out of a can, Gaby. So if you don't have any real food, tell me now and I'll go out and...and—" he looked out the window at the savagely blowing snow, then turned back to her with blind determination "—trap us something."

Peals of laughter filled the kitchen, a sound he'd never heard from her lips. And it was so beautiful, he'd almost be willing to eat cold ravioli to hear it again. Almost.

He gave her his most serious look. "I'm not kidding."

She laughed again. "I know you're not. Lucky for you Matt sent over—" she whirled around, yanked the freezer door open and snatched out something huge wrapped in butcher paper ''—this!''

''Yes! Steak!'' Bless Matt's hide. He owed big brother one.

Gaby tossed the piece of frozen meat in the microwave to thaw it and then pulled the refrigerator open and began to browse around. The refrigerator's light shone through her nightgown, showing a perfect silhouette of her body. Luke's hand stilled on Hank's ear. His mouth went dry, and his Adam's apple stuck mid-swallow. The lovely shape of her breasts tantalized his imagination until his palms itched to touch them. His fingers tightened on Hank's ear.

Look away!

Right. He might as well ask for canonization. His eyes drank in the sight before him. Beautiful. His body stirred to life and he recalled the feel of her from only hours before. Silk and sunshine. Fire and ice.

She shut the refrigerator door.

Thank you, God.

She turned to him, a guilty expression on her face. ''I don't really have anything in there except horse wormer, some butter and about twenty pounds of carrots.'' Suddenly her eyes lit up and she spun back to the freezer.

He closed his eyes as her gown wrapped tightly around her at her quick pirouette, showing him every curve he was trying to forget. He gritted his teeth against the blood rushing to his groin and tried to think of other things.

Gaby pulled a small box out of the freezer. ''I've got a box of vegetables left and—'' she pulled a cabinet open and snatched out two boxes ''—blueberry muffins and rice pilaf. Sound good?''

He just nodded, afraid to try for a verbal response. His throat was as tight as his jeans. Her gown hung loosely around her now. If she didn't move too quickly, he'd be all right. He took a slow breath and forced his thoughts to different matters.

He cleared his throat. "Tell me how you got into horses."

She lifted a shoulder as she dumped the muffin mix into a bowl. "I don't know. I just fell into it. Twin Oaks, the barn I worked at until I came here, was just five miles from my house. I discovered it when I was eight. The horses fascinated me."

She held the bowl under the faucet, added water and stirred the mix. "The first day I stumbled upon the barn, a man was putting his jumper over five-foot fences. From my hiding place in the bushes, I thought they were flying." Her expression turned wistful, and a small smile of remembrance touched her lips.

His heart ached at the thought of an eight-year-old five miles from her house, all alone, hiding in the bushes.

She opened a cabinet and pulled down a muffin tin. "Anyway, I think I hid in those bushes for a year before Trisha pulled me out and threw me on a horse's back." The gentle smile turned to one of brilliance. "When that horse started moving under me, I *was* flying."

He smiled with her. When he raced his horses across the open pasture, he felt the same way, even today. "Who's Trisha?"

"Trisha Deanne. She owns Twin Oaks, and after throwing me on that horse, she became my teacher and mentor. She always made sure I had the opportunity to ride. Lord knows my parents never could have afforded it."

Or would have, Luke thought, even if they had the funds. But he didn't say it. He didn't want to stop the story's flow.

Gaby stuck two pots of water on the stove. Then she

stuck half a stick of butter in a skillet and put it on the burner in front of them. "Trisha taught me in exchange for work I did around the barn. Then, when I was fifteen, she let me move into the room above the barn. I trained one young horse a month for her in exchange for rent, and a second one in exchange for my lessons. And she let me do it as long as I took a commission off the horses when they sold. Hence the partnership between Deanne and Richards."

For the next several minutes, Gaby busied herself getting the veggies and rice onto boil. Taking the steak from the microwave, she removed the paper and dropped it into the skillet. The sizzle of searing meat filled the room.

She turned to him. "How do you like your steak done?"

"Medium rare."

She busied herself at the stove for a few minutes and he continued to rub Hank's ear. When he looked up, Gaby was poking at the meat with a fork, a worried look on her face.

After another poke or two, she turned that worried look to him. "Look, I hate to disturb you and Hank there, but do you know how to cook a steak medium rare?"

With a quick apology to Hank, he jumped to his feet. No one appreciated a perfectly cooked steak more than he, and from the look on Gaby's face, she didn't have a clue how to go about it. Besides, he was proud of his family ranch and the prime meat they produced. He wanted her to enjoy this largess from Seven Peaks.

He took the fork. "Here, let me do that." He poked at the meat, testing its doneness. "This will take a few minutes. How is everything else doing?"

She looked at the timer. "The muffins have another ten minutes." Being careful not to touch him, she checked under the rattling lids. "The rice needs about the same, but the brussels sprouts are done."

He looked at her in horror. "Brussels sprouts?"

She laughed at his expression. "Yes. Brussels sprouts. They're good for you."

"So's castor oil, but it should never be taken voluntarily."

Gaby laughed harder and leaned in to lift the lid from the simmering vegetable. Intent on her teasing, she didn't realize her breast pressed against his forearm.

But he noticed. Gritting his teeth, he concentrated on what she said, because if he thought about how good she'd felt snuggled against him, all would be lost.

"Luke, see how good these look? And smell that wonderful aroma." She drew in a deep breath.

He took a deep breath just to clear his senses, then swung his head away from the stove. If the nauseating smell of brussels sprouts didn't take his mind off how badly he wanted her, nothing would.

"God, Gaby, give a man a break. Put that damned lid down."

Laughing gently, she left the stove and moved back to her chair. For several minutes silence reigned as Luke turned the steaks and kept an eye on the other parts of dinner. When the buzzer finally sounded for the muffins, Gaby started to stand, but he waved her back.

"Just stay where you are. I'll get them." For his own sanity it would be best if he kept her as far from him as possible. At least until this damned storm blew over and he'd put in one full day of work.

He took the muffins from the oven, pulled two plates out of a cabinet, and started to fill their plates. He placed two muffins on each plate, thinking they were a sad replacement for the real thing. Their rubbery texture and dried blueberries made him think of the big, fluffy muffins with fresh, juicy blueberries that Shanna made. The instant rice dish didn't look any better than the boxed muffins. The brussels sprouts he refused to deal with.

The steak, however, was cooked to perfection. But then, he'd done that. He handed Gaby her laden plate and lowered himself back onto the makeshift bed with his. All three dogs immediately converged on him. He laughed at their expectant faces. Cutting off a piece of steak for each one, he tossed it to them and sent them back to their beds.

He watched the dogs greedily wolf down the steak, and bit into one of Gaby's boxed muffins. He chewed mechanically and swallowed hard. The dogs could have the muffins, too. He tore them into equal parts and lobbed them in the canines' direction.

"Luke!" Gaby gave him an appalled look. "I have dog food, you know. In case you haven't noticed, the cupboards are pretty bare. That's your dinner. And anything left over is breakfast. If you feed it to the dogs, we're going to run low on food. And I guarantee you won't like sharing the dogs' food nearly as much as they like sharing yours."

"Don't bet on it," Luke mumbled, and cut into his steak. He popped another bite into his mouth and chewed with relish. Now *that* was a fine steak. He took another bite before turning his attention back to Gaby.

"Do you eat everything out of a box or a can?" He hadn't meant to whine, but he didn't want to spend all his free time with Gaby over the next few weeks in restaurants. He wanted them to have quiet, private time together. Which meant they'd be spending a good portion of that time right here in this kitchen, and the thought of eating canned and boxed food for that time was a dismal one.

Luckily Gaby didn't seem to notice his whining. She

just shrugged and popped her first bite of meat into her mouth.

Her whole expression changed. Her eyes widened in surprise. No, something much closer to revelation. And then, pure bliss filled her face. Closing her eyes, she chewed slowly, and her face became a mask of sensual delight.

Luke's heart shifted into overdrive. His blood raced through his veins and his jeans tightened painfully. Was that how she'd look in the throes of passion? He forced himself to look away. Staring down at his plate, he dragged his mind from such dangerous thoughts until Gaby's voice brought his gaze back up.

"This is incredible!''

He could tell her in a heartbeat about incredible. And it wasn't a piece of steak. It involved tangled sheets and sweaty skin, arching backs and a climb to heaven that would keep that look on her face from dusk until dawn if he had his way about it, but he reined in his imagination and reminded himself Gaby wasn't ready for that. Yet.

He took a deep breath, rerouted his carnal thoughts and promised to bring more steaks in the future. Then he repeated his earlier question about whether or not she ate everything out of a box or a can.

She chewed another bite of steak with equal pleasure—something he ruthlessly ignored—and nodded. ''In Chicago I crawled on my first horse before dawn most mornings, and off my last one around seven. Then I worked Crash and Susie until nine or ten. By then, if I had the energy to pour a bowl of cereal and eat it, I felt lucky. Besides, my apartment wasn't equipped for cooking. I had a little tiny stove with one burner and an oven the size of a TV dinner. And even if the apartment had been equipped, I don't know how to cook. My mother never taught me.''

His first clue to her past. Had the mother been too busy

protecting Gaby to teach her the mundane? Or had she simply not cared enough to bother? The trick would be to phrase the question diplomatically enough that Gaby wouldn't know exactly what he was asking.

He kept his tone casual. "Didn't you ever help your mother fix supper?"

"Are you kidding? My mother never cooked *anything*. When I whip up a box of muffins, like those you just tossed to the dogs—" she gave him a pointed look "—I think I'm being downright domestic. A TV dinner is a culinary delight to me."

He gave her a horrified look, and she laughed outright. God, he loved to hear her laugh. But her bad eating habits were beginning to make sense. If a warmed-up TV dinner awaited him, an irritating hangnail would keep him away from the table for hours. No wonder she'd been transported to Mars and back when she'd bitten into that steak.

But he mustn't get sidetracked. Her eating habits weren't what he wanted to know about. He wanted to know why her mom hadn't cooked for her and her little sister. And if she hadn't cooked for them, what had she done?

"If your mom never cooked anything, what did you eat growing up?"

Something in his voice must have tipped Gaby off because she carefully laid her fork down on her plate and fixed him with a steady gaze. Quietly she waited for him to get to the point.

He laid his own fork down and met her eyes squarely. "I'm not very good at games."

"Neither am I. Why don't you tell me what you really want to know."

He set his plate down beside him, drew his knees up

and rested his wrists on them, clasping his hands between his open knees. "I had a few beers with Tom last night."

Gaby raised a single brow. "And?"

"And he told me how your sister died and why you went after your brother-in-law."

Anger flashed in Gaby's eyes. Anger and betrayal.

Luke's stomach wound in a knot. Gaby never talked about her past, and she wouldn't be pleased Tom had breached a sacred trust by telling Luke about her sister.

But before he could explain Tom's reasons for divulging the information, Gaby raised her chin and gave Luke a defiant stare. "What else did Tom tell you?"

"Nothing," he reassured her. "He said if I wanted to know anything else about you, I'd have to ask you." He caught her gaze and held it. "So I'm asking."

A humorless laugh burst from within her, and a sad smile turned her lips. "What exactly are you asking?"

He took a deep breath and put his cards on the table.

"This isn't going to work, Gaby, if I scare you spitless every time I touch you. I think if I know where you're coming from, I can avoid a lot of pitfalls."

"Pitfalls?" She laughed again, that dry humorless laugh. "Luke, my past isn't full of pitfalls. It's full of great big yawning pits that go on and on forever. You want to know why I jump when you get too close? Why my sister ended up in an abusive marriage? You want to know why my mom never cooked for us? I'll tell you."

She put her plate on the floor and pulled the covers up over her shoulders, pulling them tight around her like a protective coat of armor. "My mother never fixed us anything because she was always drunk by eight in the morning. And she drank so that when my father started pounding on her, she wouldn't feel it."

Her eyes slid away from his for a moment and took on

a glazed look as though she were seeing past experiences. Her expression gentled but held such sadness it broke his heart.

"Sometimes, when my dad was gone, my mom would snuggle with us on the couch and read us stories about dragons, damsels in distress and rescuing princes. I think I was eight when I figured out the rescuing prince part was bogus. The dragons were real enough. My father in a rage would convince anyone of that. And Zoey and I were certainly damsels in distress. But the rescuing prince never appeared on the scene."

She pulled the covers tighter. "I learned to hide Zoey and myself in the closet. And when I couldn't make it to the closet, I learned to endure the dragon's wrath. And believe me, I endured the dragon's wrath a lot more often than I made it to the closet." Now her voice shook with remembered pain, remembered fear. She rolled her eyes toward the ceiling, trying to ward off unwanted tears.

But a single tear spilled down her cheek. Brushing it away, she lowered her gaze back to his. "That's why my mother never cooked. As for Zoey, she married a man as brutal as our father because she never understood it wasn't her fault my father hit her. And me, I jump when people get too close because I'm afraid of being touched, and I don't ever remember a time when I wasn't."

Pain squeezed his heart as if a strand of barbwire was being drawn tight around it. Had he thought just knowing about Gaby's fears would give him the leverage he needed to cure them? What an arrogant ass.

He closed his eyes and pinched the bridge of his nose, an ironic laugh echoing through his head. The poor girl. She'd waited her whole life for a prince to show up, and all she'd gotten was him. A disillusioned cowboy, battle scarred and world-weary.

But, the other day in the barn, with innocence and hope shining in her eyes, she'd asked *him* to kiss her. Him. That had to count for something. He opened his eyes and caught her gaze. "I can't change the past for you, Gaby. But—" he gave her a crooked smile "—I can definitely give you a different perspective on the human touch."

A pink flush bloomed on her cheeks, and she quickly looked away in embarrassment. But an answering smile slowly crept over her lips and she found the nerve to peek at him from the corner of her eye. "I like the sound of that."

So did he. He gave her a devilish smile. "Then take a deep breath, Gaby girl, and eat that steak and get a good night's sleep. Because tomorrow, you're going to get your first lesson in what touching's all about."

Chapter Ten

The storm had blown through sometime during the night, leaving behind mountainous snowdrifts and a pristine white terrain that reflected the sun with blinding intensity. To Gaby the scene displayed nature's fickle character with a master's touch. Savagery and beauty splashed across the canvas until it was impossible to tell one from the other.

She yanked the curtains shut and paced the small confines of the kitchen. Edgy. That was how she felt. As edgy as the sharp ridges cresting the huge snowbanks. And she didn't have to look very far to find the source of her uneasiness. In the bathroom the source of her worry shaved with her razor and some water he'd heated on the stove.

What *had* she agreed to last night? Her stomach rolled for the thousandth time this morning, and a cold sweat broke out on her palms. She knew exactly what she had agreed to. She'd agreed to let that cowboy try to seduce her.

She spun on her heel and paced back to the window. Snatching the curtains open, she stared unseeing at the scene before her. The frigid temperature of the icy pane chilled her face and hands. She grappled with her roiling emotions, her grip on the curtains tightening.

She wanted him to seduce her. *She did.* But, oh, God, she was afraid. Not of Luke touching her. Well, that, too. But mostly she feared making a fool of herself.

A twinge of anxiety plucked at her stomach. She didn't know how to play at this game. She didn't know how to bat her lashes or flirt with a coy line or even how to purse her lips for a kiss. Good Lord, her cheeks flushed just thinking about it. She cupped her burning face in her icy hands and stared at the closed kitchen door. Luke would come walking through that door any minute and what would he find? Her, blushing like a schoolgirl.

She dropped her hands from her face and began to pace rapidly. This was ridiculous. She could do this. She just had to refrain from screaming when he touched her, not purse her lips before he pursed his and remember not to faint when that giant tidal wave of heat hit her.

A distant buzzing caught her attention and she glanced out the window. She didn't see anything, but the buzzing got louder. Dragging the comforter with her, she walked to the window and peered out. Nothing. Maybe she could see something from the front window? She wrapped the comforter tighter around her shoulders and headed to the front door, the dogs at her heels.

Luke had swept the porch this morning, so she and the dogs stepped out. A snowmobile popped over the rise, and the dogs bounded off the porch into the snowdrifts to greet the visitor. Gaby shielded her eyes against the sun.

Tom.

Anger ran through her veins. He'd had no business telling Luke about her sister.

The door opened behind her and Luke stepped beside her. Bare-chested, as usual, he had his towel draped over his neck. He glanced at the snowmobiler and then back to her. He took one look at her expression and his lips thinned into a solemn line.

"When he told me about Zoey, he didn't intend to hurt you, Gaby." She started to protest, but he held his hand up to stop her. "Listen, life would be wonderful if we could all say and do the right thing all the time. But it doesn't work that way. In fact, we're so damned fallible, I don't know how man has survived this long. But I do know this. Tom is a good man. And it would be a shame if he lost a friend over doing what he thought was right."

Gaby thought of all the things Tom had done for her. The home he'd opened to her during her search for Timmy Danner. The nights he'd stayed up with her, when worry for the little boy hadn't let her rest. And the support he'd given her since she'd moved in. He was a good man. And a good friend.

He no doubt thought he'd told Luke about her for her own good. In which case, yelling at him would be useless. Like the man beside her, once Tom made a decision it took a better man than she to change his mind. She glanced at the towering majesty of the Rockies. It must be something in the water.

She gave her head a wry shake. "You win. I won't shoot him. This time."

Luke smiled. "Whew. I can't tell you how glad I am to hear that." Pitching his voice above the ever-increasing whine, Luke pointed toward the snowmobile. "Look what he's carrying."

She glanced around, and for the first time noticed that

Tom pulled something behind him. Closer inspection showed a sled loaded with firewood.

"Yes!" She jumped up and down on the porch, jigging with the comforter pulled tight around her until Tom pulled up to the porch and stopped.

Releasing the strap on his helmet, he pulled it off. "Is this jolly welcome for me?"

Gaby stopped dancing. "If that wood's for me, it is."

Tom's mouth crooked in a teasing smile. "And if it's not?"

Luke stepped up to the porch rail. "We'll probably have to shoot you and take it anyway."

Tom turned to Luke, speculation crossing his face.

A flush climbed Gaby's neck at what he must be thinking. Turning to Luke, she felt the flush turn into a blazing fire. She was so used to seeing his chest exposed for God and country, she hadn't noticed his bare feet. And his jeans weren't snapped! Embarrassment seared the very ends of her hair. She glanced at Tom. And then back to Luke.

Her toes curled at the purely male exchange going on. Luke, damn his hide, with his shoulders drawn back and chin thrust high, challenged Tom to refute his position. And Tom, curse his soul, had a smile of such superior satisfaction on it, Gaby wanted to give them both the old heave-ho. But she didn't. Because she'd kill for the stack of firewood on that sled.

"When you two gentlemen finish beating your drums, we could use that wood inside." She turned on her heel and retreated into the house, her face still burning.

Trying to ignore the chill in the house, she stomped upstairs and pulled on a pair of jeans and a soft, hip-length sweater. Desperately she tried to block the picture of Luke standing on the porch half-undressed. But she couldn't erase the image any more than she could stop the burn in her cheeks. And most disturbing, beside the embarrassment, ran another emotion.

Excitement?

Yes, that would be the one. She stepped into a pair of hiking boots and quickly brushed her hair. What was so sexy about a barefoot man standing in subzero temperatures in a pair of unsnapped jeans? He should have looked like an idiot.

But he hadn't. He'd looked proud and invincible and purely male.

She shook her head. She'd never make it through the day. Luke hadn't made a single seductive move yet, and her heart pounded like a jackhammer. She tromped down the stairs, prepared to meet Tom's knowing smile and Luke's proprietorial manner.

By the time she rejoined them, the wood had already been stacked neatly by the stove, and Tom spoke his goodbyes at the door.

Catching sight of her, Tom held up a basket before handing it to Luke. "Eggs. Nancy sent them over for you. Said the chickens went nuts in the blizzard. Laid up a storm. I talked to the highway department this morning. They said it would be tomorrow afternoon before they got out here—"

"Bye, Tom." Luke placed his hand in the middle of Tom's chest and gently but firmly pushed him out the door. "Thanks for the wood, thank Nancy for the eggs, say hi to the kids, have a nice day, drive safely, we'll send one of the dogs over if we need anything else."

Closing the door behind Tom, Luke turned to face Gaby. With the slow deliberation of a lion lounging in territory unmistakably his, he leaned against the door. He crossed one ankle over the other and his arms over his chest. Her eyes flew to his feet. Still bare. And why did that make her heart pound harder in her chest? Was it his denial of the elements? His fearlessness in challenging nature itself? Or the implication that he was above it all?

She dragged her eyes up his denim-encased legs. She took in the strong thigh muscles outlined in stone-washed denim, and her mouth went dry. Her palms began to sweat, and she warned herself not to look any farther. But she couldn't stop herself. Her eyes inched higher. And when they found soft denim cupping…her breath caught in her throat. What was she doing?

Like millions of tiny little springs, every nerve in her body began to coil tighter and tighter. Her eyes moved on. He'd snapped his jeans, but it did nothing to slow the pounding of her heart. Her breaths came in short, quick gulps of air that did little to assuage her need as her eyes moved over the smooth bare skin of his stomach.

The springs drew tighter. The broad planes of his shoulders and chest caused a flutter in her stomach, and a heat began to build in a place she didn't even want to think about. The soft hair covering his arms and chest caught her attention. She remembered how that strong chest had felt against her back, its heat branding her. Goose bumps raced over her skin, and all those tiny springs began to vibrate with a slow hum that sent her blood racing.

Nervously she wiped her sweating palms on her jeans and forced a swallow past the constriction in her throat. She dragged her gaze from his delectable body to his face. Pure male deviltry turned the corners of his mouth, and his blue eyes smoldered with such heated promise, she went up in flames. The springs exploded with a snap. Heat surged to every part of her body, and liquid fire flowed through her veins.

A provocative look. Was that all it took? A negligent pose and a cocky smile, and she went up in smoke?

Suddenly she could hear her father's words and picture him standing over her mother with his fists clenched and that ugly sneer on his face. The sneer he reserved for the nights he wanted to humiliate her mother, not just hurt her.

Gaby blinked against the ugly memory, trying to dislodge it from her mind. But she couldn't. She could still hear her father's angry and disgusted words that it didn't take more than a glance from a man to get a woman hot and bothered.

Except her father's description had been much more vulgar and crudely put. She shifted uncomfortably. Her body had responded just the way her father had described with such contempt and loathing.

Her stomach did a slow roll and the fire died. Her fingers turned icy cold. Embarrassed and uncertain, she looked away.

"Gaby?" Concern laced Luke's voice and he pushed himself away from the door.

She spun away from him, intent on making the kitchen where she could shut him out. But she hadn't gone three strides when he caught her shoulders and turned her to face him.

He must have seen the panic on her face, because he released her immediately. "I'm not going to hurt you. But I'm not going to let you run away, either. What just happened back there?"

Panic screamed through her veins. She couldn't tell him. She didn't want him to know how her body had reacted. Didn't want him to know she was exactly what her father called all women. Easy. She didn't want to see the same repulsion on his face she'd seen so many times on her father's.

She didn't want him to leave.

"Nothing," she answered too quickly, and even to her own ears the denial sounded false.

He shook his head, his brows pulled together in a determined scowl. "No, we're not playing that game, girl. If this is going to work, you're going to have to stop hiding behind your fears. Now *what just happened back there?*"

Despair and anger twined in her breast. Her already-raw nerves snapped at his goading. "You want to know what happened back there? I'll tell you. My father was right. He said all women were whores at heart. That it didn't take more than a look to have them panting and wet. And guess what? He was right!"

Hysteria threatened, and she waited for his lips to curl in disgust. Waited for the loathing to come to his eyes. But it didn't happen.

Instead, he gave her a gentle, almost shy smile. "I did all that with a look?"

She groaned and spun away from him, heat scorching her face. But she didn't run. Something in his expression kept her rooted to the spot. He hadn't seemed repulsed. He seemed almost…tender. Something twisted in her heart and, before she could stop it, a single tear splashed onto the floor.

Quickly she dashed the others away and took a deep, fortifying breath.

"Gaby."

Despite his gentle and coaxing tone, she couldn't bring herself to turn around. Her face still burned hotter than a wood-burning stove and she didn't want him to see the evidence of her tears. Or her pain, if he decided to leave.

He stepped closer behind her. His heat warmed her back, and his soft sigh of disappointment whispered across her nape. "Okay, maybe it's better if you don't look at me. What I'm about to say will probably embarrass you down to your toes. I wish I had a more poetic way to say it. But I don't. It's been too long since I've talked to anyone who had any innocence left, and a lifetime since I lost my own. So bear with me.''

He shifted behind her, and she thought she heard his hands being shoved into his pockets. ''First off, it's not a bad thing, or a dirty thing, for a woman to get aroused. In fact, it's a very sexy thing. I know it makes me hard as hell. And if I can evoke that response in you, I'm thrilled to death. It means you're as attracted to me as I am to you. And nothing but good could come of that.''

She heard the rasp of denim as he removed his hands from his pockets and rested them on her shoulders. ''I hope to God your heart pounds when I touch you. I want your palms to sweat and your nerves to tingle. And most of all, I hope you're aroused in your bed at night when you think of me.''

He moved up behind her, so that they were touching from hip to shoulder. ''And I'm thinking of you, Gaby. All night. Every night. I'm not ashamed of it, and I would be disappointed if you were ashamed of your thoughts for me. Now, I'm going to go out and start digging out the drive. Why don't you reheat the steak you left last night and holler when it's ready.''

She waited until he stamped into his boots, pulled his coat from the rack, and pulled the door shut behind him. But when the soft snick of the door sounded behind her, she unlocked her knees and sank to the floor. Folding her legs Indian-style, she placed her elbows on her knees, and buried her face in her hands. The man might not be very poetic, but he didn't have any trouble making the blood sing in her veins.

The sun hovered just above the mountain peaks when Gaby pulled her snow boots on, called the dogs and headed out to the barn. The day had not gone exactly as she'd planned, but at least Luke hadn't dashed over the mountain in an attempt to flee after her scene in the living room this morning. Actually, he seemed extraordinarily content to remain right here, working on the barn and teasing her.

With a cocky, arrogant smile that stopped her heart.

A warm shiver ran through her, and an answering smile turned her lips. She shook her head at her foolishness, and a tiny sliver of warning ran through her. She needed to be careful not to let this dating thing get out of hand.

Emotions she'd never experienced beat inside her, and she worried at their implications. She could see now the allure a man could have. If she was going to play this game, she would have to be careful her emotions didn't become too entwined with Luke Anderson. She could enjoy herself, just not too much. Her mother and sister were prime examples of what happened when women let a man become too important in their lives.

Bracing her feet, she pulled the barn door open against the snow, waved the dogs in and followed them into the dark interior.

One good look at Luke and goose bumps ran over her skin. For pity's sake, didn't the man ever wear a shirt? Stripped to the waist in these temperatures, he should be the one with the goose bumps. But not a one marred that gorgeous skin. In fact, closer inspection revealed a fine sheen of sweat. She pulled the door shut and moved into the barn.

"I thought I told you to stay in the house today. I don't want you in the cold."

She shrugged a shoulder. "I know, but it was boring in there and I wanted to see how you were doing on the pump." *And I wanted to see you.*

"Mmm." His eyes sparkled with a knowing glint.

She wasn't fooling him a bit. A slow flush crept up her neck, but she ignored it. Looking away from his sensual gaze, she regarded the miner's pick in his gloved hand.

A pick? She peeked around him. She'd expected to find a huge hole around the pump by now. Luke had been out here for three hours. But only a shallow ring, a foot deep and a foot wide, circled the pump's shaft.

Glad for the diversion, she raised a brow. "Frozen?"

"Some. Mostly just packed. Years and years of cattle running in here."

She winced and shook her head. "Why aren't you swearing a blue streak? If I'd hefted that pick for the last three hours and only had that to show for it, I'd be fit to be tied."

His eyelids dropped to half-mast, and his eyes took on a smoky hue. A slow, lazy smile settled on his lips. The kind of smile that promised secret moments and endless pleasures. He leaned the pick against his leg and pulled his gloves off. One finger at a time. "I don't mind the work. In fact, I revel in the challenge."

His blue-eyed gaze bore into her. He *wasn't* talking about that well.

"By the time I'm finished here, this…well and I will be so intimately acquainted there won't be a secret between us. I'm going to uncover it all the way down to its source and then I'm going to go over it with a fine-tooth comb. I'm going to plumb its depths and prime it until the waters are aching to burst free. And by the time I taste its sweet waters, Gaby girl, it'll be part of me. Just as my labors have made me part of it."

Her pulse raced wildly and her head spun with his seductive words. She grappled for a glib reply. One that would keep her safe, or at least make her appear more worldly, but nothing presented itself. Finally she settled for candid honesty.

She held up her hands so he could see her palms. "You'll be happy to know, sweaty palms."

He smiled wide. "Good. We'll work on the other parts after dinner." He grabbed the pick and set it against the wall. "And speaking of dinner, what did you manage to come up with?"

She wrinkled her nose, letting him know he wouldn't like it. "Canned stew."

He narrowed his eyes on her. "Are you going to serve it on plates?"

She gave a little laugh. "I even heated it."

"Glad to hear it." Chuckling softly, he grabbed his shirt, pulled it on, snatched up his coat and pushed the barn door open.

She stepped by him, absorbing his heat and smell, and signaled the dogs to follow. Purple shadows blanketed the landscape as they all made their way to the house.

"The phone lines came back up. I called the gas company. They'll be out tomorrow to find out what my problem is and fix it. And then I called Matt to let him know you were all right, and to check on my horses."

Luke nodded. "You probably just have a leak in your gas line. They shouldn't have much trouble finding it and fixing it. And I'll bet Matt said your horses were fine."

"Yeah, but I worry about Glock."

Luke scooped up a handful of snow, packed it and threw it for the dogs. "He's looking almost good these days."

"Yeah, he's putting on weight. But he has a long way to go in the trust department. I like him to eat from my hand."

Luke opened the back door and held it wide. "I know

you do. But I still don't like when you make that poor starving horse come to you.''

She shook her head at the sharpness in his voice and stepped into the warmth of the kitchen. They'd been over this ground a hundred times. "I know you don't. But it's a noncombative way to develop trust. They'll almost all come for food, and when my hands never offer anything but grain, they eventually figure out I won't hurt them.''

Luke closed the door, grabbed the towel by the door and started drying off the dogs' feet. "Yeah, but it took Glock *two* hours to come to you a lot of those nights in the beginning, and he barely had the strength to stand up.''

Gaby had to laugh. He was practically whining. "It took Killer four, and it never did work with Dreamer.''

He looked up from wiping the snow off Hank's feet. "Your black mare?''

She nodded.

"Yeah, I believe that. She's like you. She only eats when there is nothing else to do. And then she loses half her grain. Have you had her teeth floated lately?''

Gaby shook her head. The man couldn't stand the thought of someone missing a meal. "Her teeth are fine. She's a slob when she eats because she doesn't have a tongue.''

He whipped his head around and stared at her. "What happened to her tongue?''

"Her last trainer cut it out. Apparently, she had a habit of sticking it out of her mouth when she worked. So he cut it off.'' The thought of the cruel act still turned her stomach.

And from the horror on Luke's face, it did the same to him. "I'd like to meet that bastard in a dark alley.'' He shrugged a shoulder. "Or a lit one would do.''

He went back to cleaning the dog's feet. "So Killer and

Dreamer were abused too, huh? Where do you find these animals? Do you have an ad in the paper? 'Know an abused horse? Call me.' Or did you just have a sign out in front of Trisha's barn. 'Gaby's halfway house for abused horses'?''

No. No advertising and no sign, but she had developed a reputation in the business for being good with an abused horse. And she did get calls. She gave the stew a stir and then turned back to Luke. ''Something like that. Now, if you're going to wash up, do it. Dinner's ready.''

Luke slung the towel back on the hook, shucked his coat, hung it up, and then walked toward her with slow deliberation.

Excitement raced through her. No man should be that good-looking. And that easy cowboy gait? Someone should outlaw that for sure.

Luke didn't stop until she could feel his breath on her cheek. Then he leaned over and put his lips right next to her ear. ''Dish it up, darlin'. We've got better things to do.''

Her breath stuck in her throat, and her lungs refused to work until she heard the bathroom door snap shut after Luke's retreat. Then she sucked in a reviving breath, and with shaking hands dished out the stew—onto plates—and brought them to the living room. She'd returned the sofa's cushions earlier and kept the wood-burning stove stoked so they'd have a nice cozy place to eat dinner. She had just sat down, her back resting against the armrest and her knees pulled up in front of her, when Luke came out of the bathroom.

She looked once, and then again. Not only did he have his shirt on, it was buttoned and tucked neatly into his jeans. ''You *do* know how to button a shirt!''

He gave her a wry laugh as he picked up his dinner and sat down. "Yes, I do. Now eat your dinner."

Gaby tried to eat, but her stomach wouldn't cooperate. If she managed to get a bite in her mouth, she had to chew on it *forever* to convince her stomach to take it. So after a few futile attempts, she placed her plate on the floor.

Luke watched the move with a knowing smile, quickly polished off his own dinner and put his plate beside hers. Then he kicked off his boots, swung around to face her and reached up behind him to switch off the light. Drawing his knees toward his chest, he set his feet wide, opened his knees, and held his hand out to her. "Come sit with me and we'll watch the fire."

Gaby's pulse kicked into double time. She'd waited for this moment all day, but now she felt awkward and...and...oh, she didn't know what. But her heart felt as if it would explode, and her ears rang with tension. She stared helplessly at his hand.

"Don't chicken out on me now," he gently coaxed, lowering his hand back to his knee. "Come on, we're just going to watch the fire."

A hysterical laugh bubbled up. "No, we're not."

He laughed with her. "No, you're right, we're not. But we'll start there, and if you're not comfortable with going any further tonight we won't."

All she had to do was crawl across the sofa and she'd be there. Quickly, before she chickened out, Gaby scrambled to Luke.

As if he knew her dilemma, he quickly settled her between his knees. Pulling her back against his chest, he clasped his hands loosely over her stomach.

"Relax."

Gaby wanted to laugh at that suggestion. With his warm breath caressing the sensitive spot under her ear, it was a ridiculous demand. Delicious shivers raced over the surface of her skin, and she squirmed against him.

His hands tightened on her belly. "Sit still." His voice was tight and strained.

She stilled immediately. "Am I hurting you?"

A whisper of laughter tickled her scalp. "You're killing me. We're working on old-fashioned courting, remember? Keep rubbing against me like that, and we're going to jump to the nineties in a damned short minute."

She jerked away from him. Ramrod straight, she sat between his knees, not moving, not even breathing, as she tried desperately not to touch him anywhere.

His easy laughter surrounded her and he pulled her gently back to him. "Come back here. You're okay. Just take it easy on me, all right?"

His laughter relaxed her in a way his quiet reassurance wouldn't have, but at the same time it pricked. "Are you laughing at me?"

"No."

"Liar."

He laughed again, his breath moving the strands of her hair. "Yes, ma'am. I am."

"A liar, or laughing at me?"

"Both," he admitted unabashedly. "But it wasn't a bad laugh, Gaby. You know how you feel when you're about to teach a pupil, someone you really care about, how to jump a six-foot fence for the first time?"

Now she laughed. "I don't teach people to jump. I'm a dressage instructor."

"Okay, then, what's really special that you would teach a dressage rider? Something that would be new and exciting and...extraordinary."

The answer took no thought. "Passage. That's where the horse suspends himself in the air in between each trotting step. The first time you feel all that power under you lift you straight up and keep you hovering in the air—'' she shivered, remembering her first steps of passage ''—it's amazing.''

Luke must have felt her shiver, because he gave her a gentle hug. ''Let's use passage then. When you're teaching someone passage for the first time and you can see the excitement in their face, don't you laugh sometimes at their...I don't know, maybe it's their obvious enthusiasm. Or maybe you're just laughing because you're as excited about the magic of what they're about to learn as they are.''

Luke dropped his head onto her shoulder. ''Do you know what I'm trying to say here?''

She understood. ''Yeah, I know what you're saying. I do laugh at my kids when I'm teaching them something new. I think I'm laughing because I know how much they're going to like it, and I want to share it with them. Sometimes I wish it was my first time again, so I could feel that surge of adrenaline bubbling through my veins.''

Luke nodded his head without lifting it from her shoulder. And then he turned his head, and his lips caressed her nape. A caress as quick and delicate as a hummingbird sipping nectar.

''I'm excited for you, Gaby. It's probably egotistical and arrogant and unforgivably sexist, but I can't wait to show you how much pleasure awaits you.''

His head still rested on her shoulder, and his lips moved provocatively against her neck when he spoke. Goose bumps tingled over her heated skin. A soft sigh escaped her lips. Another kiss followed. This one as soft as the first.

He moved his hands to her shoulders, and then stretched his fingers inward until they grazed the sides of her neck.

The touch was soft as a feather, but, unlike the kiss, it kindled unease and the beginnings of fear. She stiffened in his hold.

He stopped kissing her, and his hands stilled in her hair. "What's wrong?" he gently whispered.

She fought the rising panic as his fingers stroked her neck, but she wouldn't last long if he didn't take his hands away from her face. And, oh God, how did she tell him that? You can kiss me, but whatever you do don't touch me. Right. He'd listen to that and then call it quits. What man wanted a woman he couldn't touch?

When she let the silence stretch out, he whispered to her, "Gaby, you liked it when I kissed you there, didn't you?"

She nodded, unable to speak. Tears closed her throat. She'd reached the end. No man wanted to be around a woman who cringed every time he touched her.

One of his fingers lightly stroked her again and before she could stop herself, her spine stiffened more.

"You don't like it when I touch you, do you?"

No point in denying it, or dragging the moment out any longer. She shook her head and sniffed against the threatening tears. One got away and splashed onto her jeans. She waited for Luke to set her away. Waited for him to end it before it had even gotten started.

Slowly he took his hands away and lowered them to his knees.

Pain lanced her heart. He was letting her go. Her head dropped in defeat. "I'm sorry."

"Don't be sorry." Gently his lips touched the top of her spine. "I like this better, anyway."

The touch startled her and she gave a little jump, but the words were like a healing balm that reached deep down to soothe wounds so old, she'd grown accustomed to their ache.

He continued to rain tiny, delicate kisses on her neck and shoulders.

She reveled in the soft, warm touch of his lips. The blood slowed in her veins. A new sensation. With Luke near, her blood usually raced. But she liked this slow, languorous feeling, the heat creeping through her veins, tantalizing her with a promise of more to come.

Just as she settled into the gentle ebb and flow of the sensuous tides, his lips settled more firmly on her neck, and his tongue flicked her skin. A shiver ran through her and a soft moan fell from her lips. He tasted her again, bolder this time, his tongue lingering on her skin. And then the taste turned into a full-fledged love bite.

Flames licked at her insides, eliciting soft groans and demanding needs. And suddenly she didn't want Luke's hands on his knees anymore. She wanted them wrapped around her, as they had been when she'd first come to sit with him. She whispered her need. "Hold me. Please."

Slowly Luke wrapped his arms around her, his fingers curving possessively around her rib cage and then, as though he couldn't resist it, he pulled her tight against him.

She could feel his arousal against her back, but this time it didn't frighten her. It excited her. And when his hands crept upward, his thumbs brushing the underside of her breasts, all reason left her. Sensations burst inside her and she arched against him.

Then, just as she began to get the hang of it, Luke set her firmly from him. Closing his knees to prevent her return, he ran a distracted hand through his hair. His expression was tense, and his nostrils flared with an emotion she hesitated to name.

When he spoke his voice sounded like ten tons of

gravel. "Gaby, if you have any intention of me sleeping on this sofa instead of following you up those stairs to your bed, now is the time to stop."

When she didn't move fast enough, he gave her a final warning. "Gaby, I'm not kidding. And forget about the bed. We'd never make it that far."

She'd been fighting her way out of a sensual haze, but those words cleared the fog with a bang. She leaped from the sofa and flew up the stairs. Her heart pounded in her ears as she slammed the bedroom door behind her. Then, as a last thought, she threw the bolt home.

A very masculine laugh floated up the stairs. "Good girl."

She made her way to the bed and collapsed on it. Her pulse still raced out of control, her neck still tingled from the touch of his lips, and her breasts…her breasts ached for more. Just as her heart did.

Chapter Eleven

Luke came slowly awake. Gaby's scent pulled at his senses and he drew in a deep breath, savoring it. It came from the quilt beneath him. Gaby's quilt. He smiled into its folds. He liked waking up under her roof, with her things around him.

It reminded him there was more to life than battlefields and the stench of gunpowder and death. It reminded him how nice it was to wake up feeling peaceful and contented in a cozy house with a beautiful woman under the same roof.

A sliver of warning tapped at his heart. He'd reveled in those feelings once before only to have his heart ripped from his chest when he realized none of it had been real.

He burrowed his face into the quilt and reminded himself this was different. He didn't love Gaby, and she wasn't pretending to love him. They liked each other. A lot. But still, it was just *like*. Neither of them was interested in happily ever after. They had simply agreed to spend some time together between now and when he left. He needed it, and she wanted it. Simple. Uncomplicated. Easy.

And to keep it that way he shoved his dark thoughts aside and concentrated on something much more pleasurable. Last night. Gaby had been wonderful. Brave and shy and so damned sexy. When had he ever been so excited just necking? Hell, when had he ever been so excited?

The answer came to him with undeniable clarity. Never.

How would he ever keep this old-fashioned dating up? At sixteen, he hadn't been any good at it. At thirty-five, it would kill him. But he wanted it for Gaby. Her life had been one stint of survival after another. And by necessity, survival offered nothing more than the barest of essentials. He wanted her to have one set of memories that had a full set of details.

And if yesterday morning and last night had been any indication, she couldn't handle more than a little necking and petting, anyway. And if that meant he had to exist in a perpetual state of arousal, so be it.

Footsteps sounded overhead. He lay quietly, listening to her move around in her bedroom. Drawers opened and closed. He imagined her dressing—something he would have been much better off not imagining. Actually, if he'd been smart, he would have slept upstairs last night and let Gaby sleep down here. They still didn't have gas, so the upstairs bedrooms had to be frigid. Exactly what he needed to keep his blood below the boiling point.

Her bedroom door creaked open and her soft tread sounded on the stairs. Well, he might as well get up. He flattened his hands against the sofa and pushed up. Pain exploded in his shoulders and back. He collapsed onto his stomach with a groan.

The soft footsteps picked up their pace. They stopped

at the doorway to the living room. "Luke, are you all right? You sound like you're in pain."

"I am in pain." His words were muffled by the quilt, but he hoped Gaby heard them. Because he had no intention of ever moving again.

Her footsteps moved into the living room and came around to his side of the sofa.

Stiffly he turned his head. Pain screamed across his shoulders. And then he saw her expression, and the pain disappeared. Her gaze traveled slowly from his naked toes to his naked shoulders, searing every inch those innocent amber eyes touched. And with the exception of the narrow strip where he'd pulled a sheet over his hips, she didn't miss a millimeter. A silent groan echoed through his head. If anyone had told him a month ago he'd be turned on by a virgin's look of stunned appreciation, he'd have laughed at them. But he wasn't laughing now.

Hard was what he was now.

And she didn't look to be in much better shape. Her lips were slightly parted, her soft breaths moving between them short and quick. Her half-mast, glazed eyes should be restricted to the bedroom. And when she finally met his gaze, she gave a little start. Self-consciously, she wiped her hands on her jeans.

His fingers flexed against the soft quilt. "Let me guess. Sweaty palms."

She nodded, but her eyes didn't even blink. She looked like a woman who'd just come from her lover's arms, all warmed-up and ready to go. He ground his teeth, trying to direct his attention from the pressure in his groin.

And then her tongue darted out to moisten her lips.

His imagination went wild. What he'd like to do with that tongue.

He buried his face back in the sofa, groaning his sexual frustration into the quilt.

Gaby's quick footsteps brought her near. Her feather-light touch settled on his shoulder. "What's wrong?"

He flinched at her touch. "My shoulders are on fire." *And another part of me you'd rather not know about.*

She gave a cluck of disgust. "Stupid! I should have known how sore you'd be today and given you a rubdown last night. But, better late than never. Don't move, I'll be right back."

Valiantly ignoring the pain of protesting muscles, he pushed himself up. "Gaby, don't worry—"

A determined hand pushed him back down onto the sofa. "Don't move. What is it with guys and this macho thing? There's no need for you to be sore all day just to prove you're a man." With those admonishing words, she padded out of the room.

He collapsed back down on his belly. A hidden smile played across his lips. Lying on the hard evidence of it, he knew the last thing he needed to prove at the moment was his manhood. But the idea of having to lie quietly under her touch, supposedly unaffected, might prove more than he could handle.

He looked quickly around. Every muscle in his upper body protested, but if he could get into his clothes before she got back, and skip this back rub thing altogether, he'd be in a lot better shape. The microwave bell went off in the distance. He eyed the rumpled form of his pants and shirt in the far corner. Now why the hell had he thrown them clear over there?

"Okay, arms at your sides. And relax."

Damn. Now he was in for it. Lying obediently on his stomach, he placed his arms at his sides and closed his eyes. Stoically he waited for her to begin.

The sound of a bottle being opened came to his ears. She squeezed something into her hand and rubbed them together. He took a deep breath, praying for the scent of horse liniment.

No such luck. Instead of the pungent smell of horse liniment, a sweet, powdery fragrance tickled his nose. And then hot, oily hands settled on his shoulders, and strong fingers began a slow, deep massage. Every nerve ending in his body exploded. Blood surged to his erection, and a groan of need escaped his lips.

Her hands stopped mid-stroke. "Am I hurting you? This should feel good."

Too *damned* good. He should stop her before things got completely out of hand. But he wasn't going to. No way in hell.

"No, it's fine. You just surprised me. It feels great." Great, hell. If it felt any better, they'd both be embarrassed by the result.

He buried his face into the quilt and concentrated on relaxing his shoulders. And he tried desperately not to think where he would much rather have her hot, oily hands.

Thirty seconds later he admitted defeat. His voice still rough, he gave her the only warning she was going to get. "That's it, Gaby. I'm getting up and putting my pants on. So unless you want a complete lesson in male anatomy, I suggest you get your cute little butt out of here. How about scrambling those eggs Tom brought over?"

She hesitated only until he started to push himself up. Then, she was off like a shot. With a dry laugh, he pushed himself to a sitting position. Old-fashioned dating? Whose idiot idea had that been?

Battling sore muscles and tenacious desire, he managed

to pull his clothes on. Then he cleaned up in the bathroom and joined Gaby in the kitchen.

He peeked over her shoulder as she worked at the stove. Were those scrambled eggs? "Gaby, did you beat those eggs with milk before you put them in the pan?"

She glanced at him as if he'd lost his mind. "No. I just threw them in the pan and stirred them up as they cooked. Providing I had milk, why would I put it in with the eggs? That sounds gross."

Gross? This from a woman who ate cold ravioli out of a can. He shook his head sadly and pulled two plates from the cupboard. "Never mind."

He held the plates, and she spooned the unappealing mess onto them. Plates and coffee in hand, they moved to the living room and sat at their respective ends of the sofa. Copying her posture, he faced her, pulled his knees up and balanced his plate on top of them.

He took a bite of eggs, chewed quickly and swallowed. Edible, but just barely. He polished off half his plate before breaking the comfortable silence. "What do you want to do tonight?"

She looked up from her plate, which she'd been studying but not eating from since they sat down. "Do you think the roads will be open to town?"

"We're at the top of the mountain, so once the plows get to us, we can get anywhere. Why?"

"There's a movie playing that I want to see. Can we go to the movies?" A light blush stained her cheeks.

His heart skipped eagerly in his chest. A teenage slasher film was playing at the local theater. No way did she want to see that. In fact, he'd bet his best horse she didn't know what was playing there. But he'd promised her secret kisses in the back of the theater, and now she wanted to try them.

Great. But not with a slasher victim's screams bouncing off the walls. "I have a better idea. Let's saddle a couple horses and take a moonlight ride up to Eagle's Peak and neck."

She blushed a furious shade of red, and her glance slid away. But she didn't chicken out. With a shy smile, she looked back at him and nodded her head. "Yeah, I'd like that."

He gave her a conspiratorial wink. "Me, too." He pointed his fork at her plate. "Are you going to eat those eggs, or just push them around on your plate?"

He should prod her to eat. But he remembered how queasy his stomach had been when he took Becky Sue out to the barn to steal *his* first kiss. He hadn't had butterflies in his stomach; he'd had an army of hornets.

Gaby shook her head. "I'm not very hungry."

He gave her an easy smile and traded his empty plate for her full one. "It'll get better after tonight. And, Gaby—" he waited until she looked him right in the eye "—it'll be special. I promise."

Perfect.

That was what Luke wanted Gaby's first real kiss to be. Sweet, and gentle, and infinitely tender. His fingers tensed around the wooden brush cupped in his palm as he ran its stiff bristles over his horse's coat. He was out of practice with tender.

Since Tanya's betrayal, his liaisons with women had been along the quick-and-functional line. He'd been polite, and he hoped kind, to his partners during the short interludes, but he knew he'd been little else.

This evening was a whole different exercise. Tonight was about seduction. A slow-and-easy seduction that would fall far short of the end his body had grown accustomed to.

He clenched his jaw and worked the brush over Buck's back, taking extra time to get the area as clean as possible. He could do this. He could ignore his own desire in order to give Gaby what she needed. And, dammit, he was going to. Even if it killed him. He would grit his teeth and go slow. Slow enough to give himself time to remember the little moves, the subtle touches meant to calm and reassure instead of invoke the sharp, heated side of passion. There would be plenty of time in the future for the rest.

Passion would have its turn. It simmered in Gaby like an underground hot spring, hot and roiling and just waiting for someone to tap its waters. But he would have to uncover it gently if he didn't want to frighten Gaby away.

Slow and easy, those were the watchwords for the night.

He tossed the brush aside, picked up his bridle and slid it over Buck's coppery head. "Okay, son, let's take the lady for a ride."

Luke grabbed the big blanket he'd thrown over the stall wall earlier and tossed it over Buck's rump. Made of several sheepskins sewn together, it would keep Gaby and him as toasty as a couple of hot dogs roasting on the grill. And for convenience, he'd cut a hole in the middle of the thing, turning it into a poncho for two. He smiled ruefully. Now if he could just talk Gaby into sharing it with him.

He led Buck into the aisle, grabbed a handful of mane and vaulted onto the horse's bare back. He'd suggested two horses this morning when he'd first brought up the midnight ride, but he'd changed his mind. He wanted to share a horse with her, to feel her body against his.

As much as Gaby needed him to go slowly, he needed to feel her warmth and softness against him. To feel her wrapped within the close circle of his arms.

He nudged Buck up the aisle to where Gaby was doing her thing with Glock and peered into their stall. Glock was doing better these days. Though still thin, he no longer looked like a living skeleton. His ribs had almost disappeared and a healthy covering of meat was beginning to round out his massive haunch.

His fear seemed to be abating as well. Gaby wasn't even feeding him by hand tonight. The feed tray was on the ground with Glock's head stuck in it while Gaby stroked and petted the horse from shoulder to hip. The animal was allowing Gaby to touch him without keeping a close eye on her. A marked improvement in trust for Glock.

Luke smiled at the picture of quiet triumph. Now, if he could only convince Gaby to be as bold.

"Are you about done in there?"

Gaby peered over her shoulder, her hands coming to a standstill. "Anytime. You have the horses ready?"

Luke scooted back toward Buck's haunches and waved a hand over Buck's withers. "Your coach awaits."

Gaby's brows pulled together in puzzlement. "But you're riding him."

He curled his lips into a smile. "Yes, I am."

Knowledge dawned in Gaby's eyes. With a final pat for Glock, she turned to face him, crossing her arms over her chest. "You said we'd saddle a *couple* of horses."

He nodded. "Yes, I did. But the more I thought about it, the more I thought this would be better."

She stood quietly, looking at the horse's back where he'd made a spot for her. Curiosity, excitement and wariness danced a frantic jig in her eyes. She wanted to share the horse with him; he could see that in the excited sparkle in her eyes. But she knew how dangerous men could be, and she was wary of trusting him on a dark path high on a lonely mountain peak.

With two horses, she would have an avenue of escape should the situation go sour. But if she shared his horse, no avenue would exist. His gut clenched as he waited silently for her decision. Would she trust him? Or not? Had he done as good a job in calming her fears as she'd done with the recovering Glock?

Finally she raised her eyes to his. "No saddle, either?"

Triumph bubbled through his veins. Despite the fear, she was going to give him a chance. He reached down behind his leg and gave Buck's haunch a pat. "This is better. I promise. Warmer. Cozier. More comfortable."

Gaby gave him a knowing look. "Uh-huh."

He smiled his sexiest grin and shrugged a shoulder. "Among other things."

Shaking her head at him, she gave Glock a final pat and left his stall. "I can't believe I'm letting you talk me into this."

He had to admit, he was surprised himself. But he wasn't going to let her back down now. He pointed to a wall of hay. "Climb up those hay bales and slide on."

Gaby climbed up the grassy steps, a nervous smile playing across her lips. Once she was high enough that she could easily lower herself onto Buck's back, she waited.

Luke sidled Buck over, dropped the reins onto the horse's neck and rested his hands on his thighs, giving Gaby an open field to get on the horse.

Resting her hands over the reins, Gaby braced herself on Buck's neck and threw one leg over the horse's withers. Her body slid against Luke's as warm and soft as he'd imagined. Quickly she settled her seat, the backs of her thighs resting against his and her tight little butt snuggled into his lap. Pure pleasure washed through him as he settled his hands on her hips. Perfect. Except for the bulk of her down coat.

He leaned forward and pointed to the top of one of the hay bales. "Now take your coat off and toss it over there."

Her head snapped around. "Have you totally lost your mind? It's all of ten degrees out there. By the time we get back, it's going to be that many degrees *below* zero." She turned a little farther on the horse and gave his chest a quick scan. "And where is your coat, Mr. I'm-Above-The-Elements?"

Smiling at her chagrin, he grabbed the blanket resting over Buck's haunches and brought it forward. "I already chucked it in favor of this."

Gaby eyed the heavy sheepskin blanket skeptically. "How is *that* going to keep us warm?"

"I'll show you. Come on, toss your coat."

Shaking her head as if he'd lost his mind and she hers, since she was going to go along with him, Gaby shrugged off her coat and tossed it up on the hay. "Okay, cowboy. Now what?"

Before the cold had a chance to seep into her bones, he snapped the blanket out, threw it over them, and settled the large cut over their heads. The heavy sheepskins fell around them like a butterfly's cocoon. Their combined heat pooled beneath the heavy folds, swirling around them, warming them, reminding them that they were not alone.

The closeness, the intimacy of the tiny space was impossible to ignore. In front of him Gaby shivered and swallowed hard. "Luke Anderson, you're a wicked man."

God, he wished. Because what he really wanted was them both buck naked with Gaby facing him, her legs wrapped around his hips, the neediest part of him buried deep, and Buck's easy gait rocking them to a mind-blowing pinnacle of shattering pleasure. But he wasn't going to get it. Not tonight.

Tonight wasn't about him. It was about Gaby. It was

about shared whispers and soft touches and sweet kisses. Period. End of discussion. There wouldn't be a damned wicked thing about it.

He cleared his throat, trying to loosen the tension there, and rerouted his thoughts. "Do you want to handle the reins, or do you want me to?"

"You."

He chuckled at the way she all but jumped on the suggestion. Obviously she thought if his hands, or at least one of them, was occupied, she'd be safer. Nuzzling through the hair at her nape, he placed a small kiss on the sensitive spot where her shoulder met her neck. "Don't sound so smug. Once we hit the trail, old Buck can make his own way up. Then I'll make up for lost time."

A delicate shiver ran through Gaby, and she drew a shaky breath. A breath that was tinted with passion, not fear.

Excitement ran through Luke. More than anything in the world, he wanted to make this night special for Gaby. He slid his hand through the slit he'd made in the blanket and grabbed the reins. "Ready."

At her quick nod, he twitched a calf and sent Buck out of the barn into the night.

Moonlight enveloped them. A sharper cold than the live-stock-warmed air of the barn hit their faces and froze their breath as it left their mouths. Gaby shuddered at the drop in temperature and snuggled closer to him.

He tightened his one free hand at her hip, but he didn't pull her closer. In fact, he scooted back far enough to keep her from realizing just how much he was enjoying this whole thing.

He dropped another kiss on her nape. "Hang on, it'll warm up fast."

A nervous chuckle escaped her lips. "That's what I'm afraid of."

He laughed gently at her panicked humor. "Relax, you're going to love it."

Their shared laughter floated through the crisp night air as they made their way across the ranch yard and headed toward the path leading to Eagle's Peak.

Luke drew in a deep breath, dragging Gaby's essence in with it. He kneaded her hip gently with the hand he had tucked inside the blanket and drew the arm holding the reins ever-so-slightly closer, tightening his subtle embrace. Perfect.

He guided Buck onto the Eagle's Peak path. The narrow trail had been cleared to allow two horses to walk side by side. The heavy line of trees flanking the path made it easy for a horse to pick his way without getting lost and without rider assistance. Buck had taken Luke up and down similar paths by himself for years.

Luke dropped the reins on Buck's neck. "Okay, son, take us up." He drew his hand back into the blanket and settled it on Gaby's waist.

She jumped as if she'd been hit with a cattle prod and drew a sharp breath through her teeth. She sucked her tummy in as far as she could to get away from his icy touch. "Luke!"

He chuckled wickedly. "Cold?"

"You rat." Her teeth practically chattered with the epithet.

"Come on, don't be a spoilsport. Warm it up."

Gaby growled her protest, but wrapped both her warm hands over his icy one and pressed it harder against her stomach. "Is this your idea of fun?"

A smile curved his lips. He was having fun. Since Tanya, he hadn't indulged in long hours of foreplay with the women who shared his bed. And until quite recently, Gaby's fear had kept him from touching her. Now to feel her warmth beneath his hand, the soft pliancy of her skin, the tiny circumference of her waist felt a little like heaven on earth. God, he'd forgotten how much he liked to touch.

He flexed his fingers beneath hers, savoring the simple pleasure of the moment. Leaning forward, he whispered in her ear, "Sit still and I'll make it fun for both of us."

She stilled immediately, clutching his hand tighter to her, though whether in apprehension or excitement, he couldn't have said.

He moved the hand he had resting on her hip to her waist and gave her a gentle squeeze of reassurance as he nuzzled the silken strands of her hair aside and settled his lips against her nape. "This is where we were the other night, isn't it?"

A soft sigh soughed through Gaby's lips, and she dropped her head forward, allowing him better access. "Your lips are so soft." She snuggled his arms against her. And this time he knew she was savoring the contact, not fearing it.

He tightened his hold, giving her a hug and drawing her tighter against his chest as he brought his tongue into play at her nape. God, she tasted good. Sweet and salty and, if he wasn't mistaken, a bit like molasses.

His lips turned up at the edges, and he tasted again. Yep, molasses. She must have scratched her neck after handling Glock's feed. Still smiling, he gave her a gentle nip.

She shuddered in his arms, and a soft purr vibrated in her throat.

The sound of her pleasure sent a fresh surge of desire through him. Call him a chauvinist, but he loved hearing her sigh in pleasure, and he loved the fact that the pleasure had come from him.

And he couldn't wait to give her more. Much, much more. But slowly, he reminded himself. Slowly.

Surprisingly he found no desire to hurry. Need ran through his veins hot and heavy, but he felt no urgency to appease it. Only a need to savor each touch, each taste. Like a starved man falling upon a feast, he wanted to revel in each little intimacy. Stretch each second of moonlight magic to its fullest.

Depositing tiny kisses from her nape to the sensitive spot behind her ear, he moved his hands from beneath hers and stroked her from rib cage to hips, reveling in the touch. Reveling in the simple act of touching. God, she felt good. Soft and womanly and so damned right, as if her planes and curves were made for the express purpose of filling his hands.

She stretched into his caress, encouraging him to continue the gentle ravishment.

He stroked back up, stopping at the soft expanse of her belly. His fingers sank gently into the malleable flesh as he opened his mouth over her shoulder and drew sharply on her skin.

Like a kitten mewling for attention, she emitted a tiny sound as she moved her hands back over his, pressing his fingers harder against her.

She was ready for more.

Carefully he pulled her shirt from her jeans and moved his hands beneath the material. Fire sizzled under his fingers as skin touched skin.

Gaby gasped. Arching against him, she dropped her head back on his shoulder, offering more of herself to his touch.

He stroked his hands up her rib cage, taking pleasure in each heated inch until his fingertips grazed the soft underside of her breast. Drinking in her quick, shallow breaths of arousal, he ran his fingers across the slick satin of her bra. Stroking back down, he stopped again at her belly to enjoy the fragile area that seemed suddenly feminine.

What was wrong with him? He'd never been fascinated by a woman's belly before, but touching Gaby's...he couldn't get enough. He moved down a little farther, tucking his fingers under the band of her jeans. Just a bit, not enough to scare her, but enough to remind her of her feminine core.

Just enough to tantalize his already-throbbing imagination.

Moving restlessly against his touch, Gaby turned her head to him. The moonlight reflected the need in her eyes. "Luke, kiss me. Really kiss me."

Absolutely.

He took hold of her shoulders, pushed her upright and started to turn her. "Throw your leg over Buck and sit across him like you would if you were in a sidesaddle." Laden with need, his voice was as rough as a hoof rasp, but he had a feeling Gaby would never notice.

And indeed, she obeyed without question, so drugged by passion she thought only of the kiss to come.

Helping her around, he kept the heavy sheepskin blanket from tripping her up and rearranged it to keep them covered. Not that they needed its protection. They were both hot enough to incinerate anything that came within a mile of them, but he didn't want it tangling around them now. Beneath the furry folds, he placed his hand behind her shoulders and lifted her arms around his neck.

Her eyes locked onto his, the amber depths filled with moonlight, heated curiosity, a maiden's innocence and a plea. A plea for him to give without hurting. A plea for a single memory of pleasure.

His heart clenched in his chest. She was so incredibly fragile. And so beautiful. So very, very beautiful.

Somewhere, deep in his head, a distant warning bell clanged its alarm, whispering for him to be careful, not to get carried away by a sad pair of eyes and his own seduction. It was one thing to decide to start living again, and quite another to let his soul get tangled up with anything more demanding than an innocent seduction and a sweet kiss.

But tonight, for the first time in five years, he wasn't going to listen to the warning. He wasn't going to bring the pain of the past into the present.

With a reassuring smile, he lowered his lips to Gaby's. Soft as a feather's touch, gentle as a lover's caress and tender as a baby's heart, he moved his lips over hers, savoring the warmth of her lips and each tiny sigh that slipped between them.

Moonlight and magic.

No, he wouldn't worry about getting carried away tonight.

Not tonight.

Chapter Twelve

Gaby placed the small bouquet of hothouse flowers on the blanket's corner. She had a picnic set up on the floor in front of the wood-burning stove with all the fixings. Fried chicken, potato salad, barbecue beans, chocolate chip cookies. She'd even splurged and bought a watermelon.

Luke would be thrilled. She hadn't cooked any of it! It had all come from the local grocery store's deli. She placed the basket of food down on the blanket and rubbed her hands together in delight. Everything was ready. She even had the watermelon cooling in a tub of ice and packed snow on the opposite side of the room. Now she only needed Luke.

She dropped onto the sofa and stared at the flames leaping in the old Franklin stove. She had left the doors open so they could see the logs and fire. She wanted this picnic to be romantic. So romantic he'd forget his promise of old-fashioned dating.

Her stomach gave a nervous flutter. Was she really ready for the next step? Not that the past two weeks had been tame. In fact, they had been far from it.

When he took her to dinner, a fresh bouquet of flowers awaited her at their table. And their table was always the most secluded one in the restaurant so his intimate touches would go unnoticed.

The food on his winter picnics was mediocre, but his tactics for hand warming were extraordinary. She still marveled that a cold hand on an equally cold breast could make her blood boil.

And the movies he'd taken her to! She couldn't have said what either was about, but she *could* give detailed lessons on stolen kisses now.

The midnight ride where they'd shared a horse and her first kiss, she refused to think about. It would only make her blood run hot and heavy and *that* would lead to another sleepless night. Another long, lonely, sleepless night where she would lie in bed, aching for something she couldn't even describe because a certain blue-eyed cowboy had been a pillar of restraint during yet another evening of necking and heavy petting.

Yeah, she was definitely ready for more.

The sound of scattering gravel brought her out of her reverie. She gave her setting one last glance, raced to the front door and opened it just as Luke stepped onto the porch. His teasing smile stopped her heart.

It always did.

He stepped up to the door, stopped, tilted his head and waited. She angled her head to avoid his hat and placed her lips on his. He pulled her closer and deepened the kiss, his tongue boldly staking his claim. Her pulse pounded in her ears, and her world spun out of control. And then, his stomach rumbled.

She pulled away with a laugh. "I guess that means I should feed you. Come on in. I have a picnic planned."

His brows went up at that. "A picnic? Inside?"

She gave him a mischievous smile and pulled him across the threshold. "Yeah, just imagine, fingers that stay *warm* while you eat the chicken."

He gave her a mock scowl. "What fun is that?"

But she caught his grin as he turned to shuck his coat and hang it up on the peg. His hat went on the peg next to it and then he turned back to her.

He drew in a deep breath, slowly dragging the air through his nostrils. His eyes lit with relief. "Smells good. What did you cook?"

She had to laugh. Her dismal cooking skills were the biggest bone of contention between them. He not only wanted lots of food at his disposal, he wanted it to taste good. Well, tonight he would have no complaints.

She pointed to the basket by the fire. "That's the best part. I didn't cook. I zipped to the deli while you went home and cleaned up."

Now his eyes sparkled with true pleasure. She laughed as he homed in on the picnic basket. It had been a long day for them. They'd skipped lunch in favor of getting the new well casing in. It had been a project that had dragged on much longer than either of them had expected, and they were both relieved to have it done.

Like hungry beasts they descended on the fare. She had to admit, the crispy chicken was good. Something she never would have noticed two weeks ago.

When the bounty had dwindled and everyone, including the dogs, had had their share, she leaned back on her elbows, her legs stretched out before her. "That's it. If I eat another bite, I won't have room for the watermelon."

"Watermelon?"

Luke's question held such a hopeful note, she laughed and pointed out the tub in the corner.

Pure delight washed over his features. "You thought of everything. Are we going to have a seed-spitting contest? I always won those when I was a kid."

"I hadn't thought of that. But I suppose we could. In the house we'll have to go for accuracy instead of distance, though. We'll spit them at the top of the wood stove and watch them pop and sizzle."

His easy expression changed. His eyes darkened and the corners of his mouth turned up in that slow, lazy smile that made her palms sweat and her heart race. With slow deliberation, he removed everything from their blanket, creating a clear playing field. Then, his heated gaze locked onto hers, he crawled to her with the sensuous power of a great cat stalking his prey.

Her mouth went dry, and a coil deep in her belly began to tighten as he closed the distance between them. His heat enveloped her.

With careful calculation, he stepped over her with his hands. His smoky gaze full of sin and promise, he nudged her knees apart, and settled one of his own possessively between them. "Darlin', I fully intend to watch things pop and sizzle tonight. But it ain't gonna be watermelon seeds."

Her heart leaped at the promise, and the inside of her knees tingled where they touched his. But she didn't have long to think about the provocative position he'd put her in. His lips descended with an undeniable purpose, pressing her gently down until she lay flat on the floor. He stretched out on top of her, his leg firmly settled between hers. His rock-hard thigh made contact with her most intimate part.

Her breath caught in her throat, as a sharp, delicious

tingle ran through her. Of their own volition her hips lifted against him. Another tingle ran through her, sharper this time. A moan of need sounded in her throat as she arched against him, seeking more.

Luke lifted his head. A fine sheen of sweat beaded his upper lip, and the hand that pressed her hip back to the floor trembled slightly. "Easy, darlin'. Slow and easy."

Frustration nearly choked her. Right now she did *not* need a pillar of restraint. She pushed at his chest with an angry growl. "Stop it!"

He reared up on his knees, and she wanted to groan at the expression of concern on his face. Not only had he been a pillar of sexual restraint during the past weeks, he'd been a prince during the times when the new touches had elicited old fears. But she didn't need that now.

He rested his hands on his thighs, where he knew she could see them. "Easy, you're okay."

"No I'm not okay! Look, I appreciate this old-fashioned dating thing. Really I do. But you're killing me. You kiss me until I'm screaming for…for…I don't even know what. And then you pat me on the head and send me to bed and expect me to *sleep!*"

Relief that he hadn't hurt or frightened her flashed briefly on his features, but it didn't linger. A sweet, sexy smile full of pure male pride turned his lips. "That bad, huh?"

She flushed crimson, but she wouldn't deny it. She ran an anxious hand through her hair and nodded. "Yeah."

Now that sweet, sexy smile turned suddenly serious. "Unbutton your blouse."

Her heart jumped in her chest, and an answering throb pulsed where just moments before she'd felt that wonderful tingle. Under his old-fashioned dating rules, her clothes had remained fully buttoned and on her body. It hadn't kept him from touching some of her more intimate parts, but it did leave a safe barrier for her to retreat behind if she felt the need.

If he wanted her to unbutton her blouse now, the rules had changed. Her heart beat faster, and her blood began to simmer. She stood on the edge of the cliff. One direction offered the predictability and safety of land. The other offered uncertainty and the unknown. And the chance to fly.

She raised a shaking hand to the first button. Clumsy with uncertainty and anticipation, her fingers struggled to free it. Finally it slipped from its hold.

Luke's eyes darkened with desire.

She moved to the next button.

His eyes darkened more. And more. And more, until by the time the last button slipped free, their smoky depths appeared almost midnight-blue.

Fire raced through her, but her nerve deserted her. She clasped the edges of her blouse tightly in her hands, holding them together. She had no experience in this game, and to lie unclothed beneath him while he kneeled above her fully clothed left her too vulnerable.

She wet suddenly dry lips. "Take yours off first."

Desire exploded in his eyes, and then his hands were a blur. He yanked the snaps open at his cuffs and the snaps from the front with a rapid-fire *rat-a-tat-tat*. He jerked the tail out of his jeans, and then with a shrug and yank the shirt became a wadded-up ball of material he sent sailing into the nearest corner.

And never once did his midnight gaze leave hers.

Heat pooled between her legs. He was giving her permission to touch, as he would expect to receive it. She held her breath and slowly pulled her hands apart.

His eyes held hers until she'd opened the blouse completely. Then his gaze moved down. He drew a sharp breath through his teeth.

Slowly, almost reverently, he reached down and ran the back of a single finger over the top of her breast. "Beautiful."

Sensation exploded through her. Goose bumps and heat waves. Tingles and shivers. Fire and ice. All that from just a touch? Would she survive her step from the cliff?

She closed her eyes and arched up. Her pelvis bumped against his knee. This time the tingle was so sharp it hurt and tiny pinpricks of light exploded in her head.

"Luke?" Question or plea? She couldn't have said. But she needed him in a way she couldn't name.

"Shhh. Just feel."

Stretching over her, he insinuated his other leg between hers. His lips traced the path his finger had taken over her breast. Fire raced over her skin. The coil deep in her belly wound and wound and wound. She lifted her hips to him, her body naturally seeking…she didn't know what. But she couldn't get enough. There had to be more.

As though attuned to her frustration, Luke placed a hand behind her knee and brought it up around his hip. He repeated the same thing with her other knee, opening her more fully to him. And then he rocked gently against her.

The world disappeared around her. Like a giant wave, heat and need and feelings so intense she thought she'd die of them pounded through her veins. She *had* to have him closer. She cursed the barrier of their jeans, but she wasn't about to stop the action now. She wrapped her arms around him and arched against him, driving them together.

His ragged breathing sounded heavy in her ear, and his fingers dug into her hips as he pulled her closer still, rocking steadily against her.

Even through the double layer of their jeans, she could

eel the blunt proof of his arousal teasing her, stroking her ntil she couldn't bear it. Her whole world narrowed down o that tiny part of her, and she rode the crest of the wave ip, and up, and up, until the world shattered around her.

A soft kiss touched her temple, and Luke whispered in ner ear. "Magic, Gaby girl. Just for you."

She tightened her hold on him and tried to pull him into ner very being. Magic didn't come close. A tiny aftershock ran through her and she pulled Luke closer. If she could just get him into her rib cage, he'd almost be close enough.

An icy chill skated up her spine, and a giant wave of fear crashed through her, swamping her in its black, freezing waters. A picture of Zoey lying bruised and broken on her living room floor flashed in her mind. Dear God, was this how it started? With a taste of magic. And this need to make another person part of yourself?

The ecstasy from moments before whipped away. Panicking, she pushed frantically at Luke's chest, fighting to get out from under him. "Get off. You've got to get off."

His arms and legs tangled with hers, keeping her pinned beneath him. Fear clawed at her, and she cracked her head against the floor in her frenzied struggles. She welcomed the pain. It pushed what had just happened between them to a safer distance.

"Get off me!" Was that hysterical voice hers?

But it worked. Luke rolled off her, and she scrambled on hands and knees to the sofa. Crawling into its protective corner, she pulled the edges of her blouse tightly over her chest.

Concern drawing his brows together, Luke pushed to his knees and rocked back on his haunches. His intense gaze locked onto hers. "Don't panic, Gaby. Just take a few breaths and tell me what's going on in that head of yours."

Her heart raced with fear. *Don't panic?* Both her mother

and her sister had stayed with men who beat them because
they loved them. And this was the first step that got them
there.

Cold chills racked her body and she shook her head in
denial. "I can't do this."

His eyes narrowed in worried confusion. "Do what?"

She pointed toward the floor, where moments before
she'd discovered magic in his arms. Magic and a terror
that tore at her heart. "This...game. I can't play it. It's too
strong. Too powerful."

Luke raised his hands in a calming gesture, but his blue
gaze bore into hers. "I'm *not* playing with you. And if
you'll give yourself a minute to calm down, you'll realize
you're just overwhelmed. Give yourself a few minutes to
take it all in."

A bitter laugh burst from her lips. "I wonder how many
times Bill said that to my sister? Or something very similar."

Luke's eyes widened. "What are we talking about here,
Gaby? I didn't just hurt you."

She shook her head. "No, you just gave me a wonderful
gift. But don't you see, that's how it starts?"

His brows snapped together in confusion. "How what
starts?"

"The dependency. First it's a smile, then a touch, and
before you know it you can't live without him."

"Him?" The single word held a dangerous note.

"Some man you think you love. And then it's too late.
Because no matter how many times he hits you, no matter
how many times he hurts you, you'll never leave."

Silence filled the room.

Gaby's fingers were icy cold as they struggled to keep
their hold on her blouse. Fear like she'd never known surrounded her. It threatened her and screamed at her and beat

on her defenses until its racket deafened her. But worse, so much worse, was the pain in her heart. It ached as if a giant hand squeezed and squeezed and squeezed and wouldn't stop squeezing until not a drop of blood remained.

Luke closed his eyes and pinched the bridge of his nose hard, as if he could stop the pain and the words coming from her mouth. Dropping his hand to his thigh, he spoke in a voice laden with fatalism and sadness. "For starters, neither one of us has ever mentioned love. I don't think either one of us is ready for anything of the kind. And secondly, love didn't kill your sister, Gaby. A bad man did. A vicious, mean, brutal man. Please don't tell me you think I'm the same."

Gaby looked away from the anguish in his eyes and steeled herself against the unbearable pain in her heart. Confusion swirled in her head. When she'd stolen away from her father's house at fifteen with a freshly broken arm, she'd promised never to be a victim again. And there was no bigger victim than a woman enthralled by a man.

But Luke was right. Neither of them had ever mentioned love. They *weren't* in love with each other. They were just two lonely people enjoying some time together until Luke hopped on his plane and left the country.

What would happen if it turned into something more? As it was, just thinking about sending Luke away was killing her. What would she do if those feelings changed to love? And Luke became as violent as her father? Wouldn't it be wiser to end it now, before there was even a chance of that eventuality coming to pass?

Another drop of blood squeezed from her heart. God, she didn't know. She only knew the pain in her heart. The fear in her soul.

She had to think. She had to sort through the emotions

clamoring in her head. And she would need time and solitude to do that.

Taking a deep breath, she blocked the pain from her mind and said the words she needed to save herself. "I don't know, Luke. I don't think you're the kind of man to hurt a woman, but people change. Men change. There was a time when Bill had been the most charming man to walk the earth. And we both know where that ended up."

She tilted her head to stare at the ceiling, praying for divine guidance. But none came. "I need time. Time to figure out what this is all about."

Pain and anger tightened Luke's features. "Dammit, Gaby, don't send me away."

She rubbed her eyes, hoping to keep her tears from falling, but one escaped anyway, slipping down her cheek. She brushed it away quickly and shook her head. "I have to. At least until I figure out what is safe and what isn't."

"Safe!" The word practically exploded from him. "Look into your heart, Gaby. You know I would *never* hurt you. In any form. At any time. For any reason. You know you're safe with me. You're just letting your fears run away with you."

She wouldn't listen to his words. She couldn't. Not until she'd had some time to think it through. The stakes were too, too high. She shook her head harder.

"Dammit! You're going to do this, aren't you? You're going to send me away." Luke spun away from her, running an angry hand through his hair. Two steps later he spun back. "And I'm going to have to go. Because this is the one step I can't take for you. But don't take forever to make up your mind, Gaby. My plane leaves in three weeks. Please, don't let us waste all that time."

His cowboy boots pounded angrily on the wooden floors as he retrieved his shirt and shrugged into his coat. Frustration and pain ravaged his features as he pulled his hat low over his eyes, then walked out the door.

Gaby's eyes burned like hot cinders, and she closed them against the pain in her chest. She had done the right thing. She knew she had. So why did it hurt so much?

Chapter Thirteen

Luke sat in the den, in the dark, and stared out at the powerful horse moving beneath the outdoor lights in the big corral. As Gaby put the animal through an intricate set of steps and patterns, the stallion's red coat flashed with the reflection of the bright lights.

A shadow moved into the room, its presence well presaged by the sound of cowboy boots on the wooden floor. Luke remained silent, hoping Matt would simply get something and leave without bothering him.

The shadow dropped into the chair opposite him and reached up. Light flooded the room.

"Turn that off."

Matt jumped in his chair. "Damn, Luke! Why didn't you let me know you were there? You're going to give me a heart attack if you don't stop skulking around like some spook."

Luke ignored his brother's protest and glanced out the

window. Had Gaby seen him watching her? No, not yet. She trotted away from the house now. He repeated his demand. "Turn off the light."

Matt rolled his eyes. "She's not going to see you, even with the light on. For two weeks she's avoided looking at this house as if she'll go blind if she even peeks at it."

"Turn it *off!*"

Matt gave a huff of disgust and gave the light's cord a sharp yank. "I have never seen two adults act in such a ridiculous fashion. You hide around this house with such a cloud of melancholy hanging over you, I can't believe Poe's raven isn't sitting on your shoulder screaming 'Nevermore.' And Gaby—" Matt stopped, searching for the correct words "—looks like hell."

Yes, she did. The ache that never seemed to leave Luke's chest increased. With the form-fitting black sweater she wore, he could see she'd lost weight. Even if she'd had a coat on, he could have seen the difference. The planes of her face had sunk to deep hollows.

He wanted to jerk her off that horse and shake her. She wasn't taking care of herself worth a damn. Actually, he wanted to jerk her off that horse, carry her into his bedroom and make love to her until the cows came home. But that wasn't going to happen. He'd promised Gaby he would give her time.

But it was killing him.

Luke ran a hand distractedly through his hair. "She's probably been busy getting her stalls up and is forgetting to eat. You know how she is."

Matt glanced out the window. "Yeah, well, she doesn't look as if she's sleeping much, either. I've seen less-defined circles around a raccoon's eyes. Your own don't look any better, I might add."

Luke narrowed his eyes on his brother. "If this is a lecture, I am not in the mood."

"We'll call it a question-and-answer period, then."

Luke snorted with disgust.

Matt steepled his fingers together. "Which one of you broke it off?"

Lordy, why couldn't he have been an only child? "There wasn't anything to break off."

Matt laughed. "You were more convincing in junior high when you said you hadn't been necking with Becky Sue. At the time you had a hickey the size of an orange on your neck."

"Do you see any hickeys now?"

"No, I don't. I see a brother I love who's hurting. And it makes me sad."

"Well, don't worry about it. In less than a week I'll be on my plane and you won't have to look at me at all. Until then, unless Gaby comes to her senses, you'll just have to put up with it."

Matt shifted in his chair, stretching his legs out and crossing them at the ankles. "So, Gaby broke it off."

With angry determination, Luke spat out the reality. "The truth is, she lost her nerve. She doesn't trust me enough to believe I won't start breaking her bones at some point in the future." Despite his best efforts, his bitterness at Gaby's decision crept into his voice.

Matt looked out the window. His brows knit together as he watched Gaby work Klaus. "You know, she has the best instincts I've ever seen in anyone who works with horses. When she's working with Glock and Dreamer, she anticipates their fear and panic before they do. When she's riding that guy—" Matt pointed out the window "—I think she knows when he's going to buck for joy before he gets the first tickle of anticipation. I think that's why she's such an exceptional rider.''

Luke raised a sardonic brow. ''Your point being?''

''My point being, I think in her heart she knows you're not going to beat her. But she's had a lot of conditioning contrary to that opinion before she ever met you. Painful conditioning. I think it's reasonable to assume it might take her brain a while to catch up to her heart.''

''You think I'm pushing her?''

''I think it's a little early to call her a coward.''

''I didn't call her a coward. But facts are facts. One second she's in my arms, and the next she's chasing me out the door saying she needs time to figure out if I'll turn into her...her...*brother-in-law*.'' God, he could barely get the word out, the thought was so repugnant.

Matt's brows rose in question. ''So, how does giving her all this time to think about who and what you are convince her otherwise?''

''It doesn't. But I promised I'd give her the time. So at the moment I'm doing my best to suppress my caveman tendencies to drag her by the hair to some secluded cabin until she figures out I'm *nothing* like that bastard.''

''Personally, I'd lean toward the caveman tendencies. Because the reality is, no one overcomes a fear by running away from it. She's never going to figure out you're not going to hurt her if you're in here skulking around and she's out there starving herself to death.''

Luke looked heavenward. ''Are you going to come visit me after she has me arrested for kidnapping?''

Standing up, Matt looked him straight in the eye. ''Brother, if you're in a secluded cabin with only a bed between you, and your powers of persuasion aren't any better than that, you deserve to rot in jail.''

Matt sauntered out of the room, and Luke slumped deeper in his chair. Damn.

He glanced back out the window. Gaby looked so fragile sitting on top of the brawny stallion, he wondered why the horse listened to her at all. But he didn't wonder for long. He knew why they bent to her will. They trusted her.

They trusted her to feed them, to water them, to keep their beds clean, to let them out to play, and not to hurt them. They trusted her not to ask what they couldn't give and as a result gave freely of what they could. Yes, she had spent hours patiently teaching them a language of touches and gentle pushes that told them when to walk, trot, canter and turn, but that was not what created the beauty in the harmonious picture before him.

The amazing part of the picture was not that the horse trotted sideways across the ring, but that he did it with such eagerness, such lightness of being, it became a dance of joy instead of an exercise of servitude.

And yet, many of her horses had been as abused as she before they came into her gentle hands. He marveled at her skill. Through empathy and endless patience she had brought them back to a world of joy.

Frustration surged through him. Why wouldn't she let him do the same for her?

And then it dawned on him. Glock hadn't *let* Gaby show him she wouldn't hurt him. Gaby had forced the knowledge on him. She'd stood in that stall with the very thing that horse needed to sustain his life and demanded that he come to her to get it. He'd received nothing but reward and pleasure once he'd come, but the tactics to bring him there had been ruthless.

A slow smile curved Luke's lips. Matt was right. Waiting wasn't the answer.

* * *

"Well, I'll be—"

Gaby screamed at the unexpected voice, her grip tightening on the hammer in her hand as she spun to confront the intruder. Until she saw his face.

She slumped against the stall in relief. "Good Lord, Tom, don't sneak up on me like that!" She tossed the hammer to the ground. "What brings you here?"

"Nancy asked me to stop by. Said she saw you at the store the other day and you looked like hell."

Gaby swallowed an ironic chuckle. "Well, tell her thanks."

"She's right."

Now she did laugh. "Well, thanks again."

Tom walked over and checked out the stall she'd been working on. "Nice job."

She inclined her head. "Thank you. So, what brings you here?"

"I brought dinner. Let's get in the house before Crash finds out I left it on the kitchen table."

Oh, God, dinner. The man had a mission. This would take forever. And she didn't have forever. She'd been working on these stalls like a madwoman for the past two weeks so she could get her horses home. Having to be at Seven Peaks to take care of them knowing Luke was there was simply too hard.

She mentally shook her head. She'd been trying to make a decision about Luke and her for weeks, but she couldn't do it. The pain and fear held her by the throat, paralyzing her.

Reason told her the only safe thing to do was to call it quits before her emotions were so tangled up with Luke she'd never be able to walk away. But the pain in her heart wouldn't let her do it. She couldn't face the reality of never seeing him again.

She *wanted* to believe he would never hurt her. Wanted to believe they could remain friends for years and never worry about it. But she knew better. She *knew* better. Men were dangerous, unpredictable creatures.

And so it went, the needs and thoughts and beliefs swirling in her head until she didn't know up from down.

The last thing she was fit for was company. Maybe she could forestall Tom. "Dinner?"

"Yeah, dinner. You know, food. It's a substance you put in your mouth, chew up and then swallow."

Irritation pulled at her. She'd fed herself since she could crawl to the pantry and open a box of cereal. Why did everyone suddenly think she didn't have the knack? She gave Tom a warning look. "I know what food is, Tom."

"Really? It doesn't look as if you do." He sauntered to the barn door and held it open for her, waiting patiently for her to walk through.

With a sigh of defeat, she doused the lights and walked by him. With a few quick steps he caught up with her and matched her step as they made their way to the house.

She turned to look at him. "Dare I hope you came here only to feed me dinner? That you'll deliver your cheerful 'Hi, you look like hell,' feed me and then be on your way?"

He gave her a brilliant smile. "You can always hope."

She gave her best martyr's sigh. "That's what I was afraid of. So tell me, is this going to be a short tête-à-tête or a long-winded one?"

"That depends on how mule-headed you're going to be."

Great. Opening the door, she stepped into the house. She took off her coat, hung it up and peeked into the living room. The flames flickering in the wood-burning stove caught her attention. She turned to Tom with a look of accusation. "You built a fire in the stove? How long have you been here?"

"About ten minutes. And don't look at me like that. You should be thanking me. Poor Hank was shivering when I came in."

Gaby walked into the living room where Hank's bed resided. His big bloodhound head and floppy ears draped over the basket's edge. His face carried his usual baleful look. His body was wrapped in her best sleeping bag.

She narrowed her eyes on Tom. "He looks warm enough now."

The chastisement went right over Tom's head. He hung his coat by the front door and disappeared in the kitchen. Resigned to her fate, Gaby dropped onto the couch. A shiver ran through her. It *was* cold in here. She whispered an apology to Hank and pulled the afghan from the back of the sofa around her shoulders. Lately little details, like keeping the house warm, just seemed to slip by her.

Tom returned from the kitchen with a white takeout bag in hand. He handed her a burger from it, and then retrieved one for himself before getting comfortable on the other end of the sofa.

She set the burger in her lap. "So, are you going to start this conversation or am I supposed to guess what you want?"

Tom looked pointedly at the burger in her lap. "In order to eat that hamburger, you have to unwrap it."

A wave of exhaustion hit her. She didn't have the energy for this. She narrowed her eyes in warning. "Tom."

He only smiled, pointed to the burger and waited patiently for her to take a bite.

With a huff of exasperation, she tore the paper off and bit angrily into the meat and bread.

He opened his own hamburger. "I hear you broke it off with Luke. That true?"

She shook her head in disbelief. So that was what this was about. Well, he'd wasted a trip. She was having enough trouble keeping her own thoughts from drowning her, she didn't need anyone else's adding water to the ocean.

She looked him right in the eye. "I'm not talking about this."

"Well, I guess that answers the question about whether this is going to be a short tête-à-tête or a long-winded one. If you're going to stonewall me, this could go on all night."

A spark of anger surged through her and she jumped from the sofa. Tearing her burger into three pieces, she pitched them impatiently to the dogs. "And I suppose you have all night if I prove to be difficult."

He just smiled.

"That's what I thought." She took a deep breath and took hold of her temper. Losing her cool wouldn't get Tom out of here any sooner. In fact, the only way to get him out of here would be to get on with it. She sat back down. "What do you want to know?"

"Tell me why you came to Montana."

She ran her hands through her hair, giving herself time to think. "I came here because after losing Zoey and spending the last year tracking Bill down, I needed what that big red mountain could give me. Peace."

"Did you get it?"

She draped the afghan over her knees. "Yeah, I did, at first. Even with this place being such a disaster, I could sit under that red mountain and it felt *so* good."

"And then?"

"And then Luke Anderson barged in and everything went to hell in a handbasket."

Tom chuckled. "Yeah, well, that tends to happen when Luke's around. But he's out of your life now. Is your peace back?"

Tears stung her eyes and she blinked them back. She didn't know how to answer that question. She missed Luke with every breath she took. But with him gone she didn't fear falling into the same trap her mother and sister had, either.

She shrugged a shoulder. "Maybe."

Tom raised a disbelieving brow. "Maybe? Well, your definition of peace must be different from mine. Because when Nancy and I ran into you and Luke at the restaurant a couple of weeks ago, you looked great. Your eyes sparkled, you had gained some weight, and you were *laughing*. Pardon my bluntness, but right now you look like a cadaver out of *The Walking Dead*. And though I've heard a few dry chuckles tonight, I don't think a hearty laugh is in you."

She shrugged a shoulder. "You're talking about happiness. I'm not sure happiness and peace are connected."

Tom took a bite of his burger and seemed to think carefully before answering her. "No, I don't suppose they have to be. It's hard for me to think of one without the other, though. So maybe I should ask, what's your idea of peace?"

Agitation ran through her. Tom knew exactly what her idea of peace was.

She pinned him with a level look. "Are you being obtuse? Or mean?"

"Neither. I'd like the words from your own lips, but if you're going to be evasive, I can spit them out for you. Is your idea of peace confined to not being beat upon?"

She held her hand out in supplication. "Is that so much to ask?"

"Absolutely not. I consider it a bare minimum. But I would hate to think you'd settle for so little."

She shook her head. "Where I come from it's not so damned little."

"The question is, is it enough? And if it was enough when you came, is it enough now? Those are the questions that have black circles under your eyes. And last, I'll remind you to trust yourself a little more. If you thought for one minute Luke Anderson was the kind of man who hit women, you never would have let him anywhere near you. You separate yourself from people with a violent streak like oil separates from water. Naturally, quickly and as completely as possible."

Old panic flicked through her veins. She shook her head. "You've got it all wrong. I don't have some inner alarm system that goes off when some bad man is near. I'm afraid of being hit. So afraid that shaking hands makes me sick to my stomach. So I stay away from all men. I'm a coward! Period. And that's the way it's always going to be."

Now Tom shook his head. "You're not a coward. *That's* your problem. You left your dad's house because hiding in the closet wasn't your cup of tea. Now, thirteen years later, you're trying to crawl back in there. It won't work, lady."

He rolled up the takeout bag. "It's late, and you look as though you need rest as much as you do food. Go to bed. But tomorrow morning take a cup of coffee—hell, take a thermos—and walk out to your big red rock and figure out what's really in your heart and confront it. Because, Gaby—" he raked her with a concerned eye "—hiding from it won't solve anything."

He stood up and tossed the takeout bag into her lap. "There's another burger in there. Eat it up before you go to bed." He walked to the door and pulled his coat on. Opening the door, he gave her a mischievous wink. "Sweet dreams."

The next morning Gaby blinked hard, trying to get her eyes to focus so she could pour the steaming coffee into the thermos. Tom was right. The time for deep soul searching had come. Because if she didn't get some sleep, if she didn't get some food, and if her heart didn't stop aching, she would die.

Screwing the lid on the full thermos, she grabbed it, her sheepskin pelt, and called the dogs into the house from their morning romp. She didn't want distractions this morning.

She hiked to the knoll and laid the pelt down, fur side up. Plunking down on it, she poured coffee into the thermos's lid and took a slow sip. The steam warmed her cheeks and softened the lines on the scene before her. Fresh snow covered the ground. The sun's early rays glinted off the mountain's giant red face. Was there anyplace in the world more beautiful?

The sound of a truck pulling into her drive caught her attention. She peeked over her shoulder.

Luke?

Her heart leaped in her chest, joy galloping through her veins. She set her cup of coffee in the snow and stood. But before she went charging into his arms, she stopped herself. She was supposed to be developing perspective where Luke was concerned, not rushing in where so many fools had rushed before.

He climbed from his truck, hat in hand. Sending the door back into its frame with a snap of his wrist, he settled his hat on his head. Cocking a knee, he placed both hands on his hips and stood, staring at her.

So handsome and bold and infinitely dear.

Her heart hitched in her chest. She *should* send him packing. She hadn't resolved anything, and she wouldn't be able to with him standing in front of her, making her nerves tingle and her heart soar.

But, oh, God, she didn't want to push him back in his truck and send him on his way. At least not before she had a chance to see his face. To make sure he was doing well.

Stupid, she knew, but still the need was there. And today she didn't have the strength to fight it. So she stood and quietly waited for him to come to her.

Even with the distance between them, she could see him draw a deep breath and expel it, the warmed air turning to icy clouds as it left his lungs. And then he gave his hat brim a determined tug and strode her way, moving through the snow as if it didn't exist.

He stopped a few feet from her and ran his gaze carefully over her, taking in every detail. Finally he locked those blue, blue eyes on her. "You look good."

A laugh burst from her, and she raised a sardonic brow. "Your eyesight go bad in the last two weeks?"

He didn't laugh as she'd intended. Instead, the color of his eyes became more intense as he looked deep into her eyes. "I miss you. To me you look good."

Her heart clenched at his naked honesty. In the face of it, she could only offer the truth in return. "I miss you, too."

He nodded, a single, succinct nod. "I tried to give you time, Gaby. But I can't do it anymore. I leave in four days, and this isn't getting us anywhere."

Four days. Pain and loss squeezed her heart. In four

days he'd be far, far away. Out of touch and way, way out of reach.

She'd be safe. And so lonely.

"I'm not going to hurt you." Luke's words whispered through the frozen air, frustration spiking each one of them.

She smiled sadly. This argument had no end.

He believed in himself.

And she believed in her past.

"Gaby, I need these four days. I want them." His gaze bore into her. "I want *you*. There's a cabin up on the top of Miner's Peak. Go there with me. Four days, that's all I'm asking for. And then I'll be gone."

Her heart tightened at his request. Four days. She wanted him, too, with a need that made her soul ache.

Four days. And then he would be gone. Far away. For a long time. Long enough, surely, for this need to abate. Long enough for the pain in her heart to die and for the normality of being alone again to set in. And when he came back she wouldn't see him. She wouldn't risk it. She would stay on her ranch. And she would make sure he stayed on his.

She could have four days in his arms. And a safe future.

So tempting.

But why Miner's Peak? She tipped her head in question. "Why a cabin? Why can't we stay here?"

He shrugged. "Because I want a quiet place where no one can interrupt us. A quiet, beautiful place where I can make love to you."

Her heart stopped and then started again with a thud and a flutter. *Where he could make love to her.* Her body tingled at the mere thought. Her heart raced with anticipation. She wanted it. But was it wise?

No, she couldn't imagine it was. She hadn't resolved

anything over the past two weeks. But at the moment it didn't seem to matter. She wanted him. And for the next four days she was going to have him.

She nodded. "Okay, cowboy. Four days."

A smile broke out on his lips, and Gaby suspected he wanted to swoop down for a resounding kiss, but he didn't. He was being careful not to push his hand. He didn't want to frighten her off now.

Instead he stuck his hands deep in his coat pockets. "How soon can you leave? Matt said you could leave the dogs with him and Shanna. We can take my truck up to the cabin."

She smiled at his enthusiasm, but caution stayed her hand. She liked the idea of the cabin—it sounded romantic—but she didn't want to be dependent on him to get her there and back.

"I have some things to do around here before I can take off. And I want to get there myself. I'll meet you at the cabin when I get things settled here. Okay?"

He narrowed his eyes on her. He didn't like it, but he knew better than to argue with her about it. Finally he gave her a single nod. "Okay. Matt will show you which trail to take up. Once you're on it, you can't get lost. I'll see you before dark?"

She nodded. "Four-wheeling in the dark isn't my thing. I'll be there before dark."

Now he did lean forward and place a soft kiss on her cheek. "Don't dawdle," he whispered, his lips tickling the spot he had just kissed.

She smiled and nodded.

Without another word he turned and strode back to his truck.

She shook her head at her decision. She'd lost her mind, agreeing to this. But she needed these four days as much as he did. They would be little enough to warm the lonely years ahead.

Chapter Fourteen

Stretched out on the bed, his head propped on a few pillows and his hands, Luke watched twilight descend through the single cabin window. Though his pose was relaxed, he was strung tighter than a barbwire fence.

Gaby hadn't arrived yet. He cursed the fool notion that had possessed him to let her come up here by herself. She could be in here right now—with him—safe and cozy and warm.

Hell, they could have worked up a healthy sweat by now. Several times. Instead, she was still out there, making her way up the damned mountain. Giving up all pretense of calm, Luke rolled out of the bed and set up a stalking pace. Anticipation and need simmered in his veins like steam in a pressure cooker. It seemed as if he'd been waiting forever for tonight.

Tonight he was going to make love to Gaby. Slow, sweet love. He was going to worship her body with his.

Caress every square inch of her with his hands. Taste every square inch with his lips. He would tantalize and caress and cherish. She'd learned early in life how much pain a man could give. Tonight, she'd learn how much pleasure he could give.

A warning note sounded deep in his head. He had to show her, convince her clear down to her soul that he would never heap anything on her but pleasure. Because if he didn't, she'd never let him near her when he returned.

He wasn't stupid. He knew she'd crawl right back behind her protective walls the second his plane left the ground if he didn't give her a damned good reason not to. If he didn't convince her she was safe not to.

And he couldn't let that happen. Because sometime in the past few weeks he'd decided he wanted her waiting for him when he returned. For once, he wanted to carry more into the hellholes he was headed for than his anger and pain. He wanted to know a little bit of heaven was waiting for him when he came back.

And dammit, where was his slice of heaven, anyway? It was almost dark. Gaby should be here. Restlessly, he stalked to the door, gave the knob a twist and jerked the door open. Frigid air rushed into the cabin along with the not-too-distant whine of a pickup truck. He peered into the deepening shadows of approaching nightfall for the telltale sign of Gaby's headlights.

And there she was, her high beams ricocheting off the deep snow as her beat-up four-by-four emerged from the dark outline of trees. Slipping and sliding on the snow, the truck made its way into the large meadow and to the cabin's door.

A tight coil deep in Luke's chest loosened. He'd kept the possibility that Gaby might not come at all buried deep.

But he could dismiss that hidden worry now. She was here. Safe and sound. And soon she would be in his arms.

She turned off her engine and doused the truck's lights. Silence and darkness once again blanketed the meadow. Gaby sat quietly in the truck, debating, no doubt, the wisdom of her decision. And wondering, certainly, about the events of the night.

His body reacted fast and hard as his own thoughts ran rampant, imagining what was to come. But he didn't walk to the truck. He leaned against the doorjamb and waited patiently. Tonight of all nights he didn't want to crowd her. He wanted her to feel unthreatened and utterly safe.

Finally she mustered her courage and pushed her way out of the truck. Carrying a small suitcase in one hand, she made her way to the door.

He gave her an easy smile. "About time you made it."

She smiled back. "I almost didn't come."

He'd suspected as much. "I'm glad you did."

She blushed a priceless shade of pink and her eyes slid away in embarrassment, but she couldn't stop the tiny smile of nervous anticipation that pulled at her lips. "So am I."

For a few precious seconds he savored her innocence, then he reached out and hooked his hand behind her neck, pulling her close and lowering his lips to hers.

Fire. After two weeks of want and need and pent-up frustration, the feel of her lips under his set a brushfire in his blood.

A brushfire that seemed to consume Gaby, as well. Her suitcase hit the cabin's wooden porch. She wound her arms around his neck, pulling him closer and opening her lips for his tongue's invasion.

Flames of desire threatened his fragile control. God, he'd missed her. And now he couldn't get enough.

Couldn't hold her tightly enough. Couldn't kiss her deeply enough. Couldn't touch her enough.

His hands searched frantically until they found an area not covered in nylon and down. Her enticing bottom. He greedily kneaded the resilient flesh covered only by the single layer of denim. Blood surged to his arousal and he had to fight the need to pull her to him.

But now was not the time for mindless passion. If he scared her now, the next four days would be lost and very possibly the future. Reluctantly he pulled his mouth from hers.

A soft moan of protest fell from her lips, and she tried to pull him back down, but he grabbed her wrists and unwound her arms from his neck. He wanted to push her gently away so they could both think clearly, but her hands clung to him, wrapping tightly in his vest.

Her lips were red, her eyes passion glazed. It looked as if she'd missed him as much as he'd missed her. Good.

Stomping his own desire back into control, he gave her a minute to compose herself and then he pried her hands from his vest and snatched up her suitcase. "Come on in before we both turn into Popsicles."

She preceded him into the cabin and gave the single room a quick perusal. She glanced back at him shyly. "Pretty."

It was far from that. A simple, crude cabin, its purpose was to shelter cowboys working the upper meadows during roundup and spring calving. But that she'd put forth the effort to say something nice, no doubt just so he'd feel good, made him think she wanted these four days to be as special as he did. But it also made him think he should have brought her someplace much nicer than a lineman's shack for a night as important as this. But it was too late now.

Mentally banging his head against a solid slab of granite, he smiled wryly, mumbled an appropriate response and placed her suitcase on a chair. Now what?

He glanced around as a moment of unaccustomed awkwardness suddenly gripped him. His gaze fell on the cooler he'd hauled up this afternoon. "Are you hungry? I brought plenty of food." He almost rolled his eyes. Food. The last thing he wanted to do was eat. He wanted Gaby naked in that bed, but for the life of him, he couldn't think of a diplomatic way to get her there.

And Gaby clearly thought he'd lost his mind. She gave him a wide-eyed look, glanced away uncertainly and glanced back with rosy blooms staining her cheeks. "I'm not really very hungry."

Relief poured through him. This time he wouldn't drop the ball. Gaby certainly didn't know how to manage the little details of a tryst. If he didn't get them in that bed, they weren't going to get there.

He gave her a reassuring smile. "Neither am I. Do you want to clean up? Change into something more comfortable?"

She flushed a deeper shade of red, but managed a nod.

He pointed to the only other door in the room. "The bathroom's in there. The plumbing is uninspiring, but the water is as hot as you want it. I brought some towels up. They're already in there."

With a short nod she grabbed her suitcase. Her movements were a little awkward as she made her way across the room and disappeared into the bathroom.

He smiled to himself as she pulled the door shut behind her, and then a sudden burst of excitement raced through him. Soon she'd be in his arms.

Heart racing and blood pumping, he began to prepare

the room. At least he'd had the sense to bring a few things to make the cabin a little nicer.

A new, fluffy white comforter covered the bed. Grabbing its corner, he pulled it down to expose the lacy edges of the crisp new sheets below.

Next he pulled the bottle of wine from the cabin's small refrigerator and set it next to the bed on the little table that served as a nightstand. Carefully he unwrapped the two wineglasses he'd hauled up the mountain, and put them by the wine.

On second thought, he uncorked the wine and filled the glasses. As he topped off the second glass, the water went off in the bathroom.

With shaking hands, he opened the front doors to the old Franklin stove and threw more logs on the fire to keep the chill from the room. Picturing Gaby bathed in soft firelight, he left the small doors open and switched off the overhead light. The soft glow of the fire softened the room's utilitarian lines. It wasn't fancy, but it was pretty in its own humble way. And anyway, he fully intended to make up for the austere surroundings. Tonight would be special.

The bathroom door opened, and Gaby stepped out. She was dressed in a white satin robe that clung to her body, defining every feminine valley and curve. The soft lace adorning the top caressed the gentle swells of her breasts, making his fingers itch to touch the soft skin the low neckline exposed.

The fire started at his fingers and toes and raced to a central location that almost brought him to his knees. Only through sheer willpower did he resist the urge to reach out and drag her into his arms. He stood there, just looking at her, drinking her in like a blind man who'd just regained his sight.

A small nervous smile graced her lips, and a nervous hand indicated the robe. "I ran into town this afternoon. I wanted something nice for you."

Something pulled at his heart, something warm and a little bit painful. She'd wanted to be pretty for him. "It's beautiful."

A soft flush climbed up her chest and neck, tinting the top of her breasts a lovely rose before reaching her cheeks and settling there with fiery innocence.

Innocence. His palms broke out in a cold sweat. He'd never been with a virgin before. Had no idea how to handle one. Add Gaby's other fears to that, and he'd be damned lucky if tonight wasn't a fiasco.

With a deep breath he gathered his resolve. Tonight wasn't going to be a fiasco; it was going to be special.

He stepped closer to Gaby and ran a soft finger over the lace adorning her collarbone. "The robe is beautiful, but I want to see the woman beneath it. Will you take it off for me?"

Gaby's pulse leaped at the base of her neck. More color flooded her cheeks, and she cast an anxious glance around the room. Her eyes settled on the wood-burning stove before she raised them to him. "Can we close the doors?"

If she'd asked for the stars, he'd have given them to her. But this one small request was beyond him. He'd waited too long for this moment. He needed it too badly. He shook his head. "I want to see you."

The stain on her cheeks got deeper, and she took a backward step to put a little more room between them, but she released the knot at her waist. Before the robe could fall open, though, she grabbed the edges and kept it pulled tightly across her. Her teeth nibbled anxiously at her lower lip as she no doubt debated both her wisdom and her courage. But then she drew a deep breath and pulled the robe open, off her shoulders, and let it slide from her arms. It pooled around her feet, leaving her unconditionally, gloriously naked.

He exhaled the breath he'd been holding, the soft sound falling into the silence of the room like a benediction. "Beautiful."

She looked up at him, uncertain but wanting to believe him. "I'm too thin." Her words were the merest whisper.

He nodded his head. "Yes. But still, so beautiful." He moved across the room to touch her, to feel the weight of her breasts in his hand, but he stopped not three feet from her. Fair was fair.

He pulled his shirttail out of his pants and shrugged out of his shirt. Her eyes widened and a slow easy smile touched her lips. Amber fire crackled in her eyes.

An answering flame burned low in his belly. If he didn't get out of these jeans, he'd be permanently injured. He undid his belt and the top button.

Interest flared in her eyes, and she took a step forward, her gaze locked below his belt.

He undid the second button.

She took a step back, her tongue nervously wetting her lips. Her eyes flicked to the fire and then hesitantly returned to his fly. Curiosity and maidenly apprehensions.

She made his heart ache.

The third button came free. Apprehensions won. Gaby's gaze flew to the stove and then she glanced at him with a desperate plea.

He chuckled, the sound low and rough, and nodded. "Go ahead."

A blur crossed his vision, and then he could hear the stove's metal doors slam shut behind him. The room plunged into darkness. A half breath later he heard the rustle of covers and the crunch of bed springs.

He smiled in the dark. "If you're hiding, I have to tell you, the bed is *not* your best choice."

Silence.

And then he heard her soft female voice full of nervous anticipation. "I'm not hiding. I'm waiting."

Fire raced through him, and somewhere between where he stood and the bed, he managed to kick his jeans off without landing on his head and removed his socks. Quick as a lick, he was under the covers. Lying on their sides, they faced each other.

She jumped when his body slid along hers.

"Nervous?"

Her head moved.

"Are you nodding or shaking your head?"

She giggled. "I don't know."

Giggled! He could classify that as nervous. He reached out and ran a comforting hand down her shoulder. "Shhh, we're going to take this as slow as we need to."

Another tiny giggle filled the silence, and an anxious hand grabbed his shoulder. She pulled him closer and snuggled into his arms. "I don't know if slow is the answer. Maybe we should just get it over with."

It was his turn to laugh. "Gaby, you're hell on the ego. And, no, we're not going to rush through this. We're going to take our time and savor every stair leading to heaven." He ignored the gentle glide of her skin against his. She'd moved into his arms more for comfort than desire, and despite her words rushing her would be a disaster. Besides, he wanted her to find out how good being with a man could be. Quick would never do the job.

She moved restlessly against him. "Kiss me before I completely lose my nerve."

He touched his lips to her cheek. "Where?"

Her body arched against him. Her hand tightened on his

shoulder, and a shudder ran through her. "Luke." A gentle admonishment wrapped around a desperate plea.

He answered the plea. He closed his mouth on hers and drew her close. Another shudder ran through her and then she flowed against him as if she were his other half. Her arms and legs wrapped around him until he couldn't tell where he ended and she began. Heaven.

His control dangled by the barest of threads, but he held on to it because he wanted tonight to be pure magic for Gaby. He wanted her ready for every step they took. More than ready. He wanted her panting for the next step before they took it.

But it was damned tough to hang on to even the barest shred of control with her tongue sparring with his. Her breasts pressed against him, their softness accentuated by nipples gone hard with passion. The soft curls of her femininity teased the absolute hardest part of him. But he did it. He gritted his teeth and he ignored the ache in his groin, and he went slowly.

Gently he deepened his kiss and brought her arms up around his neck. He ran his fingertips lightly over the side of her breast. Goose bumps rose under his fingers. He stroked again. A soft moan sounded in the back of her throat. He wanted more than a touch. He wanted to feel the weight of her in his hands, run his tongue over the hard tip of her nipple, taste the sweet warmth of that soft, resilient flesh. He wanted her to know just how much a man could cherish a woman.

He trailed a path of tiny kisses from her lips to her collarbone. There he stopped to taste. He kissed and teased the soft flesh until tiny mewling sounds filled Gaby's throat, then he delivered a stinging love bite, drawing the taste and smell of her into his very being.

She arched against him, her fingers digging into his

shoulders, and her pelvis thrusting against his. He thrust back, the friction almost driving him over the edge. He needed some distance or he'd be done long before he'd gotten Gaby anywhere close to heaven. He rolled her onto her back and, with one hand, lifted her hands above her head.

With his other hand he trailed a light, teasing path with the back of one finger from her elbow to her breast. She arched toward the soft touch, a sound of need echoing in her throat. When he reached her nipple, its distended peak begged for more. He obliged with featherlike touches, stroking her need. When she couldn't arch any higher, when the soft echo had become a needful moan, he flicked her nipple with thumb and finger, his nail biting gently into her flesh.

Her body tensed as though a bolt of electricity had gone through her, and a moan most men only heard in their dreams fell from her lips. He flicked the nipple again and then closed his mouth over it. The light of heaven appeared. He'd waited so long for this moment. And it was so *much* sweeter than he'd ever imagined.

He suckled at her breast, his tongue salving the peak he'd tweaked moments before. She grasped his head, her fingers delving through his hair as she held him at her breast. He gave her a tiny nip and another bolt of electricity jumped through her. Her fingers tightened in his hair and her hips thrust upward naturally, seeking what she needed.

He moved his hand down her belly until his fingers threaded through her soft curls. He gritted his teeth against his own need and moved farther still until he found the very center of her.

She was hot and wet and ready.

He found the proof of her desire and teased the hard

nubbin until the sounds coming from her throat begged for release. He eased one finger into her.

A sharp intake of breath hissed through her teeth, and she lifted her hips against his hand.

Blood surged to his arousal as her moist heat surrounded his finger. He wanted to be in her. Now. But this was the crucial moment. She had to be ready. If he rushed her now, she would only find pain. And *that* wasn't going to happen. He was going to give her bliss.

His hand trembling with desire, he slipped a second finger in to join the first. When she didn't shy, but rose again to meet him, he gave her a few more minutes to relax and adjust before giving her breast a last draw and moving between her thighs. He pushed her legs wide with his knees, but he met no resistance. She bent her knees and welcomed him.

Grabbing his shoulders, she drew him back down to her and closed her mouth over his.

He didn't need a second invitation. His tongue dove deep and the better part of him followed. Fire raced through him.

Desperately he fought the need to bury himself to the hilt. Fought the need to drive into her again and again. Fought the need to claim her in the most primitive fashion.

And he could have done it, if her lips hadn't left his to cry their need to him. If she hadn't raised her hips to his and tried to pull him into her with a need that matched his own. Giving up all pretense of control, he sank into her until he could go no farther.

A sigh of exquisite relief fell from her lips.

And then they raced for the top. Her hands clung and grasped at him, pulling him closer. Her hips rose to meet his, not allowing him to hold back, but claiming him as surely as he claimed her with his every thrust.

He held nothing back. He gave her everything he had—his body, his heart, his soul. And with her answering thrusts and grasping hands and sensuous cries, she returned his gifts tenfold. Together they broke their earthly ties and climbed to a place so high even heaven got left behind.

The tumble back to earth was equally powerful and twice as frightening. Luke lay over Gaby, his weight resting on his elbows, his head nestled in the crook of her shoulder and a cold chill running down his spine. He'd felt this feeling once before. This feeling of need and power and a high that sent a man soaring far above the clouds. The last time, the intoxicating high had led to a hard, painful fall. And after Tanya's bitter betrayal he'd pledged never to take that fall again.

Beneath him a shiver ran through Gaby, and she tightened her arms around him. He could feel her fear as clearly as he could feel his own. Not a fear of him, but a fear of the power of the emotion that had just claimed them. She, too, he knew, had her fears of emotional ties.

He tightened his arms around her, lending what reassurance his own reeling psyche could offer. "Shhh. It's okay. It's okay. It was just more than we expected. But we're okay. Everything's okay." He drew her closer and prayed to God he was right. He prayed that by tomorrow morning the dust would settle, and their emotions would be back on an even keel, because he wasn't prepared to love her.

But he wasn't prepared to give her up, either.

Gaby sat on the big granite boulder, cold creeping into her bones. Cold and sorrow. Hours ago, just as the first rays of dawn had tinted the sky pink, she'd woken up wrapped tightly in Luke's arms. Warmth had surrounded her, and for one peaceful moment she had absorbed the bliss.

But then the wonder and fear of the night before had seeped into her peace like early-morning fog blocking the sun and chilling the air. Being careful not to awaken Luke, she'd crawled from the protective cocoon, silently donned her clothes and escaped the intimate confines of the cabin for the safer, open spaces of the great outdoors.

Now, with the sun marking midmorning, she wondered if she'd ever find peace again, or if that last moment of half sleep and consciousness in Luke's arms had been it. Pain squeezed her heart. She'd been a fool. She'd thought she could take a single moment out of time and build some memories for the future, but she'd been wrong. She'd lost it all. The home. The mountain. The man.

She'd often wondered why her mother and sister stayed with their husbands. Now she knew. No words were strong enough, beautiful enough, to describe what she and Luke had shared last night.

But she wouldn't be another victim. She wouldn't allow herself to get sucked into the beauty, only to have it disintegrate into something ugly. She would have to go. She needed only to close her eyes and see her sister's body to know it. And she would have to go much farther than the boundaries of Peaceful Shadows to escape the pull of last night's magic. She would have to leave her new home and her glorious mountain behind.

The cabin door slammed, shattering the stillness. She looked over to find Luke striding her way in a no-nonsense gait, the collar of his sheepskin coat pulled up over his ears and his hat pulled low over his eyes. So handsome. And so dear.

She closed her eyes against the pain pounding in her chest. Now was as good a time as any for this conversation. She was as prepared as she would ever be. And she had to give him credit for waiting this long.

He'd opened the cabin door shortly after she'd sneaked out this morning, looking for her in the early light of dawn, no doubt worried that she had flown the coop on him. Her heart had contracted painfully at the picture he'd presented with his mussed hair, bare feet and a partially buttoned pair of jeans pulled over his hips.

She hadn't called to him. She'd just sat and watched and felt her heart ache with sorrow, knowing today would possibly be the last time she ever saw him.

When he'd finally spotted her, relief that he'd found her had briefly smoothed the worry on his face. But then tension had pulled his features tight. He hadn't called to her, either. They'd simply stared at each other, silently, until Luke had finally gone back inside, apparently deciding to leave her alone so she could sort out her feelings in peace.

She'd suspected he'd wanted some time to himself for the same reason. She knew something about last night had frightened him, too. She didn't know what. She couldn't let it matter even if she did know. But it made her think her decision to leave was best for both of them.

Now she watched with dread and pain searing her heart as he made his way across the snowy meadow to her. She could have lived without this moment. In fact, she'd debated packing her truck and disappearing before he'd awakened. But the act had seemed unfair and far too cowardly, even for her.

Luke stopped when his boots hit the boulder's granite base. ''We're going to have to talk about it, Gaby.''

There wasn't anything to talk about really. She drew a deep breath, gathering her nerve, and gave him her decision. ''I'm leaving.''

His eyes widened in surprise before his brows pulled

down in irritation. "You can't leave. You promised me four days."

Leave it to Luke to break it down to the bare bones of the deal. She smiled sadly. "Yes. But I can't give them to you. It's too powerful, Luke. Too dangerous."

"What's dangerous?" He sounded like a belligerent little boy denying the existence of the frog in his pocket, even as the warty fellow croaked his displeasure.

But this subject was too important to be dismissed by such a tactic. She'd reiterate for him. "What we shared last night. It was everything I had hoped for, and more. It was wonderful. Too wonderful."

His face twisted in frustration, and he spun on his heel, stalking away a few steps before spinning back. "Too wonderful? Would you listen to yourself? Do you know how often wonderful comes along in a person's life? Damned seldom. Why on earth would you run away from it?"

Pain tore at her heart. "Because today I can. And tomorrow I can't imagine having the strength."

His eyes narrowed to deadly serious blue bands. "And after tomorrow you think I might start beating you, right?"

She wanted to turn away from the accusation that all but called her a coward, but she made herself hold his gaze. She had to make him understand. "I won't take the chance."

He stalked away again, clenching and releasing his fists as he tried to dispel his own tension. When he turned back to her this time, he strode up to her boulder and leaned in until he was almost nose to nose with her. "I'm leaving in three days, Gaby. Do you really think I'll start beating you in the next three days?"

She didn't back up an inch, because she suspected he wanted a lot more than the next three days. "No. But you'll be back, won't you?'' She didn't mean back to Montana. She meant back to Peaceful Shadows. Back to her when he returned from overseas.

His eyes widened again as if he were surprised she'd known, but he didn't hesitate to answer. ''Yes,'' he admitted baldly. ''And I'm not going to beat you then, either, dammit!''

A small chuckle slipped from her lips, a sad, desperate sound. ''No. Because I won't be around.''

Luke rocked back on his heel, the fact that she might be leaving more than this mountain registering on his face. ''What do you mean you won't be around?''

''I can't stay here, Luke.'' She gave him a gentle smile. ''You're much, much too sweet a temptation. I'll put Peaceful Shadows back on the market and go back to Chicago.''

He jabbed the air two inches in front of her nose. ''You'll do nothing of the kind. You love that ranch. If one of us leaves this area, it'll damn well be me.'' His words were delivered with the precision of a six-shooter. ''But there's no need for either of us to leave. I know what happened last night was a little more than either of us expected. Quite frankly, it shook me down to my bones. But if you just give it a few days to settle in, everything will fall back into place.''

He didn't get it. The path he wanted them to take was a dead end. A dead end that didn't have a happy ending for either of them. Somehow she had to make him see that.

She held her hand out in supplication. ''What happens when things 'settle in'?''

''We pick up where we left off, and things go on.''

''For how long?'' she persisted.

He huffed in exasperation. ''Until we're done with it.''

She laughed sadly. ''Listen to yourself, Luke. You know

this relationship is going to end as surely as I do. You knew it the day you proposed your deal. You were as adamant as I we not let things get any deeper than a few dates.''

He jabbed at the air again. ''Last night it got a hell of a lot deeper than a few dates,'' he pointed out crudely, his anger and frustration getting the better of him.

She nodded. ''And it scared both of us. We both got far too close to something neither one of us wants any part of. And ignoring it this morning won't save either of us. It will only make the end that much more painful.''

Trying to ignore the pain tearing at her own heart, she went on. ''I don't know what happened in your past to make you leery of relationships. Matt told me you were married once and that it ended badly. Maybe your aversion came from there. But the truth is, you aren't any more willing to get close to another person than I am.'' She waited, gave him time to deny the accusation. But he didn't.

Her heart throbbed with a deep, deep loss. Desolation, cold and lonely, seeped into every portion of her body. It was foolish of her to want him to deny the charge. Foolish of her to want to hear him say he would love her when she would never love him back. But still, a small, secret part of her ached at his silence.

''There's no future for us, Luke. Can't you see that? Last night was as good as it gets. From here it's only downhill. Just a long, dusty road with a few roses to brighten the way. But at the end, just a giant wall of thorny bushes to tear at our hides and make us sorry we ever took the journey at all. Because the bottom line is, I won't love you, Luke. And you won't love me, either.''

He paled beneath his weather-worn tan as her bleak words fell around them. He closed his eyes against the stark picture she had created, but the belief in her words was written all over his face. He got it now. He didn't like it any better than she did. But he saw the futility in it. Saw the pain at the end of the road.

Anguish squeezed the air from her lungs. Now he would let her go.

Finally he opened his eyes. Those blue, blue eyes. So beautiful. And so, so sad. He drew a breath as shaky as her own. A breath with which to say goodbye.

But before he could form the words, a loud, throbbing roar ripped through the crisp, frigid air, and they found themselves in a vicious, swirling storm of snow and wind. Both she and Luke ducked their heads, shielding their faces from the biting snow and ice as a helicopter moved over their heads at treetop level. When the aircraft had moved beyond them and the winds abated, Gaby raised her head.

The helicopter now hovered over the meadow on the far side of the cabin. Gently it settled to the ground into the miniblizzard caused by its own whirling blades. Through the flying snow, Gaby could just make out Susie's brown and black face through the helicopter's clear bubble.

Luke glanced at her, surprise clearly written on his face.

No doubt having a helicopter drop down out of the sky into his backyard was a surprising event for him, but it was old hat for her. She drew a deep breath and pitched her voice above the helicopter's throbbing hum. "Someone must be lost. Susie's in there. Tom must have asked Matt where to find us."

Luke jerked his gaze to the 'copter, his lips forming a few words Gaby was just as happy not to hear. Obviously he didn't want what little time they had left disturbed.

She felt the same way. But the more practical side of her knew this was for the best. Tom would whisk her away, and this would all be over. It would be quick. And if not painless, at least less painful.

So why did she feel as if moving from this rock was impossible? As if her limbs were leaden with pain and sorrow and far too heavy to move at all, let alone carry her to the helicopter. She looked back to the aircraft, knowing she would somehow have to get herself there. And then force herself to cover whatever ground the search required.

But Tom was already crawling out of a glass cockpit. Crouching low, he clamped his hat to his head and ran her way as quickly as the snow would allow. Though she had expected to see no one else, it was comforting to see that it was indeed Tom. With her nerves raw and aching, the last thing she wanted to deal with was a stranger. A good friend might come in handy about now.

Mustering her strength, she made herself stand.

But before she could call out a greeting, Luke beat her to the punch. "Who the hell managed to get themselves lost today?"

Gaby winced at Luke's rudeness, but she understood his frustration. He'd had four wonderful days planned, and they had just disintegrated into a nightmare.

Tom snapped back at Luke's tone, his brows pulling together in irritation. "Sorry to interrupt your party, but I've got a lost mama and toddler up on First Face."

Gaby's heart jumped in her chest. Lost adults were hard enough, but she hated when children were lost. Adrenaline started pumping into her veins, bringing her body back into fighting mode and numbing the pain in her heart.

Luke jerked his thumb toward the cabin. "Let's go inside where we can hear above that damned thing," he shouted, tipping his head toward the helicopter.

Gaby's heart pounded as she followed Luke and Tom

into the cabin. "Where and what is First Face," she demanded as soon as the door clicked into its frame.

"It's a smooth face on the next mountain north of here." Tom pointed to the cabin's north wall. "Three years ago yesterday, this couple, the Caldwells, were married on the top of it. There's a cabin up there climbers use for a base camp. Every year the Caldwells stay there to celebrate their anniversary."

Gaby couldn't stop her brows from raising in horror. "They were married in the middle of winter at the edge of a *cliff?*" What was wrong with people?

Tom shrugged a shoulder. "It's a hell of a view."

"Who reported them missing?" Luke asked.

Gaby glanced at Luke. He briefly met her gaze, and she could see his pain and frustration for having their last minutes together disrupted by this disaster. But worry for the mom and little boy also etched his face, and with a sad resolve he turned his gaze from her and centered his attention on Tom's news.

"Mr. Caldwell," Tom said. "Apparently, Anita Caldwell took their son, Taylor, for a walk last night. They were going to watch the stars come out together."

"And neither of them came back," Luke stated, his voice grave.

Tom shook his head. "Mr. Caldwell came into the sheriff's office this morning barely coherent and looking like hell. Apparently he spent the night banging around the woods and the top of the face looking for them. In his current state of panic, it's a damned wonder he didn't step off the cliff himself."

Gaby pressed her fingertips against her eyes in frustration before dropping her hands helplessly back to her sides. "And in the process obliterated any trail we might have had."

Tom nodded and then lifted a shoulder in resignation. "I'm not sure it would have mattered. There's a hell of a storm coming in from the north. Gale-force winds are running before it. By the time we get there, any tracks will be gone, anyway."

Gaby's stomach tightened. This search would require climbing, and she hated climbing under the best of conditions. It was time-consuming, hard on the dog and dangerous. With a storm breathing down their necks, it could be deadly. And worse, they would have to take time to pick up another climber. Rescue procedures didn't allow for searchers to climb alone.

Gaby nodded her understanding. "Let's get going then. How far are we going to have to go to pick up another climber? I'm assuming you brought my gear since Susie's already in the chopper."

"Not far, I hope." Tom turned to Luke and raised his brows. "I picked up your equipment when I got the dog."

Luke gave him a curt nod and grabbed his coat from the bed. "Let's do it then."

Panic raced through Gaby. "No!"

Both men turned to her, brows raised in question.

"I mean..." What did she mean?

She meant she didn't want to climb with Luke. It would be better if they just said goodbye here. Later, the goodbye would be so much more awkward. So much more painful. This would be easier for both of them.

Luke's gaze met hers, understanding and a sadness that mirrored her own in its blue depth. "I won't make it harder on you later. Let's find the little boy and his mama. Okay?"

Gaby's heart clenched. Climbing with Luke was really the only logical solution. Picking up a different climber would only waste precious time. Time the lost campers possibly didn't have.

And it would give her one more day with him. And a chance for their final gesture together to be more than the sadness of their parting. She nodded. "Let's do it."

Chapter Fifteen

At the top of First Face, Gaby kicked a chunk of ice across the cabin's rough wood floor. "Blast it."

Luke turned to her, as the small chunk of ice skittered across the wooden planking, and placed a comforting hand on her shoulder. "Well, we didn't really expect to find them here." Pain as deep as her own dulled the blue of his eyes. But like his touch, his expression offered nothing but comforting support as if he, too, wanted their last bit of time together to count for something truly good.

She closed her eyes against a wave of threatening tears. She couldn't think about how desolate her life would be without him. Not now. Not with two people's lives at stake.

Ruthlessly she pushed her ravaged emotions aside and concentrated on the problem at hand. No, she hadn't really expected the Caldwells to be here in the cabin. But she had hoped. Sometimes injured or lost victims did manage to make it back to base camp, and she'd prayed it would be so in this case. True to Tom's words, the vicious winds running before the storm had reached the mountain. No prints marred the snow's surface, and the low temperatures, combined with raging winds, put the windchill at dangerous lows.

Worse, if they looked into the storm, they could see the snow coming. Which narrowed their window for getting the helicopter in and out considerably. If they were going to find Anita and Taylor today, they had to do it *fast.*

Gaby looked around the little cabin for something she could use as a scent rag. They needed every edge they could get. An array of clothing lay on the only bed in the room. Picking through it, she found a pair of little pajamas that had a milk stain on them. With any luck Taylor had been wearing them when he spilled his milk.

Snatching them up, she turned to Luke. "Let's go."

Luke pointed to the pajamas. "Are those going to help? Can Susie still scent in these winds, or are we better off to make an educated guess?"

Gaby rolled her eyes at the question and reached down to pet Susie. "Trust me. She's a lot better than a guess, educated or otherwise. If they're upwind, the winds will just carry the scent to us. If they're downwind, it's going to hurt us. But we shouldn't be dead in the water. Taylor and Anita should be close. Taylor's only two. I can't imagine they walked far. If we get close to them, even with the winds, Susie should be able to pick them up."

She started to leave, but Luke grabbed her arm. "Before we go out there, let's set up some ground rules. Visibility sucks, which means we're going to have to stay close. If one of us goes over an edge, or into a deep gully—and there are lots of them up here—I want the other one to know about it. Agreed?"

It would drastically reduce the amount of ground they could search, but Luke was right, it was the only sensible thing to do. She nodded her head. "Let's get going."

They pushed out into the blowing snow, and Luke pulled the door closed against the howling winds. Gaby grabbed the retractable line from her belt and hooked it to Susie's harness. It would reduce the area the dog could search, but if the dog went over an edge, she wouldn't go far.

She ruffled Susie's scruff and held the pajamas, decorated with a cartoon hero, under Susie's nose. Then, she injected a note of fun into her voice. "Find him, girl. Find him."

Excitement lit Susie's eyes and she lifted her nose into the air. Her head swiveled in both directions before she moved south, heading for the edge of First Face. Luke gave Gaby a hopeful, questioning look as the dog moved away so decisively.

She pitched her voice above the howl of the wind. "She's got something. It's not a true alert. Which means she hasn't got Taylor's scent. But she's got something. It might be the mother. Or the father," she qualified, on a slightly less hopeful note.

Luke nodded his understanding and they set off behind the dog. The eager German shepherd worked a forty-foot, side-to-side pattern in front of them, all the retractable line would allow her.

They'd been walking along the edge of the face through the savage weather, battling freezing winds and icy missiles for about ten minutes when a large, gray outcropping of rocks loomed out of the blowing snow about a hundred yards ahead of them. Over fifty feet high and taking up a space as big as a football field it would take them a good fifteen minutes to move around them.

Next to her, Luke's head jerked up with a start. Stopping dead in his tracks, he grabbed her shoulder and swung her to face him. "I know where they are."

Absently she gave the line in her hand a gentle tug to stop Susie's forward motion. "Where? How do you know?"

"Because I know where I'd go to watch the stars."

She hesitated for just a moment, uncertain about taking Susie off the scent. But Luke knew the area, and so did the Caldwells. If he was familiar with a particularly good spot to watch the stars, maybe the Caldwells knew of it, too.

"How far is it?" she hollered above the winds.

He pointed to the mass of gray rocks in front of them. "It's in those rocks. Well, below them actually."

She gave him a questioning look.

He shook his head. "I'll show you. Come on."

Luke broke into a jog, lifting his knees high to move through the snow. She followed suit, her backpack pounding a steady tattoo on her back. A quick whistle brought Susie to her. The big dog loped easily by her side.

Luke stopped in front of the mass of rocks where a huge fissure cracked the granite facade and ran deep into the small mountain. The end result was a large, closet-size room similar to a small cave. Drifting snow blocked the entrance, but it didn't take them long to kick through and get into the small area.

Gaby stopped short when she saw the huge hole in the ground right in the middle of the room. Large enough for a man to walk down, it descended at an angle toward the mountain's smooth face. Good Lord, a natural staircase. But where did it go?

Her stomach gave a nervous jump as she realized it very possibly went far enough to dump any adventurous traveler into a four-hundred-foot free fall at the mountain's face. So when Luke shrugged out of his backpack, slung his climbing ropes over his shoulder and headed down the staircase, she grabbed at his shoulder, stopping his descent.

"You can't go down there. It doesn't look safe." She pointed down the "stairs" and gave the narrow tunnel a distrustful look. "Do you know where that goes?"

He gave her a reassuring smile. "Of course I do. Come on, there's a ledge down here. And not only can you see the stars from there, you believe you're in them."

Without another word, Luke disappeared down the tunnel. Shrugging out of her own backpack, Gaby snatched her climbing ropes, draped them over her shoulder, gave Susie a quick sign to stay and followed Luke down into the dark abyss.

Sharp rocks bit at her shoulders and knees as she made her way down the narrow passage, thoughts of Poe's "Cask of Amontillado" wafting hauntingly through her mind.

The touch of Luke's hand, helping her out, brought a wash of relief through her. Then the icy winds hit her, her head spun, and the world fell away from her feet. She grabbed for Luke and hung on tight, sinking her fingers into the tough leather of his sheepskin coat.

Slowly the world righted and she realized her feet were planted solidly on the ground. The sky wasn't moving after all. It just surrounded her. She blinked a few times, to acclimate herself, and then released her hold on Luke's shoulders.

He pushed her gently away so he could see her face. "You okay?"

She nodded, noting his grim look. "They're not here, are they?"

He shook his head, his lips pulled tight in disappointment.

Ignoring the stinging bite of the snow, she took stock of her surroundings. They were standing on a tiny ledge. It stood out a scant eight feet from the mountain's face. Its width was a little more generous, ten feet perhaps. And it sported an impressive four-hundred-foot drop. Only an *idiot* would bring a two-year-old out on a ledge like this! She spun back to tell Luke just that when she caught sight of another ledge sticking out from the mountain's face, not twenty feet from them.

Grabbing Luke's shoulder, she spun him in that direction and pointed to the ledge. "Look, there they are!"

Quickly she surveyed the situation. Neither of the two bodies were moving. The little boy lay on the mother's chest, as if he'd crawled there for comfort and fallen asleep. Gaby could only hope. She glanced up to the top of the mountain to get an idea of how far they'd fallen. Her stomach took a sharp dive. The ledge sat a good thirty feet down the smooth face.

She turned to Luke, hoping there was another way to that ledge. "Is there another natural staircase over there?"

He shook his head, tension sharpening the angles of his face.

She pulled the radio from her belt and hailed Tom. When his voice crackled over the airwaves, she filled him in on Anita and Taylor's position.

"How are they?" Tom's voice came to her over the radio.

Gaby held the radio close to her mouth to reduce the interference from wind and depressed the talk button. "I don't know. They're not moving. Bring an EMT when you come."

"Okay, Gaby, listen. I'm only going to be able to make

one trip with the helicopter before that storm hits. Once it's here, we're going to be grounded. With the mother, child and an EMT, I'm only going to be able to bring one more person out. You or Luke will have to stay in the cabin until the storm blows over.''

Luke locked his gaze onto hers and gave his head a single, succinct nod. ''I'll stay.''

They would have a quick goodbye, after all. The wound in her chest bled a little harder. She nodded and tore her gaze from his. Concentrating on the radio in her hand, she forced her words beyond the lump in her throat. ''Luke says he'll stay.''

''Okay, we're on our way. Our ETA is about twenty minutes. How long is it going to take you to get there? We'll need help to get them up.''

Gaby glanced to Luke. ''We're going to have to go back up and around those rocks, aren't we?''

Luke studied the opposite ledge and then pointed to a finger of rock that stuck up from the ledge's base. ''On a better day I'd lasso that sucker, tie off here—'' he pointed to a similar rock protrusion at the far end of their own ledge ''—and climb straight over. But not in these winds.''

No. Not in these winds. ''How long will it take us to get over there?''

Luke looked up to the top of the mountain as he mentally calculated how long their trek would take. ''About the same as Tom's ETA, twenty minutes.''

She lifted the radio to her lips and snapped the answer to Tom. Hooking the radio back on her belt, she cast another look at the opposite ledge. The tot had pushed himself up and now he toddled around the narrow ledge. Gasping in fear, she grabbed Luke's arm and pointed frantically at the little boy.

Cupping his hands to create a makeshift megaphone, Luke hollered over to the little boy. "Sit down."

Startled, the toddler looked up. His pained and worried expression turned to one of relief, and he began to toddle toward them, heedless of the fact that he was about to step into empty air.

Gaby filled her lungs and hollered against the wind. "N-o-o-o-o!" Frantically she waved her hands, indicating that the child should stop.

Beside her, Luke reacted quickly. Grabbing his heavy climbing ropes, he swung them over his head and hurled them at the approaching child. The weight and power with which they flew through the air caught the child dead center, driving him back and knocking him down.

Relief washed through Gaby, but she knew better than to hope the ropes would keep him there forever. Already the little boy struggled against them. She dashed for the tunnel. They had to get over there. *Now.*

She felt a sharp jerk at her shoulder and her ropes slipping free. Spinning around, she found Luke tying a knot in the end of her climbing rope. Before she could ask what he was doing, he starting swinging the rope over his head. The small knot he'd formed turned into a large round circle. A lasso.

Cold fear raced through her. He wouldn't! But even as she thought it, he sent the rope flying through the air, the big round circle leading the way. It sailed through the open space between the ledges and settled neatly over the protruding rock. A hell of a feat, considering the howling winds, but she felt no sense of triumph. Only a cold knot of terror as he strode to the other end of their ledge and quickly ran the rope around the rough protrusion of rocks there.

For an instant the fear immobilized her, but then she

sprang into action. She'd made it halfway to Luke when he turned to her.

He tossed her the end of the rope. "Hang on."

Automatically, she grabbed the rope as it came flying at her, but even as she did so, she screamed her protest to Luke. "You can't do this. It's too windy."

She tried to grab his arm as he ran by her back to the edge closest to the Caldwells' ledge, but she wasn't strong enough to stop him. He just strode by and crouched on their ledge's edge.

Her heart racing, she quickly tightened her grip on the rope and passed it around her back as she turned toward the ledge where Anita and Taylor lay. The rock Luke had wrapped the rope around to help anchor it was now behind her. She would have the greatest leverage this way to hold the rope secure. And she could watch Luke's progress across the windy span. Clamping down with her hands, she looked up in time to see Luke lower himself from the ledge.

Her heart froze until she felt the rope jerk taut against her, telling her he hadn't dropped into nothingness. Then her heart slammed against her chest as she realized he hadn't taken time to attach safety lines. He was going to cross the windy span hand over hand, with nothing but his damned arrogance to keep him safe.

Her stomach turned over, and a cold sweat beaded her brow. She should have stopped him. She should have grabbed hold of him and tied him to the damned mountain.

A humorless, half-hysterical laugh fell from her lips. Stopped him? Rambo couldn't have stopped him. Not with a little boy's life at risk. Luke couldn't stand by while someone came to harm. Any kind of harm. As she well knew, someone missing a meal would provoke his protective instincts.

No, she couldn't have stopped him. Luke had to save the world. He had to make sure everyone was safe and fed and warm and happy. And she knew it.

Her body went cold at the sudden flash of insight.

Oh, God, she *did* know it.

If she lived to be a hundred, Luke would never hurt her. Not today or tomorrow or a thousand years from now. Not for love or hate or anger or power. Not in any way. Not at any time. Not for any reason.

Her world turned over, and in that instant she knew two things. One, she would find nothing but safety and love in Luke's arms. And two, if he made it to the other side without falling to his death, she was going to kill him.

And then she was going to love him until heaven gave up its stars.

If he'd let her.

But first she had to get him safely to the other side. And with him getting heavier by the second, that would take all the strength she had. She tightened her hands on the ropes and dug her feet farther into the snow, anchoring herself against the winds.

Her nerves drew tighter and tighter as she waited for him to come into view. Right now she saw only the rope disappearing beneath the lip of the ledge.

Her hands began to burn as the rope bit viciously into them with every move Luke made, but she thanked God for the pain. It proved Luke still hung safely from the rope. The tension on the rope increased as he approached the middle where he would be the heaviest. Her feet slipped in the snow and she fought to hold her ground, hanging on with all her might.

Finally Luke hit the middle of the rope and came into view. Her breath caught in her throat. The wind blew him as easily as a child twirled a rag doll, twisting him this way and that as he clung to his meager lifeline. Icy fingers of dread wrapped around her, but she clamped her hands tighter and held on.

And on. Until the tension on the rope began to ease and he reached the far ledge, pulling himself up to safety. Relief poured through her and she sank to her knees. Hot tears tracked down her cheeks and fell steadily into the snow.

On the other ledge Luke untangled the child from the ropes and scooped him into his arms. Keeping the toddler tucked safely under one arm, he knelt beside the mother, stripped off a glove and pressed two fingers over the pulse point under her jaw. Then he gently shook her. Twice. The second time, Gaby thought she detected some movement, but through her tear-filled eyes, she couldn't be sure. When Luke turned to her with a smile and a thumbs-up, relief washed through her.

Injuries were a certainty with the distance the mother and child had fallen. It hadn't surprised Gaby to find the victim unconscious. But that Luke had been able to revive Anita with a gentle shake was a good sign. Mother and son would make it.

And if she had anything to say about it, so would she and Luke. Together. Forever and ever. Pushing herself up, she spun on her heel and sped to the tunnel. Somehow, she would convince him they did belong together. That she'd been wrong earlier. So, so wrong.

She scrambled up the dark stone staircase with urgency pounding in her breast and a tiny ray of hope lighting her way. She would convince him. She *would,* even if she had to tie him to the mountain to do it. At the top Susie waited anxiously for her in the small rock enclave, a soft whine humming in her throat.

Gaby gave her a reassuring pat. "It's okay, girl. We

found 'em. Now come on. We've got a cowboy to lasso before he gets away.''

Gaby came around the far side of the rocks to find the rescue helicopter sitting in the middle of the open meadow at the top of the face. Its blades beat slowly overhead so that the engines remained ready to go, but it didn't cause a frenzy of flying snow on the ground beneath it. Surprisingly they were in a temporary lull in the storm. The winds had died down somewhat, and visibility had vastly improved. It wouldn't last long, but they only needed a few minutes to get the helicopter out of here.

She peered into the helicopter as she got closer. The pilot sat at the controls, ready to lift off on a moment's notice. In the back, the EMT kneeled over a thrashing Taylor. She glanced quickly at the cliff's edge. Luke and Tom were hauling simultaneously on separate ropes as they lifted Anita up in a basket. Gaby wouldn't be of any help there.

She jogged to the helicopter and climbed in. ''How's he doing?'' She looked over the small two-year-old, whose arms and legs were moving at a rate designed to make the EMT's job as difficult as possible. But there was a smile on his face.

''It's amazing,'' the EMT answered. ''He seems fine. His blood pressure's good, and he certainly isn't lacking any animation.''

Gaby tickled the boy's tummy. ''That's right, Taylor. Give him hell.'' She grasped one of the little boy's flailing hands and looked at his fingers. ''He's got some frostbite.''

The EMT nodded. ''Yes. But it won't kill him.'' Gently taking the tiny hand from Gaby, he gave the boy's fingers a closer examination. ''They're going to hurt like the devil once he starts to warm up, but I don't think he's going to lose any."

A commotion at the helicopter's door hailed the arrival of Luke and Tom with the mother. As the EMT strapped Taylor in, Gaby grabbed the end of the rescue basket, pulled it in and secured it to its moors. Finishing, she glanced up to find Tom already strapped into the copilot's seat and Luke moving away from the helicopter so it could take off.

Her heart clenched in her chest. He looked so alone, moving into the storm by himself. But he wouldn't be alone for long. Not if she had anything to say about it.

She called Susie into the helicopter, vaulted out herself, and hollered back to Tom. "I'm staying with Luke. Will you take care of Susie for me?"

A wave of relief washed over Tom's face. "Boy, am I glad you said that."

She pulled her brows low in question. "Why?"

"Because Luke told me to push you out of the helicopter if I couldn't convince you to stay any other way."

Her eyes popped wide. Push her out of the helicopter! She snapped her head around and stared at Luke's retreating figure. He was moving away from the helicopter with the arrogant assurance that Tom would naturally do what he'd requested. She shook her head at his audacity, but the tiny ray of hope growing in her breast got just a little bit wider. He wanted her to stay. At least for a little while. Now she only had to convince him to stretch a little while into a lifetime.

She turned back to Tom and moved her finger in a circular motion slightly above her head, indicating Tom should take off. "Go. We'll see you in a couple of days."

Tom nodded, and the helicopter's blades whirred to life. Ducking low, she moved away from the machine as it lifted into the air. When it lifted high enough that she no longer had to fight its vicious gale, she straightened up. And faltered in her step.

No longer obscured by the blowing snow, the peaceful red mountain that had so clearly pulled her to its sheltering domain rose proudly behind First Face's dramatic edge. And standing not ten feet from that edge, silhouetted against that majestic face and nature's raging glory, stood her destiny.

He stood tall and proud with one knee cocked to the side and his hands shoved deep into his jacket pockets. His cowboy hat was pulled low over his brow, but not low enough to hide those arresting blue eyes. Good Lord, even from this distance, those blue eyes stood out like a perfect summer day.

And he was waiting for her.

Butterflies ricocheted around in her stomach with the same frenetic energy as the snowflakes that hurled through the crisp mountain air. Her heart pounded in her chest. If he wanted her badly enough to have Tom push her out of the aircraft, surely she had a chance to convince him to give them a real chance. A real chance at a real future.

She was certainly going to give it everything she had. And then some. She raised her chin for battle and tromped through the snow with conviction and purpose in every step she took. And she didn't stop until her hiking boots clipped his own. Locking her gaze onto his, she raised a single brow in challenge. "Push me out of the helicopter?"

He didn't back up an inch. He met her gaze head-on and gave his shoulders an unapologetic shrug. "Crude. But effective. I wasn't about to watch the best thing that ever happened to me disappear in a flurry of snow and whirling blades."

The best thing that ever happened to him.

Her heart expanded in her chest, and a giddy tendril of happiness brightened her ray of hope. Desperately she clenched her fists, trying to keep her rapidly escalating emotions from getting ahead of her. He might want nothing more than the next three days. And if that were the case, she still had a battle on her hands.

She reined in her swirling thoughts and tried to put them in order. But before she could manage, Luke stepped back. He kept his penetrating gaze on her, though, as if to make sure she didn't miss a word he was about to say. "You were right about my marriage. It was bad, and it soured me on anything that even remotely smacked of commitment. But there's nothing like hanging off a rope with nothing under you but air and a very painful fall to clear a man's head."

Gaby's breath caught in her throat, and that ray of hope got just a little bit bigger. A little bit brighter. She waited with bated breath and her heart hanging by a thread to see what he would say next.

He looked away for a second, his eyes seeing a distant past. "I realized hanging out over that chasm that there was no love between Tanya and me. There was lust and pride and an endless struggle for power, but no love."

He swung his gaze back. Bold and true, it reached into her until it touched her soul. "I love you, Gaby. And I have a lot more to offer than a few straggly roses to brighten the way and a bad end. And if I have to keep you up on this mountain for the next hundred years for you to figure it out, so be it." Pure cowboy determination rang in his every word.

Joy and jubilation burst in Gaby's heart, and before she thought better of it, she launched herself into Luke's arms. "I thought I was going to have to tie you to the mountain to get you to stay." She rained tiny kisses all over his face as Luke scrambled to keep his footing.

When he had his balance, he swooped in and caught her mouth for one hard kiss before disentangling their limbs and setting her away. He cocked his head, his blue-eyed gaze boring into hers. "Get me to stay? You don't think I'm going to start beating you tomorrow?" Disbelief gilded with hope colored his words.

She met his gaze squarely and shook her head. "You save people, Luke. You don't hurt them. It took me a little while to figure that out. But I got it."

A smile as gentle and life affirming as a bubbling mountain stream curved his lips. "Thank you."

Her own smile was threatened by tears, but she managed to keep them at bay as she pushed the words past the constriction in her throat. "Anytime, cowboy."

Luke took her hand, his expression turning serious. "I want it all, Gaby. Marriage. Babies. And happily ever after."

Happily ever after. And *babies*. Her heart hitched in her chest and a wonder so pure it warmed her from the inside out washed through her veins. She'd never thought about babies. Never dreamed they'd be in her future. But, oh, she wanted them. Little cowboys and cowgirls with blue, blue eyes. Her smile trembled with happiness. "Lots of babies."

Luke smiled wide, his grip tightening on her hands as if he would never let her go. "Say it."

She tightened her fingers around his. "I love you."

"And you'll marry me," he prompted.

"I'll marry you." Laughter fell from her lips, tears of joy christening her promise.

Luke caught each and every one of them with the soft warmth of his lips. And then he closed his mouth over hers and deepened the kiss until there was no doubt in Gaby's mind he was staking his claim.

Wrapping her arms around his neck, Gaby drew him closer and met him thrust for thrust, making her own claims as clear as the love in her heart.

Her home.

Her mountain.

Her man.

* * * * *

If you enjoyed what you just read,
then we've got an offer you can't resist!

Take 2 bestselling love stories FREE!

Plus get a FREE surprise gift!

Clip this page and mail it to Silhouette Reader Service™

IN U.S.A.
3010 Walden Ave.
P.O. Box 1867
Buffalo, N.Y. 14240-1867

IN CANADA
P.O. Box 609
Fort Erie, Ontario
L2A 5X3

YES! Please send me 2 free Silhouette Special Edition® novels and my free surprise gift. Then send me 6 brand-new novels every month, which I will receive months before they're available in stores. In the U.S.A., bill me at the bargain price of $3.57 plus 25¢ delivery per book and applicable sales tax, if any*. In Canada, bill me at the bargain price of $3.96 plus 25¢ delivery per book and applicable taxes**. That's the complete price and a savings of over 10% off the cover prices—what a great deal! I understand that accepting the 2 free books and gift places me under no obligation ever to buy any books. I can always return a shipment and cancel at any time. Even if I never buy another book from Silhouette, the 2 free books and gift are mine to keep forever. So why not take us up on our invitation. You'll be glad you did!

235 SEN CNFD
335 SEN CNFE

Name	(PLEASE PRINT)
Address	Apt.#
City	State/Prov.	Zip/Postal Code

* Terms and prices subject to change without notice. Sales tax applicable in N.Y.
** Canadian residents will be charged applicable provincial taxes and GST.
   All orders subject to approval. Offer limited to one per household.
   ® are registered trademarks of Harlequin Enterprises Limited.

PAMELA TOTH
DIANA WHITNEY
ALLISON LEIGH
LAURIE PAIGE

bring you four heartwarming stories
in the brand-new series

So Many Babies

At the Buttonwood Baby Clinic,
babies and romance abound!

On sale January 2000: **THE BABY LEGACY**
by Pamela Toth

On sale February 2000: **WHO'S THAT BABY?**
by Diana Whitney

On sale March 2000: **MILLIONAIRE'S INSTANT BABY**
by Allison Leigh

On sale April 2000: **MAKE WAY FOR BABIES!**
by Laurie Paige

Only from Silhouette SPECIAL EDITION
Available at your favorite retail outlet.

Silhouette®
Where love comes alive™

Start celebrating Silhouette's 20th anniversary
with these 4 special titles by
New York Times **bestselling authors**

*Fire and Rain**
by Elizabeth Lowell

King of the Castle
by Heather Graham Pozzessere

*State Secrets**
by Linda Lael Miller

*Paint Me Rainbows**
by Fern Michaels

On sale in December 1999

Plus, a special free book offer inside each title!

Available at your favorite retail outlet
**Also available on audio from Brilliance.*

Silhouette®
™ *Where love comes alive*™

Special Edition is celebrating Silhouette's 20th anniversary!

Special Edition brings you:

• **brand-new LONG, TALL TEXANS**
Matt Caldwell: Texas Tycoon by **Diana Palmer**
(January 2000)

• **a bestselling miniseries
PRESCRIPTION: MARRIAGE**
(December 1999-February 2000)
Marriage may be just what the doctor ordered!

• **a brand-new miniseries SO MANY BABIES**
(January-April 2000)
At the Buttonwood Baby Clinic,
lots of babies—and love—abound

• **the exciting conclusion of ROYALLY WED!**
(February 2000)

• **the new AND BABY MAKES THREE:
THE DELACOURTS OF TEXAS**
by **Sherryl Woods**
(December 1999, March & July 2000)

And on sale in June 2000, don't miss
Nora Roberts' brand-new story
Irish Rebel
in **Special Edition**.

Available at your favorite retail outlet.